The

Sugar
Inferno

Lyle Garford

Except where actual historical events and characters are being described for the storyline of this novel, all situations in this publication are fictitious and any resemblance to living persons is purely coincidental.

Copyright © 2019 by Lyle Garford

All rights reserved. No part of this book may be reproduced or transmitted in any form or by any means, electronic or mechanical, including photocopying, recording, or by an information storage and retrieval system, without permission in writing from the publisher.

Published by:
Lyle Garford
Vancouver, Canada
Contact: lyle@lylegarford.com

ISBN 978-0-9952078-6-8
Cover photo by PHB.cz (Richard Semik)/Shutterstock.com
Book Design by Lyle Garford
www.lylegarford.com

First Edition 2019
Printed by Createspace, an Amazon.com Company.
Available on Kindle and other devices.

Dedication

This one is for my first draft reviewer Margaret Penner. Her sage advice makes the final product better every time.

Chapter One
February 1798
London, England

His instincts honed from long practice, Evan swiveled his head without conscious thought to look in all directions as he stepped out of his lodgings and made for the waiting coach. He had served in enough dangerous, covert situations over his career to make being cautious as a matter of course well worth it.

The problem was wearing his full dress uniform as a Commander in the British Royal Navy in the open for all to see. His instincts were on edge, because for him doing so was far from the norm. Evan struggled to remember the last time he wore the uniform and could only remember doing so at his wedding over four years ago. While pulling on the unfamiliar clothes in his room he fought the irrational urge to tear them off, for with each piece of clothing he put on his sense of being exposed grew in magnitude. But he kept telling himself the uniform would actually help him to blend in and not stand out, for men in full uniform were everywhere in London and particularly so where he was going today.

As he made his way to the coach the other unfamiliar sensation he struggled with was the blast of frigid air biting him the second he walked outside, making him pull his heavy winter cloak as close as possible. A light skiff of snow fell overnight, enough to make the air seem crisp and the streets slippery with icy slush. Evan knew the temperature was probably hovering around the freezing mark and it could have been far colder than it was, but the thought was of little comfort. Having been stationed for well over fifteen years in the warmth of the Caribbean without having been back to England until now, he felt woefully unready for the chill of London in February.

The driver was holding the door to the coach open for him and as Evan approached he saw the man had one of the sleeves of his own heavy coat pinned to the shoulder. The two men locked eyes and Evan knew his driver had been staring with equal interest at him. One sleeve of Evan's cloak was pinned up too, because of having lost his left arm to a smuggler's gunshot in 1783. The driver saluted with his remaining arm at the same time and Evan nodded acknowledgement. Under other circumstances Evan would have taken a moment to probe the man's past, certain he was an invalid out of the Navy, but the light wind was far too biting to contemplate standing outside engaging in conversation.

"Whitehall, please. Admiralty House," said Evan, certain the man would be well aware of where his destination was.

"Aye, sir," said the driver, closing the door and climbing up to his bench to grasp the reins.

The inside of the coach wasn't much warmer, but it at least had the benefit of keeping the sting of the wind at bay. As the coach began to move Evan settled back into the cushions and tried staring out the window at the scenery, but was soon foiled by the warmth of his breath fogging the windows.

Evan was staggered by how everything had changed so much in the years since he was last in London and seeing it all had not lost its novelty in the three days since he had returned. Clothing styles had changed significantly and he was forced to spend a larger sum than he wanted to update his wardrobe, but this wasn't all he found different. Everywhere he looked old, familiar buildings were gone and new ones had appeared. Evan was stunned to find his once favorite inn and pub was now a warehouse.

With little else to do as the coach jostled through the streets Evan's mind drifted back, not for the first time, to the mysterious orders he had received from spymaster Captain Sir James Standish in Barbados. Evan knew him well, as Sir James had served as Evan's superior officer in charge of all covert activities Evan and his men undertook throughout the Caribbean for many years. Much had happened since the day Evan was given command of the Royal Navy Dockyard on the Caribbean island of Antigua in 1784 as cover for his covert activities and Sir James became his superior.

On many occasions over the years Sir James had cause to be deliberately cautious about what he communicated in letters, but this was different. The letter Evan received ordered him to take ship and sail for England right away to attend a meeting at Admiralty House. Nothing other than the date and time for the meeting was given. With not even a hint offered as to who would be present or what it was about meant something highly unusual and significant was happening. Evan had stewed on it every day since receiving the orders, but the possibilities of what was behind it all were endless. As his career as a spy for the Royal Navy and the Foreign Office progressed Evan had learned much about himself and he knew being active was when he was at his best. Fortunately, the inactivity and waiting was finally over.

Ten minutes later Evan alighted from the coach and eyed the two guards at the entrance to the courtyard of Admiralty House before turning to his driver. Evan looked closer and saw his driver was perhaps twenty years older than his own thirty-five years of age. He also saw the man's clothes appeared well worn and seemed a little frayed. Evan tipped him well and turned to go, but the driver forestalled him with eyes still wide from Evan's generosity.

"Sir? Would you like me to wait for you?"

"Hmm, I can't say how long I'm going to be here, you understand."

"I can wait, sir."

Evan stared at him for a long moment before offering the man a grim smile and replying.

"What ship?"

"*HMS Worcester*, sir," said the man, giving Evan a gap-toothed grin and a side nod to his missing arm. "Lost this back in '83 to the Frenchies."

Evan nodded. "I'll look for you when I finish. I may well be wrong, but I don't think this will be more than an hour or two at most."

Evan turned, went to the waiting guards, and announced himself. The one in charge nodded on hearing the name and looking carefully at the uniform Evan was wearing underneath the cloak.

"Sir, you are expected. The entrance is through the courtyard on your left."

A well-dressed servant met Evan inside a small outer alcove and took his coat. Once Evan finished straightening his uniform he was ushered further into an inner reception hall past a wonderful, grand staircase to his right and into yet another room. Evan surmised this was for dining, as a large table with several chairs around it filled the room. Pictures of warships at sea adorned the walls of the room while a fireplace set into one of them blazed with welcome warmth. Sir James Standish was seated at the table with another man Evan did not recognize, but they both rose from their seats to greet him.

"So very good to see you once again, Mr. Ross," said Sir James. "I am pleased to present you to the First Lord of the Admiralty, Earl George Spencer. My Lord, this is Commander Evan Ross."

Evan saluted before taking their proffered hands to shake.

"My Lord, I am honored to be here."

The First Lord stared hard without smiling at Evan for what seemed an eternity, but was in reality only a few seconds before he grunted noncommittally and spoke.

"I've heard about you. Read plenty of your reports, too. Well, we shall have company soon and we have things to discuss before they arrive. Why don't you fill him in, Sir James? Please take your seats while I arrange some refreshments for us."

As the First Lord walked over to a side door to

pass orders to his servants Evan turned back to Sir James.

"Certainly. So, Commander, I expect you are most curious about all this. I'd apologize for the lack of detail in your orders, but the nature of the business before us today is so sensitive that putting anything about the subject of it in writing was deemed an unnecessary risk. This is also why we are meeting in the First Lord's residence today instead of in the Admiralty itself. The possibility of French spies or informers in the capital is also always a concern. The thought was meeting here could attract less notice and this would be good, for we will be joined by some very senior people shortly."

"I understand, Sir James. If I may, what is the subject of this meeting?"

Sir James smiled. "Our presence in Saint Domingue and, most importantly, what we are going to do about the island from this point on. What else would it be?"

Evan gave him a rueful smile in return. "Yes, I shouldn't be surprised. It has been commanding rather a lot of my time."

A servant had anticipated his master's order and he appeared with a large tray bearing a pot of tea and several cups as he followed right behind the First Lord. Earl Spencer lifted a hand to signal for silence until the man had served them. As the door closed behind the servant the First Lord turned to Evan.

"Sir James recommended we bring you here for this meeting, given the depth of your involvement with Saint Domingue. Your role here is to provide context and, if asked, your recommendations. Aside from this, there is one other matter that is for us alone. Sir James, over to you."

"I am retiring, Commander Ross. After over thirty five years at sea and having now served the Foreign Office for almost twenty years, I think I've done my share."

"Congratulations, Sir James," said Evan, letting a heartfelt smile appear on his face. "Your retirement is certainly well earned, but I will miss you and your sage advice. What are your plans? Are you returning to England?"

"Good Lord, no. After all the years I've been in Barbados I couldn't possibly contemplate spending winter in England. The arthritis slowing me down would be even worse if I was here. No, I have acquired an estate on the island and that is where I intend to spend my remaining days."

"I understand, sir. I confess the winter here has been a shock to the system."

"You'll be back in the Caribbean soon enough, Mr. Ross," said the First Lord. "We need to discuss—ah, I think our other guests have arrived. Please remain behind after the meeting, both of you, as we have other matters to deal with."

Moments later the three of them rose to greet a group of four men as the servant ushered them into the room. The First Lord ordered more tea be brought before turning to do introductions all around as they all took places at the table.

Three of the men were in civilian clothing while the fourth wore the uniform of an obviously high ranking Army officer. The Army officer was introduced as General Thomas Maitland, whom Evan knew by reputation as having extensive experience in the Caribbean. Evan struggled to keep his face bland as the first of the civilians was introduced as William Pitt, currently Chancellor of the Exchequer and a former British Prime Minister. Seated beside him was Baron William Grenville, the current British Foreign Secretary.

The last to be introduced was Roger Bonds, presented as an assistant to Baron Grenville in the Foreign Office. Evan knew at once the man was anything but a mere assistant, as was obvious from the ugly scar running from the side of his forehead to his ear. Evan studied the cat like grace Bonds displayed which spoke of a man in peak condition, complemented by broad shoulders, and was absolutely certain this man had seen military service somewhere in his past. He also found himself glad the two of them were on the same side. The man sensed Evan's attention and the two of them locked eyes, but the First Lord cleared his throat and began speaking.

"Gentlemen, thank you all for attending. Well, the day has come to make a decision and we are the ones tasked with making it. I know we all have opinions on this, but we must find a way forward."

"Lord Spencer," said the Foreign Secretary. "As I've said before, we've made too great an investment to stop now. My thinking is unchanged."

Chancellor Pitt drummed his fingers on the table for a moment before speaking.

"My thinking isn't any different, either, Baron.

But something does have to change here and it needs to be for the better."

"Hmm," said the First Lord. "Perhaps before we go further we should take a moment to bring these other gentlemen up to speed on how we got to this meeting today."

Chancellor Pitt shrugged while the Foreign Secretary waved a hand to proceed and the First Lord turned to the others at the table.

"I will be brief with a little history, which I expect maybe you all know at least some of the details. We were invited by the French royalist plantation owners to bring order to the chaos of Saint Domingue and we first attempted to do so in 1793. The force we landed at the time was insufficient for the job at hand and no, gentlemen, that is not a criticism. It was the best we could do back then. The reasons also all made sense at the time as well. Put a stop to the flood of money from the island to France, push the meddling Spaniards out of the way, and while we were at it hopefully add to our own coffers. Of course, as Prime Minister at the time Chancellor Pitt here saw the problem and we made the decision to send another 30, 000 troops in 1795 to wipe the frogs out of the Caribbean altogether and Saint Domingue in particular."

The First Lord paused to sip at his tea and grimaced as he continued.

"But then, from what I can see, yellow fever and a rather determined resistance from the slaves on the island are forcing us to make a difficult decision. I gather we also have issues with our coffers, but Chancellor Pitt can speak to that."

"Well, if the Army had done their bloody job we wouldn't be in this position," said Pitt. "I still can't believe a bunch of ragtag slaves continue to best us in the field."

General Maitland made no attempt to hide his scowl as he sat forward in an aggressive stance.

"Chancellor, that is unfair and you know it. A soldier has no ability to fight while he's busy puking yellow vomit."

This time the Foreign Secretary rolled his eyes and put a hand to his forehead.

"God Almighty, gentlemen, we know this. The question is what are we going to do. As I said, I think we've made too great an investment to simply toss it all away."

The First Lord cleared his throat again, a little louder this time to signal his displeasure.

"So yes, we all know we are in a hard place and the question is obvious. Perhaps then we can move on to a more in depth assessment of the situation as it stands now, which is why Sir James and Commander Ross are here. Commander, as the one man here who has been physically closest and most directly involved with this mess, you were brought all the way here to give us your first hand thoughts on where we stand in Saint Domingue and this is perhaps a good point to have you do that. So you know, these gentlemen are aware of all aspects of your role. My Cabinet colleagues at the table have seen copies of more than a few of your reports and I daresay even General Maitland here has seen some."

Having seen the discord around the table and the direction the conversation was going Evan had already surmised it was a certainty he would be called upon for this exact purpose at some point. Having such an august audience for the thoughts of a lowly commander felt surreal, but Evan resolved to simply have at it.

"Of course, My Lord. There are many factors at play here, but were I to be pressed I don't think I could be very optimistic about our future there. I am a Navy officer and not schooled in land based military tactics, so I cannot speak to whether better military decisions could have been made. I will say I respect the men on the ground and I think they have done the best they could in difficult circumstances."

Evan saw Chancellor Pitt's face darken, but pressed on.

"Yes, illness has been a major factor, but our foes have proven far more resilient and determined than anyone, including myself, expected them to be. Having a seemingly endless supply of men to throw at our soldiers helps. No one knows for certain exactly how many runaway slaves are hiding in the mountains and serving in the black armies, but my men and I estimate it is in the many thousands and perhaps even well over a hundred thousand. These slaves on Saint Domingue have made the collective decision the island belongs to them as their home and, in my experience, people fighting to keep a home they think belongs to them alone have serious motivation. I expect you've all heard the reports of screaming hordes of blacks armed with little more than machetes rushing the walls of our forts. Well, they are true, because I've seen those hordes up close."

Evan looked around the table, but saw no one wanting to challenge him on anything he had said to this point so he continued.

"So, my assessment is there are three problems we face. Yellow fever is obviously one and I think we all know there is nothing to be done when it strikes. You either live or you die. The second problem is the thousands of foes we face and, more importantly, the leadership they have. I realize this could be hard to accept, but I'm going to be blunt here. Their leaders are not stupid and, in fact, they are extremely devious and highly intelligent."

Evan paused for another brief second in case they wanted to argue about this too, but no one spoke so Evan took a deep breath and carried on.

"They may not have formal military tactics training, but they have seen how our army operates and learned fast. I have no doubt many hard lessons were learned by watching the French and Spanish before us. In particular, they have learned to strike hard and fast and then leave equally fast, especially when faced with a larger number of foes. They have many captured weapons and have learned quickly how to use these too. When you combine it all with the sheer number of motivated men at their command they are formidable. This is the reason our forces are basically confined to holding a thin strip of land along the coastline."

The First Lord rubbed his chin in thought before speaking.

"And the third problem, Commander?"

"The third, and to my mind, most challenging problem is Saint Domingue is a swamp, sir. There are so many different factions on all sides, all willing to align with each other if the situation warrants it, and all willing to stab each other in the back, if the situation warrants it, that plotting some way through it all is fraught with peril. God knows we've tried to build various alliances before, but they all fall apart because interests change in an eye blink on this island. I've been racking my brains for some new combination to try, but the allegiances change so fast the ink hasn't even dried on my plan before I have to throw it away."

"Factions, you say?" said General Maitland, sitting forward with interest. "Elaborate, please."

"Certainly, sir. The whites on Saint Domingue are divided into two basic classes, the grand blancs and the petit blancs. As one might expect, the grand blancs are the wealthy plantation owners. Most of these men are staunch former royalists, but their true loyalty is to themselves and the ability to make staggering sums of money from their plantations. They command a small, but well paid and trained crowd of thugs and overseers to look after their properties."

Evan paused to sip his tea before continuing. "The petits blancs are the tradesmen, the small business owners, government bureaucrats, and a number of fortune seekers and street scum of all stripes. This is a much larger group with a mixed bag of royalists, revolutionaries, and people loyal only to themselves. They will fight only when necessary, by and large. Naturally, the grand and petit blancs all want the plantation system to continue as is, with the exception of the revolutionaries who strangely somehow think they can both free the blacks from servitude and still make a mountain of money. The last group consists of a little more than two thousand, at best, French soldiers who have a wary coexistence with the blacks in areas we do not control. Most of these are stationed at Cap Le Francois in the north."

Evan paused to sip his tea once again while across the table Sir James nodded in silent agreement and encouragement.

"If this sounds like a complicated relationship, the situation with the blacks in Saint Domingue is worse. They can be divided into those with some degree of white blood in their veins, who are generally known as mulattoes or gens de coleur in French, and those who are pure black, brought straight there from Africa or are children born to pure black parents. The pure blacks are at the bottom of everything in the world of Saint Domingue, while those with a mix of parentage have the power. Within the mulattoes there are different people struggling for sole leadership and, despite a lot of tension, the pure blacks on the island continue to support them."

"Mr. Ross?" said the General. "I've heard rumor the mulatto leaders are in favor of keeping slavery. Why would the blacks support them if this is so?"

"A good question, sir. The answer is likely they have to trust someone and they would prefer it to be men who at least look more like them than we do. This and the fact the mulatto leaders are competent at what they do."

"I see."

"There are two leaders most prominent on their side. One is a fellow whose name you will have seen in my reports. Toussaint L'Ouverture is a mulatto plantation owner, who was once a slave himself, but now keeps his own slaves. From what I've seen he is the most skilled of the black leaders. The strange part is Toussaint professes to want no slavery and he has proclaimed an end to it, but it continues in areas he controls. His rival is Andre Rigaud, another mulatto who wants to keep slavery and has no time for anyone thinking of ending the practice. My understanding is this man has little sympathy for white or black people either. He apparently thinks mulattoes should be ruling the world, let alone Saint Domingue."

Evan held up his hand to emphasize he had no explanation for the contradictions before he continued.

"So these men have proven adept at switching their allegiances when it suits them and at somehow convincing the pure blacks to support them, on Toussaint's side, and the mulattoes to do likewise in the case of Rigaud. The French Governor Sonthonax and his administration was also a problem until last year when Toussaint forced him out. With him gone the situation was a little simpler, but it is only a matter of time before France sends someone else to take charge. Our sources inside the French administration have told us France is most unhappy at the disruptions to the flow of money the revolutionaries desperately need. This makes me fear the newcomer, whoever it is, will be much worse and will be especially so if he brings more troops from France to back him up."

"And lets not forget the Spanish on the other side of the island, gentlemen," said Sir James. "They may be puppets of the French in theory, but we think there are many in the Spanish administration there who would love nothing better than to take control of the entire island and loosen the French grip on the place. And last of all we should not forget the Americans here. They aren't strong enough to engage in military action, but their traders are everywhere and would dearly love to steal business from anyone and everyone."

"Commander?" said Baron Grenville. "Let me see if I understand correctly. You are certain there are no other possibilities for a successful alliance which could serve our interests best?"

"There are always possibilities to try, Baron. Whether they will prove successful is another matter entirely. The simple problem is everyone involved in this situation, including us, wants to be in sole charge."

The Foreign Secretary's assistant leaned forward and spoke for the first time.

"Commander, if the people we are dealing with are too obstinate, why not simply install the right people in the right places to be happily on our side? There are ways to do it, you know."

Evan locked eyes with the man once again and gave a small shrug.

"Of course there are. As Sir James can attest, we've made several judicious attempts to suborn key people with our gold. The problem is they are all too happy to take it and then ignore anything we or anyone else wants them to do. For example, Toussaint at one point was allied with the Spanish. As soon as he got the arms and gold he wanted from them he promptly switched allegiance to the French. The other option for dealing with someone too obstinate is to find some means to have them removed and to install someone more amenable. But the thing about this island is no one trusts anyone, meaning removing someone is easier said than done."

"Come, Commander. I think you know what I'm talking about here. Have you tried it?"

Evan glared at the man in exasperation.

"You are referring to the expedience of a knife in the back and, yes, I assure you the thought has crossed our minds. To date we have not, though. The difficulty is these men Toussaint and Rigaud are extremely well protected and they are both suspicious in the extreme we might try something exactly like that. The odds of anyone accomplishing the task and living long enough to enjoy their success is incredibly slim."

"Isn't risk a part of our business, sir?"

This time Evan scowled and couldn't keep a hard edge from creeping into his voice.

"Of course it bloody is, and I can assure you my men and I are not afraid of risk. We've employed such approaches plenty of times elsewhere. I just see little sense in sending a valuable man to his almost certain death without a guarantee the sacrifice would be worth it. What you need to understand is even if we succeeded in removing either of these black leaders there are others who would step into their shoes in a heartbeat and the possibility is strong they could be even worse."

"I agree with Commander Ross, gentlemen," said Sir James Standish. "A good example would be one of Toussaint's senior generals, who is a vicious brute named Jean Jacques Dessalines. Were we to dispose of Toussaint I wouldn't be surprised at all to find Dessalines immediately in charge. The difference between these two men is you can actually negotiate with Toussaint. Hard bargaining, but you can work on him, whereas Dessalines absolutely hates all white men and wouldn't even try to talk. Were it up to him, every white man on the island would be fed to the sharks."

"Commander," said Baron Grenville, although he glanced sharply at his assistant for a moment. "Mr. Bonds here means no offence, right? We've come to realize having men in the same line of business as you is useful and this is what he is doing for the Foreign Office. I just wanted his thoughts to be certain all options are being considered, hence his presence. Have you thought about employing someone other than one of your own men to do the job? Someone who couldn't be traced back to us? Or what about finding something someone doesn't want revealed and using it as leverage?"

Evan was about to reply, but Sir James broke into the conversation once again.

"Baron, we've looked at everything. Nothing has come to light we could use to gain leverage, as you suggest. As for using a cut out to do the job we stayed our hand on that approach because, as Commander Ross says, it is not clear we could feasibly arrange succession to be more favorable to us and the probability is too strong we may even be in a worse position than before. Better the devil you know, what?"

Sir James paused and looked at Evan. "Commander? Despite what I just said, I think you should tell them."

Evan sighed. "Sirs. What you may not know is I have been successful in infiltrating one of my men into Toussaint's inner circle of advisors. We've taken the long approach to this by attempting to influence Toussaint in a slow, but sure manner. If it is considered necessary, we can direct my agent to make an attempt such as we have been discussing."

"Hmm, thank you, Commander Ross," said the First Lord. "Gentlemen, I apologize for this, but I deemed it necessary to ensure we all had the necessary context before we considered the latest news I have just received. I think you will all understand when I tell you."

"News?" said Chancellor Pitt, his face darkening once again. "What news, Earl?"

This time it was the First Lord who sighed.

"A packet ship came in direct from Saint Domingue and word reached me only late last night of its news. The black armies are on the move, gentlemen. Notice I am talking about two armies, not one, and the report is both are large in the extreme. One has focused on our forts defending Mirebalais while the other went for Jeremie in West Province. Our men beat back a major assault on Jeremie with heavy losses on both sides, but Mirebalais has been a bloodbath. The situation was still fluid when the report was written, but the way I read this, I think it likely our defenses have fallen and the road to Port-au-Prince is open."

"My God," said Evan.

"Shit," said Chancellor Pitt, hammering the table with a fist.

Baron Grenville groaned and put his face in his hands.

"Quite, gentlemen," said the First Lord. "I am assured every effort will be made to defend Port-au-Prince, but my understanding is it will be most difficult to defend a city of this size against a determined assault. I expect our forces will have to abandon even the coastal areas we hold and consolidate in our forts. Does this make sense, Commander Ross?"

"My Lord, it does. I fully expect the Army may fall back on Mole St. Nicholas in the north and Jeremie in the south."

"General? I know you've begun studying the situation. What do you think about defending Port-au-Prince?"

"Your understanding is correct, My Lord. We could certainly make them pay for it, street by street, but it would be madness to make a stand at all costs there."

"Good God, is there nothing we can do here?" said Baron Grenville. "The last thing we need is for the French to be emboldened in the Caribbean. It wasn't long ago we were in fear of losing Jamaica and I for one still think the bloody frogs were the ones agitating the slaves to rise up there. And, we don't want a fresh flow of money heading to France from Saint Domingue, now do we? Can we find more troops to send?"

Both Chancellor Pitt and General Maitland made to speak in response, but the General deferred to the Chancellor.

"Baron, I think we are in agreement we don't want to lose what we have gained to this point and God forbid we cede any advantage to the French. As much as I would like to send more men there I have to point out we cannot afford to do so. This campaign has cost us ten million pounds and we simply can't sustain that kind of enormous effort anymore. Yes, we've managed some trading gains, but there's not been near enough revenue to cover it. Perhaps the General has some miracle he can offer?"

General Maitland grimaced as he responded. The edge to his voice was harsh.

"I'm not in the business of providing miracles, gentlemen. I posed the question of more resources to the Secretary at War before I came here, as I knew he was not able to attend today, and his answer was no. Our forces are fully committed and there is nothing to spare. So yes, I have been ordered to take command in Saint Domingue and I have nothing other than what is already there to get the job done. The question, though, is what do you want me to do? Perhaps bear in mind the thousands of good men we have already lost there."

A glum silence descended on the table as everyone digested what they had heard. After several long moments it fell to the First Lord once again to keep the conversation moving forward.

"Well, the one bright spot I can offer is the Navy stands ready to do whatever we can in support of General Maitland. If the enemy gets close enough to the shore, we have enough resources in the area to make them pay for doing so. And we of course will provide aid in an evacuation if such becomes necessary."

"Sirs?" said Evan. "If I may, I don't think they will strike immediately for Port-au-Prince. As I said, this man Toussaint isn't stupid and these would be his forces that are on the march toward it. He knows exactly what our Navy can do with its cannons and he will want to rest his men if the fighting has been as brutal as I suspect. I think he will try to negotiate taking control of the city. It would fit with the pattern of past behavior. The idea is make gains to turn up the heat and hope we will despair."

The Foreign Secretary rubbed his chin in thought and turned to look at Chancellor Pitt.

"Parliament just voted against any pullout, Chancellor, but the direction matters seem to be heading is the exact opposite. What do you think, can we deal with this?"

Pitt grimaced. "If we don't want to get handed our political heads we need to find a way to gain some sort of win from this bloody mess. But I don't think this changes our interests here. Shall I elaborate?"

Pitt looked first at the Foreign Secretary and then at the First Lord. Both men shrugged to acknowledge he should proceed.

"Our original interests were to cut the flood of money from this damn place to the French. We wanted a return on our investment. We wanted to check French ambition elsewhere in the Caribbean. Keep the bloody Spanish on their side of the island and shut the door on the Americans stealing our business as much as we can. Gentlemen, I suggest none of what we've talked about today changes those as goals. If at all possible, we need to find a way to turn the tide and take control of this bloody place once and for all, without it costing us more in men and money."

"I agree Chancellor, and if anyone can achieve it for us, it is General Maitland," said the First Lord. "But realistically he will be challenged to do that. I think we should keep the objectives as exactly what you just stated and leave it to the General's discretion to do as he sees fit to accomplish them once he arrives and can assess the current situation. If it's necessary to evacuate Port-au-Prince, at least in the short term, for example, then we should not tie the General's hands."

The Foreign Secretary finally stirred in his seat and sat forward, elbows on the table to steeple his hands.

"Yes, I believe I like this. Let us not tie the General's hands. Once the General is there to deal with it first hand perhaps some other way of achieving all of this will become clear. If we leave his mandate broad enough we can perhaps spin whatever the outcome is to suit our purposes. Would you not agree, Chancellor?"

"We do what we must. Yes, I concur. Above all, though, we must have some financial gain from this, General. The Treasury has been stretched to the maximum. My fear is not for today or even tomorrow, it is for the long term, because we are not done with the French. Not by a long stretch. We need resources to find some way to do that."

Evan was a veteran of many similar meetings with senior diplomats and military personnel over the years and because of his experience he told himself he shouldn't be surprised to find cold political calculations were central to the decision making process once again. But Evan knew he wasn't a politician and never would be. Nonetheless, it was discouraging to watch the simple, cynical decision being made to give a fine soldier such as General Maitland orders broad enough he would face being the scapegoat if it all went badly. The General locked eyes with Evan for a moment as he contemplated what he was being told and in this brief second Evan knew the General was well aware of what was happening. But the General gave no outward sign and his face remained carved in stone.

"Well then, it is decided," said the First Lord. "Commander Ross, your orders are to dedicate every second of your time to supporting the General in every way possible. We will discuss the ramifications stemming from this decision after this meeting."

"Of course, My Lord," said Evan, turning to

lock eyes with the General once again. "General Maitland, my men and I will do whatever it takes to support you."

The General remained silent for a moment, but gave a brief nod to Evan before speaking.

"Gentlemen, is there anything else? If not, I have much to do before I leave and, under the circumstances, I think it best I depart as soon as possible."

"I can help with that too, General," said the First Lord. "I have a frigate taking on supplies in Portsmouth at the moment. It is scheduled to depart for Barbados in four days time. I believe the Admiral on station is planning to deploy it immediately to serve offshore of Saint Domingue, so if this works for you then there is nothing to get you to your destination sooner. Commander Ross will be taking ship on it too, but he will have to detour to Antigua before joining you in Saint Domingue."

"My Lord, this is most welcome and I accept your kind offer."

The First Lord gave details of the ship to the General and committed to warning the Captain he would have guests as he rose to signal the end of the meeting. Evan and Sir James remained behind as the others donned their coats and took their leave. When the door finally closed and the three of them were alone once again the First Lord sighed and shook his head.

"A difficult business, gentlemen. Well, we are not done just yet. Commander Ross, we must make some provision for your situation in light of this and, of course, deal with the consequences of Sir James leaving our service. So you know, I've already had a separate conversation with the Foreign Secretary about this and we are both of the same mind. This experiment to have a naval officer specialize in intelligence matters Nelson began so many years ago has proved—useful. Having Sir James lend his expertise to the diplomatic community has also been beneficial."

The First Lord paused a moment to reach behind him to a side table where some envelopes were waiting on a tray. He shuffled through the envelopes as he turned back to speak again.

"My predecessors and I noticed you have served us well in this rather unorthodox arrangement over the years and have not once complained. Others have moved up the ladder of promotion because they are on open, active service while you have toiled in secret. But heaven knows we have found need for your services. Well, I don't know why we haven't done this sooner, but better late than never, *Captain* Ross."

The First Lord handed one of the envelopes to Evan as he finished speaking and he smiled for the first time that day. Evan stared at it for a moment in disbelief before reaching out to take it.

"If you don't waste any time you can make arrangements to get a new uniform before you depart, although they will likely charge an outrageous price for it. And yes, this commission means I desire you to assume the role Sir James has so capably performed for so long. Sir James and I are in agreement your workload will now be such you can no longer carry the added burden of running the day to day affairs of the Dockyard in Antigua, which means one of these two will have to take on the role."

The First Lord passed over the remaining two envelopes and Evan saw one bore the name of James Wilton, his second in command. The second envelope was for Timothy Cooke, the other Lieutenant that reported to Evan. A smile came to his face as he saw that both envelopes referred to his men as Commanders and, as Evan looked up, the First Lord nodded.

"Yes, the men serving with you deserve rewards too. It is up to you which of them will assume the overt role of running the Dockyard. Your men also need a third ship, which I have already arranged for. When you get to Barbados you will assume temporary command of *HMS Stalwart* and sail it to Antigua. It will require a refit and perhaps a few more men, but it will serve. This means you and your officers will each have your own ship. This last envelope has the orders you need to do all this."

Evan replied as he took the proffered envelope. "My Lord, I am at a loss for words. Thank you, on behalf of my officers and myself. We will do everything we can to reward your trust in us."

"Good, because I fully expect it."

"I will be staying on in London a little longer, so perhaps we can dine together tonight Comm— ah, Captain Ross?" said Sir James, laughing at himself. "Using your new title will take some getting used to. But we have much to discuss about the transition. And before I forget about this again, I trust the trading company I set up for you as cover for your ships is still serving you well?"

"It is, Sir James, and I would love to dine with you," said Evan, before turning to the First Lord. "Hmm, a question, if I may? Do you wish me to relocate to Barbados, My Lord?"

The First Lord looked at Sir James, who shrugged in response. The First Lord turned back to Evan.

"I think this is a matter for the two of you to sort out, Captain Ross. My only interest is in getting the job done. Aside from the obvious point your duties will continue in the Caribbean, where in the area you are while you do it is your business."

"Captain Ross?" said Sir James. "So you know, I plan to make myself available if you have need of advice at any time in the future. Deciding what kind of wine to drink with my dinner may be the most important decision I'll be making in future, but I don't plan to abandon you entirely. And now, I'm sure the First Lord has much to do and we should take our leave."

Evan made arrangements to meet Sir James at his club later the same evening after the two men left the First Lord. The coach driver's face lit as Evan appeared outside the gate and signaled for him. Others appeared trying to solicit his business, but Evan waved them away, barely registering the disappointed looks on their faces.

He was completely focused on the surreal new reality of being Captain Evan Ross, with the strange feeling he was walking on air.

***

Two days later Evan left the warmth of the coach dropping him off in front of an entrance to a building in the Kensington area, not far from Hyde Park. A small walkway over a below ground level cellar led from the street to the arched doorway of what looked to be a well-maintained building giving no hint of what the interior might be like. Evan knocked and within a second of the door being opened he was enveloped in a long, crushing embrace from his sister Fran, before she finally relented and bustled him inside. After closing the door and taking his heavy coat she stepped back to look him up and down, before coming closer once again to give him another hug as the tears continued streaming down her face.

Evan knew he was holding back his own tears, because it was over twenty years since they last saw each other. Fran was only one year older than Evan, who was the youngest of the family. They were inseparable when they were young, because of the gap in ages between them and their two older brothers. Evan knew with his mother gone there was no woman Evan loved more than his sister, with the exception of his own wife Alice.

"My God, Evan," said Fran, finally stepping back to hold him at arms length. "You've grown so much, I hardly recognize you. You are not the young midshipman I remember any more."

"No, I am a Captain now, believe it or not," said Evan with a grin, as her mouth fell open in astonishment. "And you—my word, you are as beautiful as our mother was."

"A Captain? Evan, you have no idea how proud I am! But please, come in and let us sit near the fire. I'll make some tea and introduce you to your niece and nephew. It's about time you finally met them."

As they entered the sitting room Evan was grateful to see a fire was already burning on the grate in the fireplace. Sitting on chairs near the fire were two children who looked to be in their early teens and were obviously close in age. They both perked up and stared at the uncle they had never met with interest as he walked into the room.

The next two hours were a blur of conversation and reminiscence for Evan and his sister. Evan was unsurprised to hear his oldest brother John had major health issues and was not expected to live for many more years. When their parents passed away John, as the eldest, had inherited the minor family title, in keeping with the norm. What hadn't been normal was his blatant attempt to rob the rest of his siblings of their inheritance because his dissolute lifestyle demanded large sums of money to spend on gambling, women, and drink. Fortunately, he hadn't succeeded, but the dispute left bad feelings all around. Their older brother Francis would inherit some day if he survived being posted to India with the Horse Guards.

Having a chance for Evan to visit with his sister was welcome coincidence. Her husband Hugh, an officer with the 1st Foot, was stationed with the family in Gibraltar until recently. A promotion brought about an immediate transfer to Lower Canada, but Fran and the children weren't able to join him on the same ship. Arrangements for a merchant ship they could use to reunite them took longer than expected, which had meant Fran had to rent rooms in London. Fran was enormously grateful for a little time to visit family and friends in London and, most of all, to do some needed and welcome shopping for goods either impossible to get or prohibitively expensive in distant posts like Gibraltar or Canada.

Over dinner Evan regaled his niece and nephew with judiciously edited stories of his exploits in the Caribbean. The weather being consistently warm and pleasant all year round seemed a foreign concept to both of them, but his description of the fearsome wrath of a hurricane had everyone's eyes wide. Evan could see his nephew was hanging on every word of his experiences and he was certain the young man would follow his father's steps into some branch of the British military. His niece had a faraway look in her eyes as Evan talked of the crystal clear waters and beautiful beaches of the Caribbean.

The evening finally drew to a close as Evan looked at his watch and saw it was late. His sister knew he was making ready to leave and once again the tears came. She went with him to the door and they held each other in a long embrace before Evan finally pulled away and shrugged on his heavy coat.

"My God, Evan, when will we see each other again? Please tell me it won't be another twenty years."

Evan could only shake his head. "I wish I could, Fran. It is the times we live in, I suppose. This war with the French seems endless and I fear there is more to come. Such is our fates and we must face our destiny with courage. I will continue to write, of course."

Fran wiped the tears from her eyes with a handkerchief. "Hugh told me he thinks we will be posted to Montreal. I am having trouble imagining what it will be like to live in a city where the French outnumber us by so much, let alone how we will raise the children there. But you are right, of course. We do what we must. So please keep writing me, dear brother, and go now, before I start weeping like a little girl again. Remember us and remember I love you!"

"I love you, too," said Evan, embracing her one last time before walking out the door. And this time he didn't hold back the tears from flooding down his face as he stepped into the cold once again.

***

Two days later Evan found himself standing on the quarterdeck of the frigate the First Lord had ordered to carry both himself and the General to Barbados. As he watched the frenetic, but orderly bustle about him he thought back to his arrival the day before. Evan had coached down from London and taken a room in The George Inn right outside the entrance to the massive Royal Navy Dockyards in Portsmouth. He marveled at the scale of the Dockyard facilities, as by comparison the Dockyard he managed in Antigua was miniscule. This place was a hive of constant activity and he knew there must be hundreds of workers dedicated to keeping the Royal Navy afloat.

The Inn was packed with officers both coming

and going from Portsmouth. Many had brought wives and even children to stay with them while they awaited readiness of their ships. Evan had arranged to meet General Maitland at the Inn, whose Army uniform made him stand out like a peacock in flock of sparrows. They shared a laugh together as both men ordered the roast beef dinner, knowing it unlikely they would enjoy a proper English meal like this again any time soon.

Both men also knew if they were going to work closely together they would need to know each other well, which meant the real purpose of the dinner meeting was to take each other's measure. Evan was pleased to find the General was direct and outspoken, but he also possessed a keen mind and bore a deep concern for the welfare of his men. The General never said as much, but seemed satisfied Evan was someone he could work with. As both men relaxed with each other the evening progressed pleasantly enough and by the end of it they had polished off a bottle of wine. Both men were amused to find glasses of French cognac could be had if no one wanted to ask questions about the source and with much laughter they both ordered some. As they finally paid their bills and shook hands Evan knew they were both satisfied they could work with each other.

The frigate came alive with shouts of the officers who seemed to be everywhere, bringing Evan's focus back to the present. The ship began to move as the top men aloft freed the sails and more sailors along the port side let loose the lines tethering them to the shore. As the gap between the ship and the dock slowly widened the General came over to stand beside Evan, out of the way of the sailors and officers still bustling about. The two men stood in silence as the frigate was brought about into the Solent to depart with the tide. Both pulled their heavy cloaks closer as the cold breeze out on the open water bit hard. The General finally sighed and broke the silence.

"What do you think, Captain Ross? When will we see England again?"

Evan was silent for a moment as he stared at the grey skies and the stark brick buildings of the Dockyard covering a huge area along the waterfront of Portsmouth Harbour.

"It's been almost twenty years since I was last here, General. The strange part is England will always feel like and be my true home, but the reality is it isn't my home anymore. And who knows, it may be another twenty years or more before I'm back here again. Then again, perhaps it is my destiny never to return."

Chapter Two
March 1798
Antigua and Saint Domingue

The chill and snow of London were a distant memory by the time Evan sailed into English Harbour, site of the Royal Navy Dockyard on the island of Antigua in the Caribbean. Evan was grateful to gradually shed his heavier clothes the further south he sailed and, although it left him with mixed feelings about leaving England, being back in the agreeable warmth of the Caribbean in March was a guilty pleasure he reveled in. The stifling, often sticky heat of the summer months to come was another matter, but the temperature even now as it was growing close to sunset was pleasant.

As the crew of *HMS Stalwart* secured the sloop to one of the docks Evan looked to shore and saw Lieutenant Timothy Cooke walking over to take a look at the newcomer to English Harbour. The Lieutenant saw Evan standing on the quarterdeck and stopped to wait for him on the dock, but Evan waved for him to join him on deck. A brief flash of puzzlement appeared on the Lieutenant's face, but he made his way up the boarding plank once the men had it in place.

"Welcome back, sir," said the Lieutenant. "I hope your trip home was good?"

"All too brief and, yes, it was as bloody cold as you would expect. Can't say I miss that part of it. We have much to discuss. But first, I'd like your opinion of this ship."

The puzzled look reappeared on the

Lieutenant's face, but he began peering about.

Evan smiled and waved his hand. "Take a few moments to walk about. Tell me your honest thoughts on it."

This time the Lieutenant's eyes widened, but he did as he was told. He walked forward a ways, looking aloft at the sails and peering into the open hatch to the hold before stopping to examine how well the six pound cannons were maintained. After turning back and going aft for a few minutes he finally returned to where Evan was standing.

"Sir, she's a bit of a shabby old bitch, but she seems reasonably well maintained and I think she's got good bones to her. It's maybe fifteen or perhaps twenty years old? Seen some hard service somewhere over the years, though, and she needs a little tender care. I'd say she's just a little smaller than your ship the *Alice*. I need more time to give her a detailed look, but on the surface I don't see anything that couldn't be put to right with some time here in the Dockyard."

"Well, you shall have the time to make matters right, because The Leeward Islands Trading Company has acquired this as another asset and she needs someone like you to sail her. And we can't have you sailing about in your own ship unless its up to your standards, now can we? So what do you think? Now you know it's yours to command, do you still think she's a shabby old bitch?"

Lieutenant Cooke's mouth fell open momentarily before he mastered himself and peered about in disbelief, before turning back to Evan with his eyes narrowed and a questioning look. Evan couldn't contain himself any longer and simply nodded, laughing hard at the comic look on Cooke's face.

"My God—sir, thank you, sir! I can't believe this. She may be a shabby old bitch, but by God she looks like the most beautiful woman I've ever seen right now."

Evan was still laughing as he pulled the envelope from his pocket and handed it to the stunned Lieutenant.

"You know, that's exactly how I felt when I first took command of the *Alice*, which I trust you took good care of while I was away. And by the way, you'll be needing your commission paperwork in future, Commander Cooke."

This time his jaw fell open and stayed there as the new Commander reached out to take the envelope with a hand trembling a little. The wonder in his eyes made Evan laugh once again.

"Commander Ross, I don't know how to thank you. My God. This is something I've dreamt about for a long time and now it's happening it still feels like a dream."

"Well, I assure you it's not a dream and you don't need to thank me, thank the First Lord of the Admiralty. He seems to think we are useful and deserve some rewards. And by the way, you will have to get used to calling me Captain now, because I got one of those envelopes, too."

A broad smile lit Cooke's face as Evan finished speaking and he put out his hand.

"Captain! Permit me to be the first to congratulate you. I cannot think of anyone more deserving, sir."

"Thank you," said Evan, reaching out to grip Cooke's hand in return. "And now, lets get out of the sun and head for the office. I think a glass of some cool tea would be welcome while we bring each other up to speed on developments."

"Uh, sir? What about the crew?"

"Ah, yes, they are all Royal Navy. They seem a competent lot, at least based on their performance on the way here. You will have to take them out on a shakedown cruise and test their mettle, though. Also, they have no idea about the nature of our work. We will, of course, have to make some adjustments to make this look like its been turned into a merchant ship and we've got a bunch of paperwork to do for the Company to bring her into service. You will need to have the conversation with them about secrecy, too. You know what to say. You can do this once I give you some written orders to take formal command and you read yourself in. So let's disembark and you can fill me in on what I've missed."

"Thank you once again, sir," said Cooke, but a shadow fell over his face at Evan's words as they made their way off the ship to the dock. Evan had noticed the look on his face and asked about it once they were on shore.

"Yes, Captain, there is much going on as usual, but I confess there is one thing I know you will be displeased about."

"Oh? Well, out with it. What do I need to know?"

'Sir, there is no easy way to tell you, so I'm just

going to say it. An officer has shot and killed another officer in the Dockyard."

Evan's jaw fell open as he stopped in his tracks and looked at Cooke in disbelief.

"God Almighty, are you serious?"

"Sir, I am. I know how you feel, because I can't believe it myself. It all happened right after you left for England. You recall Lieutenant Wilton and I were tasked with a journey to Saint Domingue at the same time? We were thus absent too, although I'm not entirely sure our presence would have made much difference. There were only two ships in the Harbour at the time and it seems the two senior officers detested each other. The problem arose when the Lieutenant serving as First Officer of *HMS Favourite* was passed over for command, which was given to a junior Lieutenant. The First Officer apparently resented this, which was noticed, and he was given command of *HMS Perdrix* to resolve the situation. Unfortunately, a few days later it happened they were the only two ships in the Harbour and some sort of argument ensued over who was the more senior and who should take orders from who."

Cooke paused a moment to point to one of the Dockyard buildings before continuing.

"So I'm told it happened outside the capstan house. Both officers had men from their respective ships drawn up to defend themselves and the junior Lieutenant asked whether the senior was prepared to obey his orders. After being told a few times it wasn't going to happen, the junior officer accused the other of mutiny and shot him point blank."

"For God's sake, who are these bloody fools? Is the survivor still here?"

"Sir, the junior officer is Lieutenant Thomas Pitt, the second Baron Camelford. The deceased party was Lieutenant Charles Peterson. And yes, the Baron is indeed the nephew of our former Prime Minister. He is no longer on the island, sir."

Evan groaned, for all was now clear as to the source of the problem. This was not the first time a competent, senior naval officer found himself passed over for promotion by an often less competent, junior officer with important family connections. In Evan's experience, every time it happened it fostered nothing but resentment.

"So he's no longer here, you say? What happened?"

"Sir, the Governor ordered an inquest which took place the next day, but it proved inconclusive."

Cooke paused a moment for deliberate emphasis before continuing.

"The inquest determined Lieutenant Peterson's cause of death was mutiny, but they couldn't determine *who* the mutinous party was."

Cooke continued as Evan put a hand to his forehead and groaned again.

"Fortunately, *HMS Matilda* came into port soon after. The Captain took the Baron to Martinique where enough other Captains were present to convene a court martial, but the Baron was acquitted and he resumed command of *Favourite*."

"Which has obviously now left port," said Evan, unsurprised at the outcome. "Well, we will have to be careful if he puts into the Harbour again."

"Ah, but the story isn't over, sir. He did come back and, unfortunately, Mr. Wilton and I had still not returned. The Baron wanted some repairs done to *Favourite* and was unhappy it wasn't being done as fast as he thought it should be, so he assaulted our lead Shipwright. He was beaten rather severely and ended in hospital."

"What? God Almighty!"

"I'm told the Baron is a rather difficult individual to deal with. In any case, the Shipwright laid charges and this time the Governor had the Baron taken into custody. He was standing before the magistrates in St. John's and was told to post a bond to ensure his future appearance, but he rushed out of court, stole a horse, and tried to get back to his ship. They caught him, though, and he was forced to make arrangements for his bail. Meanwhile, the Governor got word of it all to the Captain of *HMS Matilda*. Soon after, he surrendered his command and was ordered to return to England, which he has done. And, perhaps needless to say, the people in the Dockyard were extremely happy to see me finally return."

Evan couldn't help a rueful, small laugh as they resumed walking to Evan's office.

"I'm sure. Well, I suspect you are right our presence might not have made any difference. When someone is a fool it usually ends badly regardless. So what else do I need to know? And by the way, where is Mr. Wilton?"

"The Lieutenant remained on station in Saint Domingue because of the fighting, sir. I assume you are aware of this?"

"I am. We got word in Barbados matters have settled down somewhat, but that the defenses surrounding Port-au-Prince were indeed taken. I suspected Toussaint L'Ouverture would hold off and rest his men. I expect the next step will be a list of his demands. We shall see soon enough. As an aside, Mr. Wilton has been promoted to Commander, too."

"Excellent news, sir," said Cooke as they entered Evan's office. "It is well deserved. So as you can see, I have attempted to keep the paperwork under control in your absence. This large pile over here awaiting filing consists of copies your clerk made of matters I have dealt with, in case you wish to review any. Unfortunately, the slightly smaller pile here are matters I would not presume to decide on your behalf. They are not urgent, but will have to dealt with sooner or later."

Evan groaned again as he sat down and surveyed the pile.

"It's all right, Commander. The pile is not unexpected, and is actually a little smaller than I thought it might be. Actually, you aren't done with it yet, I'm afraid. I neglected to mention in addition to your ongoing covert role you are going to assume the duties of Dockyard Commander I have fulfilled until now."

Evan spent the next hour with Cooke going over the details of his meeting with the First Lord and Sir James and what their new roles were to be. Evan wrote a set of orders for Cooke to take command of the *Stalwart* and the new Commander left clutching them as if Evan had given him a brick of solid gold for a gift, but not before they arranged to meet the next day to work on the transition of duties.

After another hour of sifting through his correspondence and paperwork Evan was growing tired, so he decided to wait for fresh eyes in the morning to deal with it all. But what looked like a possible letter from Admiral Horatio Nelson waited in the pile and Evan had to wrestle with the desire to read it at once instead of going straight home to his family.

The problem was Evan couldn't be certain it really was from Nelson. The envelope itself was consistent with the type and quality Nelson always used, but the handwriting on the cover of the envelope was strangely both familiar and not familiar at all. Evan sighed, unable to contain his curiosity, but as the envelope didn't seem overly thick he made the decision to read it. Using the small knife embedded on a wood block on his desk for this purpose Evan slit the envelope open and pulled out two slim sheets of paper. Within moments of beginning reading Evan slapped his forehead at his stupidity, as the letter was indeed from his former Captain.

Until recently Nelson was actively stationed for much of his career in the Mediterranean, but he had evacuated with the British forces in 1796 from the area. In the years since his reputation around the Fleet had grown exponentially because of his actions during the Battle of Cape St. Vincent in 1797, where he had left the line of battle in an unorthodox maneuver. With his 80-gun ship of the line he engaged and took two Spanish first-rate warships of superior firepower. After boarding and taking the first of the two ships he crossed from the deck of the first victim to board the second ship, which had become tangled with the first in the heat of the battle. The act became known as Nelson's patent bridge for boarding first rates and was a story being told around the Fleet over and over. Earning widespread respect from the hardened professional seamen of the Royal Navy was no easy feat, but Nelson's reputation as a fighting officer who would stand shoulder to shoulder with the common seamen in battle had now reached unheard of levels.

Word of the success and the devotion Nelson was inspiring in his men had long since reached Evan. He had cheered wholeheartedly to hear they had promoted Nelson and he was now a Rear Admiral, in addition to being made a Knight of the Bath by the King. But success had not automatically followed Nelson. In an attack on Spanish forces on the island of Tenerife in the Canary Islands a musket ball struck Nelson in his right arm. Saved by the quick action of his men to staunch the wound, Nelson was taken back to his ship and the arm was amputated.

Evan was devastated to learn of this and even more so by the irony of the two of them, connected by their shared experiences fighting smugglers on Antigua fifteen years before, now both knowing the pain of losing of a limb. When Evan was in London he learned Nelson was recuperating in Bath and word had come regaining his health was difficult, but few details were to be had.

The letter from Nelson Evan was now holding was proof he was now on the mend and adapting to his new circumstances, having to do everything including writing with his left hand. While he had obviously progressed to the point of being able to write legibly enough with his left hand, his writing style was still clearly rough and awkward. Evan had groaned aloud on first hearing Nelson had lost his right arm, for he knew Nelson was naturally right handed and he should have expected the handwriting on the envelope would be different. In his own case Evan was thankful it was his left arm and not his right he had lost, for he too was right handed. Learning how to function with only one arm was bad enough, but having to learn to function with the hand you wouldn't normally use seemed a cruel irony.

The letter filled in the gaps Evan did not know. A ligature used to close his wound had attached itself to a nerve and refused to let go for a long time. Nelson was not a man to complain about his health, but Evan knew from hard experience of his own how great the pain from such a wound could be and he winced at the thought of constant pain from the nerve.

Evan could think of no better place for Nelson to recover than Bath, though. Evan had spent time in Bath once before and he had fond memories of the beauty of the town nestled along the banks of the Avon River. The spa waters of its ancient Roman baths would ease Nelson's condition and its ancient, amazing Abbey Church would lift his spirits. As Evan continued reading he was overjoyed to learn all was now well as the ligature had finally detached before Christmas and Nelson had healed quickly after this. The other good news was they had offered him another ship and he would soon be back at sea, which helped his spirits most of all.

As Evan put the letter away and made ready to leave his thoughts drifted back over the years to 1784 when Nelson was stationed as a Captain in English Harbour. Evan and James Wilton had both been badly injured, but Nelson put them to use as spies to fight the rampant smuggling in the area. With no other options to be of service the two injured men gratefully accepted the opportunity and in the process uncovered a plot by French and American spies to disrupt the British grip on the area.

Ever since Evan and James had served on countless covert missions throughout the Caribbean on behalf of both the Foreign Office and the Navy. They had become so good at what they did no one had any thought of having them do anything else and adding Timothy Cooke to the mix in support became essential. When war with the French broke out in 1793 and the situation in Saint Domingue in particular came to the fore their workload increased exponentially. The pressure for useful intelligence was unrelenting and Evan was constantly grateful for the steadfast support of his two officers to deal with it.

Evan was also both grateful and amazed by Nelson's continued interest in him. They had maintained a steady correspondence with each other over the years and Evan long since learned Nelson's interest was genuine and unfeigned. The marvel was how a man with a workload such as his would continue to make time to correspond with a lowly officer such as himself and it spoke volumes about the kind of officer he was, for Evan had no doubt he was not alone in receiving letters from Nelson. He also knew Nelson was likely to have made representations in support of promoting Evan and his men along the way. As Evan closed and locked the door to his office he resolved to pen a reply the next day.

As he made his way to the Dockyard gate for the short walk to his home Evan's thoughts inevitably turned to Saint Domingue and his friend James Wilton. James had long since evolved from being just another colleague to become his First Officer and his closest friend. This was unique, for James Wilton was black.

With slave plantations and overt racism everywhere in the Caribbean a friendship such as this would not seem likely to an outsider, but the difference was the Royal Navy. Although racism existed in the Navy too, what mattered to most officers was whether you did your job properly or not. The professional respect you were given if you did it well was common, especially among those who had grown up in the Navy, like Evan and James. As they came to know each other they both realized they had much in common and liked each other. Having saved each other's lives on more than one occasion cemented the bonds.

But James was still on Saint Domingue and this made Evan frown as he returned the guard's salute and left the Dockyard gate. Evan knew all too well exactly how dangerous the island was, but he had little he could do until he returned there himself. The knowledge James was more than capable of defending himself gave comfort, but he also knew James had a way of finding trouble and he would need all of his skills. With little he could do for now Evan smiled at the thought of giving his friend the envelope from the First Lord. His smile broadened even more at the thought of soon seeing his wife Alice and his family.

***

Lieutenant James Wilton was immersed deep in a pile of paperwork, but the knock on the door broke his concentration. He grumbled a command to enter and scowled as he looked up to see one of the Army clerks on loan to them enter the tiny room set aside for their use as Evan's headquarters in Port-au-Prince, the capital of Saint Domingue. The clerk had yet another envelope in his hands and shrugged on seeing the look on the officer's face.

"God, must you?" growled James. "I swear, if you show up with any more of this shit for me to deal with after this I'll throw you into the harbour for the sharks."

The clerk shrugged and let a rueful smile appear on his face as he held the envelope out to show he knew James was joking.

"Sorry, sir. I promise I shall sit on whatever else shows up for the rest of the day. I was told to tell you this one apparently has some urgency to it."

James eyed the envelope with suspicion, expecting it might somehow grow fangs and bite his hand, but he sighed as he gave in. He motioned to the clerk to remain where he was as he tore it open and quickly scanned the brief, one page message it contained. James frowned as he put the message down on the desk and stared blankly at it as he considered its contents for several long moments. With a sigh he sat back in the chair as he made his decision and looked at the clerk.

"Pass word to my crew to be ready to sail with the tide this evening. If anyone asks after me I've been called to Santo Domingo and will be back in due course."

The clerk nodded and left as James resumed staring blankly into space, thinking through the ramifications of the message. James knew Evan would need to know what was happening, but the question was when Evan would be back from England to learn of it. James sighed again and shoved the paperwork he had spent the morning focusing on until now to a corner of the desk. Quickly composing his own short note he took both it and the message he had received and put them in an envelope he sealed and addressed to Evan for when he eventually did return.

As James rose from his chair and went to the door to give the envelope to the clerk he knew Evan would understand why James was dropping everything and sailing to the Spanish side of the island. They had both known this problem would appear on the horizon sooner or later and had hoped it would not be so soon. But it was happening now and information was the gold the Army needed to deal with it. Once again James and his men would have to provide it.

***

The squalls of unhappy children grew louder the closer Evan got to the home he had lived in for well over ten years now with his wife Alice. Evan smiled to himself, knowing the only reason they were unhappy was likely the fact dinner had not appeared on the table before the children as fast as they wanted it to. But the savory scent of something cooking in the kitchen was drifting on the light breeze and it made Evan realize he was hungry too.

As Evan got even closer he saw no one was in sight other than Evan's old dog Nelson. The dog lifted his grizzled head the second he heard Evan trudging up the path. The dog had been dozing in the shade on their verandah, which is what occupied most of his time at this stage in his life. But Evan's return always got a reaction and today was no exception. Nelson struggled to his feet and shuffled to the end of his leash, wagging his tail as he waited eagerly for Evan to come to him.

The fact the old dog had only three legs didn't make it any easier. He was a mongrel stray and had already somehow lost a hind leg when Evan took him in, saving him from an officer in the Dockyard who wanted him gone permanently. Because the dog was a fighter and a survivor both Evan and James had agreed he should be named after Horatio Nelson. As Evan scratched behind the dog's ears and talked to him the faint sounds of someone approaching came from the entrance to the house.

Evan looked around in time to see his wife Alice open the door and peer about with a frown which instantly turned to an expression of joy. She gave an inarticulate scream as she rushed over and wrapped herself around him in a crushing hug, rocking Evan back on his heels. Evan laughed as he held her tight with his arm, relishing in the feel of her body after so many long weeks away.

"My God, lover man, I missed you so bad! Thank God you're home. I had no idea you were back."

"Just docked a couple of hours ago, my love, and yes, I missed you bad, too."

Evan gave her a long, burning kiss, which she returned with unfettered pleasure. Both of them were used to the periodic absences from each other they were forced to endure because his duties took him frequently to other islands, but this trip was different. In total he had been away a little over two months and it was the longest separation they had ever had. When they finally ended the kiss Alice pulled back a little and gave him a direct look, her eyes narrowed.

"How long are you home?"

Evan pressed his lips together and gave a small shrug.

"Not long enough, my love. I am off to Saint Domingue again as soon as possible."

Alice sighed and frowned, unable to hide her disappointment. She simply held him tighter and was about to speak, but pandemonium broke out behind her as two small children burst through the door followed close by an older woman trying to bring them to heel.

"Not to worry, lover man," said Alice, with a quick glance over her shoulder. "I will prevail upon mother to take the children to visit her sister for a couple of days. We will just have to make the most of what little time we have, won't we?"

"Sounds like a damn fine idea to me," said Evan, making a point of caressing a breast for a brief moment out of sight of the children before they pulled away.

"You are such a beast, you know," said Alice, giving him one more sensuous, quick kiss as she whispered in his ear. "I like you as a beast."

"Evan, thank God you are home safe again!" said Alice's mother Anne as she collared the two children. "I'm sorry the children got away from me. Little imps."

"It's all right, Anne," said Evan, getting down on one knee to gather the two children into his arm and give each of them a long hug.

Being parents of these two small miracles was still a source of wonder to Evan. Little James Evan Ross, named for his best friend James Wilton, and his twin sister Manon Anne Ross, named after Alice's dead friend Manon, were almost a year and half old now and they seemed to be growing by leaps and bounds. When Evan had left for England the two of them were both still unsteady on their feet, but they were long past this now. Evan stood up and smiled at them before reaching into his pocket and pulling out a package.

"What do you think, my love? Is it too late to give them a little treat? I brought a little rock candy back with me from England."

Alice peered into the package with a questioning look on her face and Evan laughed, knowing she had never seen any before. With his encouragement she took a small piece out and put it in her mouth. Her face lit with surprise in moments.

"It's wonderful, it's so sweet," she said, smiling at the taste.

Evan doled out little pieces to the children and another to Anne, who all had the same reaction. The children liked it so much they clamored for more, but Evan shook his head and promised more tomorrow.

After dinner Evan sat on the verandah with a glass of wine to watch the sunset while Alice and her mother cleaned up and put the children to bed. Sitting outside was so pleasant Evan found his thoughts drifting while he waited for Alice to join him, feeling blessed to be at this point in his life with such a wonderful woman as his spouse.

The two of them had met years before when Evan was injured and abandoned by his Captain on Antigua. Alice was a young slave prostitute working in a tavern in St. John's when Evan met her while recuperating from his injury. When Horatio Nelson recruited him as a spy to ferret out smugglers Evan did the same to Alice, using her local contacts to gain information. With her help he succeeded and unearthed a devious plot by French and American spies to destabilize the British Caribbean in the process. Reward was promotion to command of the Dockyard, for there were no opportunities for an active commission at sea.

The even better reward was to fall in love with the most beautiful woman on the island and eventually make her his wife. Alice was the daughter of the richest white plantation owner on the island, while her mother Anne was one of his house slaves. Alice's hated father was in league with the French and American spies and she was more than happy to help Evan succeed. Evan had purchased Alice and her mother's freedom and they had lived in this house near the Dockyard ever since. In the process Alice had become part owner with other freed slaves of the Dockyard Dog Inn in the nearby town of Falmouth.

Through the years Alice had also joined Evan on several trips to other islands and had continued to help with covert activities wherever possible. She had been deeply involved in action on both St. Lucia and Grenada. The years had flowed one into the other with an endless series of missions to other islands, growing ever more dominated by the stark reality of the conflict on Saint Domingue. Evan had refused to bring her to Saint Domingue, unwilling to risk her in operations on such a volatile, dangerous place.

The consequence to marrying a black woman on an island where racism was so deeply engrained meant Evan received few invitations to local society events, but this didn't bother Evan. Although some officers in the Navy shared the prejudices of the plantation owners, most were more interested in the men under their command being competent at doing their job. Having grown up in the Navy, Evan was exposed to sailors recruited from all over the world and he had learned the folly of prejudices fast. If you were in the middle of a desperate fight and about to be cut down, the skin color of the sailor beside you deflecting the killing blow was irrelevant.

Evan was still staring at the sunset, lost in thought, as Alice finally joined him on the verandah and slipped her hand into his. He smiled and gripped her hand.

"The children are in bed, my love?"

"Took a while to settle them down, but they are now asleep. I don't think the rock candy and your return home helped matters."

Evan laughed and gripped her hand tighter, knowing it was a miracle they even had children. Alice had lost a child much earlier in their relationship and had almost died. The fear was another pregnancy might kill her, but she had wanted to try. Although the births were difficult, to everyone's surprise she had given birth to the twins. Afterwards she was warned not to risk any more pregnancies and they now used protection whenever they were in bed.

Evan looked over at Alice, seeing the fine lines and wrinkles around her eyes, and knew it was for the best they exercise care. Those same signs of age were written on his face too, and perhaps even more so, given the amount of time he spent outside on the deck of his ship in all manner of weather. A pregnant woman of her age didn't have the same endurance as one fifteen years younger. Alice returned Evan's look and gave him the broad smile he had come to know and love so well. Her dark eyes glinted as she spoke.

"We've been together a long time, haven't we, lover man?"

"We have."

"Which means I know what you are thinking. As it happens, mother knows how you think, too. She kindly offered to take the children to visit her sister in St. John's tomorrow for a couple of days without my having to ask. So we'll just have to make sure we're quiet about it tonight and then tomorrow we can be as noisy as we want."

Evan glanced at the last fading rays of the sunset on the horizon before turning back to her.

"Well, it has been a rather long time, hasn't it? Is it too early to go to bed?"

Alice let the smile on her face widen ever further.

"Hmm, I've never been to bed with a real Captain before, but I'd like to find out what it's like. Besides, those new rooms we had built for mother and the children are on the opposite side of the house anyway."

***

The harbor front of Port-au-Prince was a seething hive of ships of all shapes, sizes, and types. Evan was on edge as they sailed in, for in any other port in the world it was accepted larger ships had right of way due to their limited ability to maneuver easily, but everyone here went about their business on the blithe assumption everyone else would get out of the way. Making way to their usual berth alongside the docks set aside for the Royal Navy was thus a different experience every time the *HMS*

Alice sailed into port. Evan wasn't certain how it had evolved into this uncontrolled chaos, but the Army was too preoccupied with the situation on land to worry about what was going on out on the water. As they came closer and reduced sail Evan's sailing master grunted beside him.

"Nothing has changed about this place," he said, gesturing toward a Navy frigate and a much smaller merchant vessel making way out of port and across the course of the *Alice*. "Sir, if I may, we should consider altering course. I don't think those two—God Almighty!"

Even before the man finished speaking Evan was barking out orders to do what he suggested, as he had seen the possible collision looming too and wanted to be as far from the two of them as possible. With a deft maneuver at the last moment the frigate Captain managed to avert being struck broadside on by the smaller ship. The two Captains were now standing at the railings of their respective ships waving their arms and shaking their fists at each other. Evan couldn't hear the conversation, but well knew what they would be saying, because the same thing had happened to him on previous trips to this port.

Picking their way with care through the remaining hazards of the port they were finally able to breath easier and tie up at an open berth on the dock. As they did Evan finally relaxed enough to peer closer about. He frowned as he did, as he was trying to spot James's ship *HMS Penfold* without success as they came into port.

With the demands on their time growing every

year it had become abundantly clear *HMS Alice* wasn't enough and James required his own ship. Sir James Standish had successfully made the case and James was given command of the *Penfold*, which could have been a sister ship to *HMS Alice* they were so alike. Evan asked his sailing master if he had seen the *Penfold* on the way in and he shook his head.

Finding she was not in port was odd, but not completely unusual. The absence meant James was either off making contact with someone or something had happened to warrant investigation. Evan cursed the timing, because he was certain General Maitland would want to see him the instant he set foot on the island and being fully briefed by James on the latest developments beforehand would help.

As Evan stepped ashore he automatically looked warily about for anyone taking overt interest in his presence. Although they were within the perimeter of the heavily guarded, Navy controlled port area the possibility of prying eyes was everywhere. The *Alice* and the *Penfold* were both made to appear as if they were merchant vessels bringing in supplies for the Navy, but Evan knew on this island it likely didn't matter anyway, as everyone was suspicious of everyone else.

Two heavily armed sailors joined Evan on his orders as he made his way out of the Navy docks area and past the guards. The sailors were dressed in the same nondescript clothing Evan was. The unusually stifling heat of the morning made Evan wish for a cooling breeze, but he knew one might not appear until later in the day.

On the surface, at least, Evan and his men looked no different than a thousand other merchant sailors thronging the port. Although Evan was more than capable of taking care of himself in a fight, despite having only one arm, the two men with him were essential. A single man walking the streets of Port-au-Prince was an immediate target, but three such well-armed men gave would be thieves cause to look elsewhere.

The seething hive of activity on the water was matched a thousand times over by the chaos of the streets. The moment they were out of the Navy's domain they were engulfed by a tide of humanity going about their daily business. A polyglot of languages and accents ranging from English, French, Spanish, Dutch, American, and the local creole dialect assaulted their ears. Most of the people on the street were mulattos, but many were white. Heavily armed guards surrounded the few white women brave enough to be out. Yet more guards stood watch over the multitude of open-air shops selling all manner of savory foods or other wares. Despite the early hour taverns were packed with raucous merchant sailors coming and going with prostitutes on their arms. The only people on the streets wearing smiles were the drunks staggering in and out of the taverns.

As Evan made his way further past the densely packed, ramshackle shops and homes of the city toward Army headquarters situated on one of the nearby low hills they found the way blocked by a sudden surge of people trying to get out of a tavern in a mad rush. Close behind the surge was a large group of men clawing at and struggling with each other. The sickening crunch of clubs connecting with flesh and the screams of the victims grew exponentially as the number of combatants also grew. With no room to get away more and more people were dragged into the chaos because of the need to defend themselves. Within moments blood was seeping into the dusty street as men gasped out their last from knife wounds or crushed skulls.

"Shit," sighed Evan. "Not again. Right, backs to the wall till this mess sorts out. Swords will be useless in this. Dirks and cudgels at the ready."

A bare second later Evan was forced to smash the hilt of his dirk into the face of a man who appeared to have completely lost all control and was lashing out indiscriminately to get away. The assailant fell clutching his face and instantly paid an even worse price as another participant in the melee moved blindly backwards to avoid a blow and stepped hard on the man's crotch, eliciting a searing howl of pain. The two sailors with Evan were also lashing out with their cudgels and soon enough the chaotic crowd seemed to realize instinctively it was a bad idea to get too close to the three men.

Ten minutes later enough people had finally run far enough away to thin out the crowd, while the combatants still standing were tiring and looking around for ways to escape themselves. The need became urgent as the Army finally made an appearance as soldiers brought order to the scene with the butts of their muskets. Evan barked a command to his men to sheath their weapons and remain where they were as the tide of combatants running from the soldiers went past. As the chaos diminished and order was slowly restored a soldier saw them standing impassively against the wall and came over.

"Right, you lot. Move on, now," he said, motioning with his musket in the direction everyone else had gone.

"We will," said Evan. "Except we are going the direction you just came from. We are just waiting for matters to settle down."

The soldier scowled. "Are you deaf? You go where I bloody tell you to!"

"What's going on here?" said a young Army Lieutenant who had seen the confrontation and came over.

"Captain Evan Ross, Royal Navy, and these are my men, sir. We are on our way to see General Maitland. Got trapped by this nonsense."

The Lieutenant's eyes narrowed, as he looked Evan up and down, obviously puzzled by the lack of a uniform. But Evan had deliberately used an unmistakable tone of command in his voice, perfected from many years of use, and he knew the Lieutenant wouldn't fail to hear it. The Lieutenant nodded and stepped back respectfully as he made his decision.

"Very good, sir. Sorry we couldn't get here faster. Let's go, Jones."

As the two soldiers stepped away Evan saw they now had a clear path to move on and they resumed their journey. Minutes later they reached Army headquarters and after identifying themselves to the suspicious guards at the entrance Evan was soon on his way to the tiny office he shared with James, leaving the two sailors to lounge in the soldier's mess while they awaited his orders. On his way to the office a hail from behind stopped Evan and he turned to see General Maitland striding toward him with two Colonels in tow.

"Well met, Captain. I was not aware you had returned."

"I've not been back even an hour, General, let alone made it to my office yet. I was going to spend a little time catching up and then come to see you, sir."

The General nodded. "I understand. I am about to go into the meeting room here with some of the locals. May not be a long meeting as I suspect they aren't going to like what I have to say. Join us if or when you can. We need to talk."

Evan headed for his office as the General walked away. Thirty minutes later Evan had sorted through the pile of paperwork awaiting him, looking for the most urgent to read and deal with. The two most important were from his men. The hastily scrawled note from James was the first he opened and as he read it he understood at once why James had left. A vague report from one of his sources on the Spanish side of the island hinted at the long anticipated arrival of a senior French administrator happening. Whether he had come with additional troops or what his mission might be was unknown.

The other report of consequence was from the man Evan had insinuated into the inner circle of Toussaint L'Ouverture. One of Toussaint's senior advisors, a man named Julien Raimond, had recently been sent with little notice to Santo Domingo. Toussaint had not announced why this was happening, but it was unusual for a senior advisor to drop what he was doing and leave for the other side of the island. After quickly scanning the remainder of the reports waiting for him, Evan decided to go and join the General's meeting as the General would need to know of the looming arrival of yet another factor to consider.

Evan arrived at the meeting room as people began spilling out the door to leave. He recognized a number of the men leaving, having met several before on previous occasions. Most were wealthy members of what was known as the grands blancs class, although several others were local businessmen Evan knew had substantial interests in Port-au-Prince. None of them looked happy.

"I tell you, the time we feared is upon us, Raymond," said one man to another as they walked past Evan with scowls on their faces. "The goddamned British are doing nothing to protect us despite all their wonderful promises."

"I agree. He says the right things, but I'm not certain what to do, Pierre," replied the other. "We are still making money, are we not?"

"Yes, but for how long? The time to pull up stakes is coming fast."

More men drifted past and the snippets of conversation Evan heard echoed what the first two men said. As the room finally cleared out Evan peered in and saw the only men remaining were the two Colonels and the General. The General saw him and waved a hand for Evan to join them. Evan closed the door behind him and sat down, trying to read the General's face as he did. The General did not look any happier than the people who had left the room moments before.

The General introduced the two men with him as Colonel Francis Bains and Colonel Sydney Warrington. Both men were newly assigned to the Saint Domingue conflict, too. Colonel Warrington raised an eyebrow as the General explained what Evan's role was, but said nothing.

"So, Captain Ross, as you may have noticed the locals are not happy. Neither am I. The situation has gone from bad to worse. The capital here is not under attack as yet, but our foes are slowly making moves to put men in place to do that. Meanwhile, I've never seen such a level of—defeatism around me. I tried just now to put some spine into them, but it seems safe to acknowledge the cynics are winning the day, at least for now. I think fear of the guillotine is motivating the French émigré royalists in particular. My officers and I have been discussing options, but none of them are very palatable. So, I know you have only been back a short time, but I really hope you have some better news for me."

Evan sighed and shook his head, telling him what he had learned from the reports waiting for him. The General's face remained bland, but Evan knew it was a devastating message.

"I see," said the General once Evan finished. "Commander Ross, I need information about this and I need it fast. When do you think you will know more?"

Evan was about to respond when Colonel Warrington interrupted them.

"General, if there are even more Frenchmen on the horizon it is all the more important we regroup and pay this man L'Ouverture back as soon as possible. With respect, I don't know why we need to wait for the bloody Navy to tell us anything. Let's have at them, sir."

"Sydney," said Colonel Bains. "I can't agree. You weren't at the battle. I got here in time for the tail end of it and, I tell you, we took a pasting. Badly. The men are in no condition to face it again without more rest, reinforcements, and a sound plan."

"And there are no more reinforcements, as I have told you both," said General Maitland, with a hint of frost in his voice. "Captain Ross, your answer to my question?"

"General, it is now late March. If Commander Wilton has not returned by very early April I will go to Santo Domingo myself. I have full confidence in him, though. He knows our need and if anyone can get answers fast, it is Commander Wilton. Meanwhile, I will seek more information from my other colleague as fast as possible. We need to know Toussaint's thinking, perhaps even more than we need to know what is going on in Santo Domingo. I still believe he is going to make an offer to negotiate with you. He is undoubtedly aware you have arrived by now and you represent an unknown. But he won't make the approach until he is confident he has a winning hand. I think he knows attacking the city will make for an even worse bloodbath and this is why he is taking his time establishing a new perimeter around you."

The General nodded slowly. "I agree with you. Well, we have a little time to plan for some different courses of action. We will just have to make use of what we have. But Captain? Have you given any more thought to the idea of simply disposing of this man Toussaint? I realize it might result in someone worse appearing on the horizon, but it might also buy us more time."

Evan pressed his lips together as he considered the idea for a moment before responding.

"I will give it more thought, General. I will also raise the notion with my spy once again. I am not given to defeatism, sir, but events seem to be moving faster. We may be too late even for that."

Chapter Three
March 1798
Santo Domingo/Saint Domingue

As she settled in to wait at her favorite listening post Monique Desjardins let her thoughts drift. She knew the French Governor and the newcomer would be meeting soon and when the time came she would eavesdrop, as she had done so many times before.

She had lived in Santo Domingo long enough now the city was home and for a long time she felt it likely it would remain this way for the rest of her life. But she still wasn't ready to accept this as her fate.

The only daughter of a minor French diplomatic official and her English mother, she had come to Santo Domingo a little over forty years ago, when she was only eight years old. Her father had made bad investments and she was left with little money when both of her parents were carried away by the fever a few years after their arrival. With no one to send her back to France the Spanish Governor had taken pity and made the then teenage girl a servant in his combined headquarters and residence on the hill overlooking the river and harbor front of Santo Domingo. She had lived there ever since, serving successive Spanish and now French Governors, slowly saving everything she could from her meager wages for the day when she could escape and return home.

The question was where her home really was. She knew she was from somewhere in northern

France along the coast, but exactly where was lost, as was any record of relatives she might have there. What she did know was her English mother was from London, a place Monique had never been to. But she remembered the stories her mother told her of her far off home and, over the years, moving to London became her goal. She refused to give up hope some day she would get there.

Santo Domingo held no attraction for her whatsoever. She loathed the sticky, sweltering heat of the summers in particular. She would lie naked in a pool of sweat on many such nights and think of the cooler, pleasant temperatures she remembered from her childhood. She knew from her mother England would be the same. On such nights she also let herself fantasize of an English gentleman, perhaps even a knight, coming to take her away from the dreary routine of life in Santo Domingo.

And one day the man of her dreams appeared.

She was in the local market, shopping for a few personal items as she sometimes did, when a tall and fit looking man with light, coffee colored skin began talking to her. She couldn't remember much of their first conversation because she recognized his slight English accent right away and because she had fallen hard for his strikingly handsome looks. How he picked her out to talk to and why he did was a mystery, but he treated her with respect and seemed genuinely interested in her. By the time she came to understand he was a Royal Navy officer and was recruiting her to spy for England it mattered little, as she had already long since reached a point she would do anything for him.

Monique knew in her heart this man had no romantic interest in her. Being a rather plain, withdrawn woman meant few men had ever taken interest in her over the years and, when they did, they were in reality interested in only one thing. Being old enough she could easily be his mother didn't help. But the kindness he showed her hardened her resolve to escape her dull existence and find another kind Englishman to spend the rest of her years with. This officer was willing to pay her well, which also helped. She had saved more money in the two years since he had appeared in her life than in all of the previous thirty years as a servant combined. She hadn't quite saved the sum she thought she needed yet, but she was getting close.

In the meantime she was happy, enough she felt like a young girl again every time her handsome officer made contact with her. She was looking forward to another visit from him soon because of the report she had recently sent. Finding information to give him was easy, as Monique had lived in the Governor's headquarters so long she was like a piece of the furniture to the Governor and his minions, and may as well have been invisible. Her encyclopedic knowledge of every part of the building along with intimate knowledge of the routines of the people in it made her the perfect spy.

The sound of a door opening in the room below brought her focus back from the reverie she had drifted into. A series of small vents built into the stone of the walls allowed for air flow throughout the interior of the massive building and conveniently allowed for the transmission of sound along with it, a fact the successive Governors had not realized. As long as the people in the room below didn't whisper and no one else was making noise in the room she occupied, by listening close Monique could hear what was said. She smiled as two men began talking, knowing exactly who they were.

"So was the woman I had sent to you satisfactory, Theodore?" said Philippe Roume, the French diplomat who had assumed the role of Governor of Santo Domingo and the Spanish side of the island.

"Very much so, thank you," said the other man, who Monique now knew was Theodore Hedouville, a senior official serving the Directory, the group of men holding power in France since the French Revolution. "I confess her talents in the bedroom were enough she is coming back tonight."

The two men laughed before Hedouville continued.

"So have you had any word of when the representative from this man L'Ouverture will appear?"

"No, but I expect it won't be long now. I agree with your thinking it is best to make them come to you rather than the other way around, at least for this first meeting. I'd be surprised if he were in a rush to get here, though."

"So while we wait, Philippe, you started telling me the other day the situation here is somewhat volatile? What is happening?"

"The same as has been happening since the first

day we took over when it was ceded to us in the 1795 Treaty. These arrogant Spanish bastards still think they are in charge, despite the fact they are allegedly our allies now. There seems to be more than a few here who believe their compatriots back home are a bunch of weak-kneed incompetents who sold them out. Who knows, they may even be right. So I would like to tell you I could offer plenty of support by way of Spanish militia from this side of the island to help out in Saint Domingue, but I can't be certain of it. Getting them to actually do something they agree to is a struggle every time. I'm working on them, though."

"Hmm, you will have to work hard and fast, Philippe. The more I can bring to bear in Saint Domingue the better."

"What about you, Theodore? I saw only one troopship came with you? How many men have you brought?"

"A little over three hundred, Philippe. It was the best we could do right now, for the damned British and their allies have been pressing us. Of course, many of these are raw recruits, too. And you know this means they will need time and training locally before they are even close to being useful. The Directory has given me specific orders to use whatever resources I can muster locally and, between us, the idea and hope is to rely heavily on our Spanish allies."

"So I really must do more."

"Yes, you must, and do it fast, as I said. The British are in trouble in Saint Domingue and the time is now to make them pay the price. But what about this man L'Ouverture? Is he as arrogant as I hear?"

"I've not met him, but I've heard the same stories. He seems to be a rather devious bastard. I've heard he sees himself as a patriotic Frenchman at heart, but he also wants to rule the entire island and not just Saint Domingue. "

Hedouville grunted. "Well, no matter, he does not have the power of France behind him. He will toe the line or find himself on the outside or worse, because it is the Directory who decides who rules. And as it happens, out here right now I am the Directory. Well, enough, let's go get a drink somewhere, shall we? This room seems stuffy."

"I have a bottle of very good French wine waiting for us on the big balcony upstairs which overlooks the river. We can sit in the shade and get a nice breeze."

Monique heard the two men's chairs scrape the floor when they stood up to leave and moments later she heard the door close. She smiled to herself as she got up to leave, too. She would have plenty to report to her handsome officer when he came.

***

The first time *HMS Penfold* sailed into Santo Domingo over two years ago she was flying an American flag, giving no indication she was anything other than what she usually pretended to be, an American merchant vessel. Because of more recent tensions between France and the Americans, this time she flew a Spanish flag. To maintain the fiction of being a trader the *Penfold* maintained a supply of American dry goods and timber on hand to trade at all times, using the ruse they had smuggled it out of America. James knew no one would complain despite the tensions, as Santo Domingo needed the American goods as much as ever.

Three members of the crew were Spanish and one was tasked with pretending to be the Captain, while the others made certain the local port authorities could hear their Spanish voices at every opportunity. James had deliberately recruited them for exactly this purpose. Being loyal Spaniards, the men absolutely loathed the thought of being allied to the French and were most happy to be part of the Royal Navy.

With the formalities over and one of his Spaniards off contacting local merchants looking for interest in buying their wares, James ensured the rest of his men knew their jobs for the day and turned his mind to making contact with his spy. James knew Monique would be aware of his arrival, as the Governor's headquarters had a commanding view of the port and she knew what his ship looked like. The routine they had established was for her to leave a message in a prearranged, hidden spot only the two of them knew of, naming a choice of locations to meet along with a time. Each location had its own code name to keep the meeting place a mystery should anyone stumble inadvertently on the message. Although they had only been in port a few hours, the possibility existed she had already left him a message, so his next step was to check the location.

On the way into the harbor James saw what

was likely part of the reason for the urgent message from his spy. One of two French warships tied up at the docks was a frigate, while the other appeared to be a large troopship. Neither was present in the harbor the last time James was in Santo Domingo.

James made his way to the boarding ramp to leave the ship and with his normal caution he automatically began scanning the people thronging the docks, looking for signs of trouble. As nothing stood out he was about to step off the ship when he stopped in his tracks and swore aloud. One of his men had to step back in a hurry to get out of his way as James turned in a rush to stand behind the main mast.

"Sir?" said the puzzled sailor.

"Someone I don't want to know I am here," said James, ignoring more puzzled looks from other men on deck as he peered around the mast, staring hard at two men who were passing by the *Penfold* in deep conversation. The men carried on past the ship, giving no sign they had paid any attention whatsoever to the newcomer in the harbor. James stepped out from behind the mast and scanned the dock front with care once more before telling his bosun he would be back before nightfall. Stepping off the ship he joined the passing crowds of people in time to stay behind the two men while keeping a comfortable distance between them.

As he wound his way through the crowd, matching the pace of the two men, James wrestled with the belated thought he should have brought one of his men with him in the event his quarries separated. The response to this notion came a millisecond afterwards and James gave himself a mental shrug, knowing he had needed to act fast. But even if he discovered nothing else, simply learning of the mere presence of these two men was worth gold.

On the surface the men he was following appeared as unremarkable as James himself. Both were wearing nondescript clothing allowing them to blend easily into the polyglot of sailors, merchants, and dockhands populating the harbor front. In reality, they were French spies and deadly foes James had first met two years before on the island of Grenada. They had wanted to kill James outright and James had no doubt they would still want to try if they knew of his presence.

At the time James had infiltrated a rebel camp of local mulattos struggling to wipe their British masters entirely off the island. The rebel leader, Julien Fedon, had sympathy and ties with the French on Guadeloupe, who were supplying them with arms. The two men James was now following were the French contacts with the rebels. James had only survived because he had already established a relationship as an advisor to the rebel leader and remained under his protection.

The two Frenchmen were formidable foes to Evan and James, and likely had been for many years now. Hubert Montdenoix was the senior of the two, while Flemming Linger was his assistant. In the years following the French Revolution the new government had taken an aggressive stance, seeking to export their ideals beyond their borders. Evan and James had soon sensed they had opponents serving in the same way they did in the Caribbean, even if they had not met them. The two Frenchmen had made numerous attempts to bribe, extort, or threaten people for information on every British island. More than a few of those people had ended up dead, including sources Evan and James had recruited for their own purposes.

As James continued following them he debated his course of action. Having the two men unaware of his presence was an advantage, but exactly how he could use it was unclear. If he could somehow get one or both alone the opportunity to kill them would be too good to pass up. Removing both of them from the fight would be a serious blow to French efforts to return to a dominant role in Saint Domingue.

With every step the two men were coming closer to the area cordoned off for the two French warships in the harbor and James assumed this was their destination. He was about to stop and return to his own ship, not wanting to get too close, when the two men detoured into a waterfront tavern. They settled into a table and chairs the owner had set out front to afford patrons a view and ordered drinks from the server who soon appeared.

Their sudden detour meant James had to make his own abrupt deviation in his path to remain undetected, coming to stand just inside the shade of an alley between two nearby buildings. He remained peering around the corner and watching the two men for a couple of minutes while he debated what to do, but a voice behind him demanding in French to know who he was and what he was doing ended his vigil.

James had learned French years before and knew exactly what he was being asked, but he feigned ignorance of the language as he turned to look at the man asking the questions. The man was attired like a typical French sailor and had the telltale rough hands of one. The sailor scowled when he saw James wasn't responding and pointed at the tavern where the two men were, demanding to know if James was following them.

James feigned ignorance of the language once again and looked aside, drawing the man's attention away from him. James was relieved to see no one on the street was paying the two men in the alley any attention, so he made his move. He grabbed the sailor by the throat in an iron grip, preventing the man from crying out. As the sailor made to pry the hand away James drove his knee hard into the sailor's groin. The man crumpled before him and James pulled him further into the dark shade of the alley, looking around to see if anyone was paying attention. No one was and with a sigh James turned his attention back to his victim, knowing he had no choice because the sailor could identify and describe him.

James kept one hand over the sailor's mouth as he drove his dirk into the man's back where his heart would be. After rifling though the man's pockets he shoved the meager supply of coins he found into his own pocket, attempting to make it look like robbery was the motive. Covering him with some refuse in the alley as best he could, James wiped his dirk clean and left the alley without attracting attention.

After walking a short distance away he made a sudden stop with the ease of long practice, feigning an interest in the wares of a waterfront fishmonger. In reality he was using his peripheral vision to scan for anyone following him who had to duck out of sight, but he saw no one. James circled slowly back, coming to stop at a new spot to close enough to observe his quarries once again. But even as he settled into his new post the two French spies finished their drinks and left the tavern, heading once again for the French warships.

James remained where he was as the two men walked away, cursing his stupidity for not having brought another of his men with him. Being able to follow them and learn more of what they were up to would be a golden opportunity, but James was the only one of his crew who knew what the two spies looked like. James resolved to solve this by bringing two men who could understand French next time and by wearing a disguise to ensure the two French spies didn't see him. Whether he would get another opportunity was another matter.

But now, it was time to check the message drop and meet Monique. James smiled at the thought, as he was well aware the woman had fallen for him. He had refrained from taking her to bed, as he had learned of her fantasy to leave Santo Domingo and make a home in England with an English gentleman. The fact he hadn't mocked her fantasy and actually encouraged her to dream of a better life only endeared him more to her. He realized she was a simple, kind soul and felt she deserved better in life. James was happy to pay her well and do what he could to make her dream come true, because while her dream was not his, she reminded him of his own mother and he liked her.

***

"So you have no idea whether this murder was a simple robbery gone wrong or something more nefarious, Theodore?"

Hedouville shrugged as he stepped away from staring out the window and turned to face Philippe Roume.

"Who knows? My two advisors see plots and British spies everywhere. Of course, it is their job to ferret them out and, God knows, the damned British have been active. But the evidence seems to point to robbery and unless they find something, this is what I am going to assume. Even if the British are spying on us I don't think it would change anything anyway. We will be more vigilant, of course."

"The waterfront is a dangerous place, Theodore. Well, what do you think, have we made this pompous peacock wait long enough?"

"No. First, he took his time getting here and then when he does arrive, he acts like he owns Santo Domingo. And, my God, I've never seen anyone dressed so garish in my life. Does his master L'Ouverture dress like this too?"

"No idea, but I wouldn't be surprised. Let's take our time finishing our drinks."

Fifteen minutes later they finally made their way into the meeting room, where a tall, black mulatto man was waiting for them. The man rose from his chair to greet them, but was unable to master himself fast enough to remove the frustrated look from his face before the two Frenchmen came in. As they stepped closer Hedouville once again marveled at the man's flashy attire and realized it was a deliberate attempt to impress. Fully half of the man's apparel was styled as a French Army officer's uniform, while the rest was modified with added frills and a riot of colors.

The newcomer introduced himself as Julien Raimond, advisor to Toussaint L'Ouverture. After Roume had drinks brought to the three men and the server left, Raimond thanked the two Frenchmen for seeing him.

"Gentlemen, my General Toussaint L'Ouverture desires me to extend greetings to both of you and a welcome to our island in particular to the new representative of France. We knew some day a new man would come and we hoped it would be sooner. He seeks to understand your thinking so we may work together to defeat our common enemies. My General desires to lead Saint Domingue to realize its true destiny as the shining star of the French Caribbean and, indeed, of the entire French speaking world."

Hedouville smiled. "Excellent. I am certain we can find a role for your master in achieving this lofty goal. But first we must deal with more mundane matters, such as purging the greedy British pirates from Saint Domingue once and for all. Unfortunately, my predecessors let the overall situation in Saint Domingue get entirely out of hand. Yes, it's true; France itself had a role in making the situation what it is today. We were preoccupied with matters at home and the damned plantation owners out here, who in reality are secret royalists at heart, welcomed the British with open arms. No, Saint Domingue has been in dire need of a firm, guiding hand from France, and I have been sent to fulfill the role."

"I see," said Raimond, his face remaining bland. "And once we shove the British back into the sea, what is your role then, sir?"

"The need for a guiding hand will not disappear, of course. I am here to bring order to this chaos. I don't anticipate this will take long. There are much larger considerations than just what is going on in Saint Domingue, you understand, and we must pull together under French leadership for the common good."

Raimond frowned and sat back in his chair, silent for a moment.

"And what are these larger considerations, sir? I merely seek to understand better so I may report to my General and he may best prepare to help, you understand."

"Of course. I'm sure your General is a fine man and we will achieve much together, but his focus is solely on what he sees before him. Yes, Saint Domingue is undeniably important, but there is more to the world than this. It is the wider world France must deal with and it is full of peril. There are many who oppose the enlightenment our Revolution has brought and seek to stamp it out. We must not let them prevail."

"My friend Theodore here is right, Julien," said Roume. "As I have pointed out before in my letters to Toussaint, there is much more to the business of leadership than simply bearing arms against enemies. One must understand the realities of the larger world and the area you live in."

"And what are those realities, sirs?"

"Well, the British are an obvious reality," said Hedouville. "They have been a constant thorn in our side here in the Caribbean for a very long time. But the tide has turned against them and I think we should keep the pressure on. They crown jewel of their assets in this area is Jamaica. Can you not see this is where we should strike? The blow of losing Jamaica would be so great they would lose all interest in efforts to maintain a significant presence in the Caribbean. And once we have done that, there are the Americans to deal with."

"The Americans? What do they have to do with us?"

"The Americans are proving—difficult. France supported them with our money, our military, and by providing arms during their Revolution. And what do they do? They now refuse to pay the loans we made to them, claiming the money was owed to the old royalist regime in France. Then they sign the Jay Treaty and begin trading with our enemies the British. And now we hear they are arming their own warships to fight us! Yes, it's true our privateers have been seizing American merchant vessels and stripping them of cargo meant for the British. What do they expect? I don't know how they justify this outrageous behavior."

"So the point here, Julien, is the Americans are not your friends," said Roume. "Added to this is they are laying claim to yet more of our Spanish allies holdings on the continent. You can stay focused all you want on this small island, but the larger world will intrude on you sooner or later."

"And this means what, exactly?" said Raimond.

"It means we should be giving thought to invading them to put an end to their threat. Our possessions—I mean, those of our allies on the continent cannot be forgotten. France has a long history in New Spain and we must work together to build a bulwark against the greedy Americans there. If we fail in this it may well be they will be knocking at the door here with their warships."

"I see. You must forgive us if we have not understood. As you say, we have been focused on our own situation and have not seen the much greater picture you describe. I shall do my best to help my General understand and prepare for your arrival. If I may, I observed when we sailed in you have two warships with you, but one appears to be a troopship? Have you brought many men? Are more coming?"

"Oh, I have brought several hundred well trained men with me. I have been assured more will follow in due course, but I personally doubt they will be needed, as we have the loyal armies of your commander and those of our Spanish allies here on this side of the island. Your commander's men have proven themselves in battle and I have no doubt they will acquit themselves well in Jamaica or wherever else they are needed. Of course, if matters don't go as the Directory desires here then more resources will be found to bring about the outcomes we are looking for."

"So there you have it, Julien," said Roume. "I trust this will help your General understand. Do you have any other questions? If not, I shall make arrangements for dinner. I can also promise you arrangements for your bedroom later tonight if you wish."

Hedouville laughed. "You should take him up on the offer. I did and I'm not regretting it."

"Thank you, but my wife takes care of all my needs and more. I would like to go now and consult with my aide to ensure I can answer all of the questions my General may have. I look forward to dinner and discussing this further, though."

Hedouville sat in thought for a long moment. This man Raimond had not proved as arrogant as he had expected. Hedouville had anticipated blunt threats and haughty demands, not a relatively mild mannered, respectful composure, and a willingness to simply listen. Hedouville wondered if this man L'Ouverture was indeed more subtle and devious than he was giving him credit for, but Hedouville rose from his chair to signal agreement to end the meeting. Whether this man L'Ouverture was highly intelligent or not mattered little, as he would have to step in line or face the consequences. Hedouville was completely unaware Monique was smiling once again in the room above him as he led the other two men leaving the room.

***

James favored the local market for connecting with Monique and, as long as it was operating, it was an excellent location to meet and debrief. The market was crowded as always, with vendors selling wares of every kind. A riotous display of local fruit and vegetables, spices, clothing, hand made trinkets for the sailors, and meat of all kinds filled the tables and stalls. The fish sellers were the most noisome of the vendors, for the longer their mornings catch sat the smellier it became, making it less likely to be sold at all.

The crowds and the noise of the market meant it was impossible to be overheard unless the listener was standing right beside you. Anyone following James or Monique would also have to stay in close proximity or risk losing them in the warren of stalls and meandering paths through the market. With his years of experience, in these circumstances James could identify an opponent in seconds. By stepping to the side in the gap between two stalls they could pretend to be going about their separate business, while not looking at each other and still having a conversation.

In the two days since his arrival James had haunted the waterfront in disguise, hoping to catch either one or both of the French spies unawares. Neither of them had appeared and the two warships were now showing the telltale activity of ships being readied to leave. James was frustrated the two Frenchmen hadn't showed themselves, but he felt certain more opportunities would be forthcoming. Besides, James had what he needed.

James had felt a chill on hearing the details of what Monique overheard, despite the warmth of the day. He and Evan had discussed what they thought French intentions might be many times, but to hear confirmation the French would seek to expand their domain exactly as they feared was still daunting. James paid Monique even more than usual, assuring her the information she had provided was vital. He even gave her a quick hug of gratitude before disappearing into the maze of the market.

James had learned what he came for and if the French warships were leaving he had no need to remain longer. Evan needed to know what was happening.

***

The meeting room in Mirebalais, not far from the capital of Port-au-Prince, could have been stuffy in the heat of the day, but a light breeze came through the two large, open windows of the room. They were sitting in a room occupying a corner of the fortifications on the perimeter of the town, recently captured by L'Ouverture and his men.

"And that is everything they said?" said Toussaint L'Ouverture, rubbing his chin in thought.

Toussaint was sitting at the head of a large table. A variety of key advisors and various army commanders occupied several seats around it. They had all been listening to the recently returned Julien Raimond's report of his meeting with Hedouville and Roume in Santo Domingo.

"It is, my General," said Raimond.

The men around the table were silent in thought as they digested what they had heard, aware Toussaint would expect comment from his senior people. Although there were almost a dozen other men present, everyone was also aware there were only a few men Toussaint would in reality listen to.

Three of them were senior army commanders. Jean Jacques Dessalines, a huge black man with a forceful personality, was the most dominant of the three. But L'Ouverture had made room for a few key civilian advisors as well, in addition to Julien Raimond. Jean Francois Pierrot, a mulatto with striking good looks, owned one of the largest slave plantations in the areas of Saint Domingue not controlled by the British and was always another voice L'Ouverture paid attention to. Pierrot was a match for Dessalines with the arrogance of his character and he usually tried dominating proceedings by shouting everyone else down. Between the two of them it was often difficult for anyone else to get into conversations around the table.

But the other civilian, a man who went only by the name Baptiste, a handsome, young mulatto himself, had grown accustomed to their styles and adapted, making certain his own perspective was always heard. The others at the table grudgingly came to accept the remaining civilian advisor Toussaint would pay attention to was going to be heard whether they liked it or not. Because he was very good at his job the fact Baptiste was also a British agent and a serving midshipman in the Royal Navy had escaped all of them.

Baptiste had honed skills he had no idea he had in the years since Evan Ross and his men rescued him from a French dungeon in St. Lucia in 1793. Baptiste was the senior slave to his deeply loved French royalist family on his home island of St. Lucia and was shocked when French revolutionaries murdered the husband. When in a fit of rage Baptiste killed a soldier trying to rape the owner's wife he was thrown in jail to wait on a date with the guillotine. On a high risk mission to save a French royalist officer from the same guillotine Evan had taken a chance and freed Baptiste. Baptiste was so grateful he had sworn undying allegiance to Evan, joining his crew on *HMS Alice*.

Baptiste quickly became indispensable, learning every task set for him. He initially saw service as a cook, but with a stunning thirst for learning he absorbed in less than two years a decade's worth of knowledge in every role on a Navy warship. Men who knew their job and did it well commanded respect in the Royal Navy, and Evan's crew were soon affording him the respect he deserved. They also loved him, for his cheerful demeanor and refusal to worry about anything endeared him to everyone.

Two years before Evan had sent Baptiste in to support James in his attempt to infiltrate the rebel camp in Grenada. Baptiste succeeded beyond Evan's expectations and since had served in numerous covert roles on a variety of dangerous missions throughout the Caribbean. Being fluent in English and French along with being able to hold his own in Spanish was a boon.

His continued success and dedication led Evan to muse about finding some way to reward him. When Evan announced to his crew he was making Baptiste a midshipman, which was essentially a Navy officer in training, he was gratified to hear the men cheer loud and long enough to make Baptiste blush. Evan had no power to appoint him a Lieutenant as reward and, as Baptiste was in his late twenties now, it was unlikely he ever would be. But Evan told him he couldn't think of a more deserving or better candidate to be a Navy officer.

As matters began deteriorating on Saint Domingue over two years before Evan pondered ways to gain better intelligence than they had, knowing the need was becoming desperate. When he approached Baptiste to talk about the dangerous mission Evan had in mind, Baptiste agreed without even hearing the details.

Evan told Baptiste he would have to create a story for the black leaders on Saint Domingue to believe if he wanted them to accept Baptiste into their councils. Armed with plenty of British gold, Baptiste made a show of his arrival on a merchant vessel from St. Lucia, making an even bigger scene for all to see when he purchased a small plantation from a royalist planter who was desperate to get out of the morass Saint Domingue was becoming and escape to America.

As Baptiste settled in he also made a point of ensuring everyone knew he had run from his servitude on St. Lucia to serve as one of the rebel fighters for Julien Fedon's lost cause on Grenada. When questioned about the source of his wealth he would smile, confessing it was indeed gold he had stolen from British plantation owners in the chaos of the final days of Fedon's Rebellion. When the British finally let their guard down some months after the fight Baptiste claimed to have dug up the gold from where he had hidden it and fled to Saint

Domingue.

He brought with him a young black woman from St. Lucia he recruited to help with the fiction. Knowing if he succeeded in his task his movements could be watched, the need for someone to serve as a conduit to pass messages to Evan became imperative. Sylvia was a stunning, lithe young mulatto woman in her early twenties he had encountered on one of his more recent missions back to St. Lucia. The daughter of an itinerant English businessman trying to run a tavern on the island and one of his slaves, she found herself forced to work as a serving girl when both of her parents were killed during reprisals stemming from the declaration of war between England and France.

The two of them had felt an instant, electric connection to each other the moment they saw each other and Baptiste knew he had to have her. She readily agreed to become his woman, long before he shared the reality of who he was and what he was doing. When he did she reacted with enthusiasm, as the fury deep inside her over the injustice of her parent's murder was still burning hot. The fact she spoke both English and French fluently was an added bonus. For the purpose of their mission in Saint Domingue Baptiste began referring to her as Sylvie, the French version of her name.

Toussaint L'Ouverture took notice of this young, attractive couple, seeing a willing, intelligent supporter of his cause. Baptiste and Evan were overjoyed when within six months of his arrival a surprise invitation to dine with the black leader appeared, a certain sign the plan was working. Baptiste made the most of this and several subsequent dinners. His story of coming to Saint Domingue because he had heard of Toussaint and had hopes he could be the successful leader Julien Fedon on Grenada had failed to become was wondrous music to the ego of Toussaint. Toussaint was impressed by the thoughtful comments on the current situation Baptiste offered during the dinners and within another few short weeks Baptiste became a regular fixture at Toussaint's councils.

And, not for the first time at these councils, Dessalines slammed a meaty fist onto the table, making almost everyone give a small start of surprise.

"Toussaint," he growled. "This is bullshit! Why don't we just send this arrogant bastard Hedouville packing, like we did with Sonthonax?"

Toussaint winced and shrugged as everyone else at the table tried to speak at the same time. Predictably, it was Pierrot who finally shouted loud enough to get everyone's attention, and Baptiste smiled inside, knowing the two men would dominate the conversation for the next five minutes. As usual, Pierrot took a contrarian position to Dessalines, expressing concern over the wider implications Hedouville had outlined to Raimond. After the debate had raged on for over five minutes Baptiste saw Toussaint was looking at him directly and he smiled. At the next opportunity Baptiste interrupted and turned to Toussaint, who had still not said anything to this point.

"Toussaint, if I may? Sadly, as we have discussed before, France speaks of the equality of men, but it is not clear to me their actions are matching their words. It seems this man Hedouville obviously does not understand things have changed and that you are a capable leader. He also fails to understand you are a true Frenchman and really do support France and the revolution. Really, when you think of it, why should a white man lead an island populated almost entirely with black people? In any case, it seems to me the key to his approach is the idea he will use the Spaniards in Santo Domingo to enforce his will upon you. Yes, he has brought more French troops with him, but it is only one such ship. How could so few affect the outcome here?"

"They can't," said Dessalines, anger suffusing his face. "And neither will the damned Spanish. We beat them before and we can do it again."

"Hmm, perhaps," said Toussaint. "But we cannot rest on past achievements and assume we will prevail every time. Perhaps the Spanish have been coerced into supporting him or they have truly turned their coats and are now actively supporting him? Damn it, this complicates matters. I agree with you and I need to know if this bastard Roume will be following behind Hedouville with a Spanish army at his back. I foresee more negotiations coming and it will make all the difference if I know the answer to this. Can any of you help here? Any suggestions?"

A silence descended on the table as they all gave the idea thought. Baptiste knew instantly what his answer was, but he gave them time to come up with something. After enough time lapsed Baptiste sat forward.

"Toussaint? As it happens, I used to travel on occasion around the islands for my former master on St. Lucia and I still know good people in Santo Domingo. Perhaps I could write them, find out what the real state of affairs is there? Even better, I could send Sylvie to talk to them. No one will be suspicious of a black woman from Saint Domingue. They will tell us if the army is supportive of what this man Roume wants. In the meantime, you have consolidated your positions here now, have you not? Why not move another chess piece on the board and open direct negotiations with the British? I think the time has come. After all, you are the one in charge here, not this man Hedouville."

Toussaint rubbed his chin in thought before nodding his assent.

"Yes, send her, and do it as fast as possible. We must prepare for this man Hedouville's arrival. I will stall him as much as possible until I hear from you. I also agree with you about who is in charge and this means I must also work on the damned British with negotiations, too. Besides, if I open direct talks with them before Hedouville gets here it will be sure to annoy him. Well, lets see if I can outwit both of them."

The men around the table laughed, as everyone was well aware Toussaint was a master negotiator. Baptiste laughed along with them, but for his own reasons. He would send Sylvie to Saint Domingue for appearances, but in reality whatever he ended up telling Toussaint would be coming straight from Evan Ross.

As the meeting broke up and Baptiste made his way back to the quarters he was assigned in the fort he was already composing his report to Evan in his mind. He knew Evan would be pleased.

Chapter Four
April 1798
Saint Domingue

Evan was taking his time eating his breakfast on board the *Alice*. Although he had no lack of things to do, nothing urgent was on the horizon. The only decision of import was whether today would be the day to leave in search of James, but even as he turned his mind to the issue a knock on the door to his cabin intruded on his thoughts. He called a command to enter and his master's mate, the most senior warrant officer on the *Alice,* came in and saluted.

"Captain? You wanted to know when the *Penfold* returned to port? She is sailing in right now. She looks to have sustained some damage."

"Damage? What kind of damage?"

"Rigging doesn't look right, sir. We think she's missing a spar."

Evan frowned. "I'll be on deck directly."

As the man saluted and left Evan ate the remainder of his meal in a hurry, his mind running over the possibilities. Although hurricane season was months away, tropical storms of lesser intensity were possible at any time of the year. The weather two days before was stormy and Evan wondered if it had something to do with this.

He gained the quarterdeck as the *Penfold* was maneuvering slowly to a berth beside the *Alice*. He saw James and breathed a sigh of relief before making his way over to their berth. As a boarding plank was finally dropped to the dock Evan was the first to use it. He peered about at the obvious damage as he made his way to the quarterdeck where James was waiting.

"My God, what happened to you?" said Evan.

"Sorry, Commander. We would have been here much sooner, but what could go wrong did. Can I offer you something while we talk?" said James, pointing in the direction of his cabin.

Once they were settled and tea had appeared for them James resumed his story.

"We ran into a French privateer who took an interest in us, despite the Spanish flag we were flying. I deemed it best to run and we lost them in the night. This took me well off course, naturally. The next day we ran into an unusually heavy squall moving way faster than I thought. Apparently we had a weakness in the spar we are missing, because it split under the pressure. It was a total mess. Had to heave to at night and sort it all out. Would have been here two days ago were it not for all this. And I wish it were so, because I have urgent news."

"As do I. So let me get to what really matters first. Congratulations, Commander Wilton," said Evan, pulling out the envelope with the commission papers from a pocket and passing it across to James. "This is for you, direct from the First Lord of the Admiralty."

With eyes wide James stared at the envelope as if it contained some fairy treasure about to disappear at any moment. When he finally looked up at Evan, who was still holding the envelope out for James to take, Evan smiled.

"I assure you, it's real. And by the way, you

will have to get used to calling me Captain now, because I got one of those, too. Lieutenant Cooke is also now a Commander like you. Good news all around. If the spirit of your father is out there somewhere and somehow knows of this, I have no doubt he is unbelievably proud of you."

James finally took the envelope and stared at it for a moment longer before standing up and walking over to stare out the stern windows. Evan remained sitting where he was, knowing exactly what was going through James's mind. James's father was serving as a Lieutenant in the Royal Navy when he had died of fever in the Far East. For the son to now surpass the father in rank was a moment to savor. After a few more moments James finally walked back over and sat down again.

"Sorry—Captain. I needed a moment."

"I know you did. I did, too. We've both been through a lot together and we deserve this. Well, let's get down to business, shall we?"

Much had happened in the two months since Evan had left for England and it took them almost two hours to fully debrief each other. Evan groaned when James revealed the presence of the French spies Montdenoix and Linger.

"God Almighty, did Baptiste ever meet them when the two of you were spying on the rebels in Grenada? If he did and they follow this man Hedouville to Saint Domingue, Baptiste could be in serious danger."

"Hard to say, Evan. They didn't show up often at Fedon's headquarters on his estate, but Baptiste was certainly around when they did. I don't remember a specific time when they were in the room at the same time as Baptiste and me. It is possible they may have seen him doing whatever tasks on Fedon's estate, though. If so, the question becomes would they remember after over two years? Most of the time servants are invisible to people, but who knows? These two specialize in paying attention to things other people maybe don't and they aren't above using servants as spies, just like us."

"Well, I've got to get a warning to him about this. Your ship is in no shape to take it just yet, so I will get underway and craft a message to him along the way. In the meantime get your repairs done fast. I don't like how quickly events seem to be moving around here and we need to be ready for anything. We will have to get patrols to our contact location more often, in case Baptiste has to make a run for it."

As the two men rose from their chairs a knock came on the door to James's cabin. One of James's men came in when ordered with another man in tow who Evan knew was an Army clerk.

"Sirs? This gentleman claims to have a message for you."

"Captain Ross, General Maitland desired me to find you. I am to advise you a message has come in from this General L'Ouverture. Apparently it is an offer to negotiate. General Maitland desires to discuss this with you as soon as possible."

Evan sighed. "How foolish of me to think I would have time to do things at my own pace today. Right, advise the General that Commander Wilton has returned and we will attend him directly. James, put someone in charge of repairs while I have my crew prepare for sea and lets go. The sooner we get this done the sooner I can get a message to Baptiste."

***

Baptiste woke as the sun began streaming into his room. Still sleepy, he reached out for Sylvie, but found she wasn't there, only then remembering she was still away on her false mission to Santo Domingo. She had only left four days ago, but Baptiste was already struggling with the unaccustomed sensation of missing her company. Finding women to share his bed had never been a problem, but the thought of finding one he wanted to share it with on a long term basis had not crossed his mind until now. The fiction they were maintaining of being married for the purpose of his mission felt like it was somehow becoming pleasantly real.

The night before she left on the small merchant vessel Baptiste had hired for the trip was memorable. He sensed she didn't want to be parted from him and seemed insatiable, making efforts to please him strong enough to make him redouble his own desires to do the same for her. They had feasted on cold meats, cheese, and cool white wine from France in between trips to the bedroom and it was late by the time they both finally fell asleep from exhaustion.

He rubbed his face and got out of bed, calling out his door for a servant to prepare some coffee as he made himself ready for the day. He shoved the question of his future with Sylvie aside as he walked out to the verandah of his mansion set high on the cliff side on the north coast of Saint Domingue for his waiting breakfast, for he had far more serious matters to contemplate.

The small coffee plantation and estate he had purchased on arrival in Saint Domingue was on a remote piece of land on the north coast of the island, midway between Le Cap Francois to the east and Labadie to the west. Having managed coffee plantations on St. Lucia meant Baptiste had little trouble making it work. The property was far enough from both towns on a little travelled and remote branch road and it afforded an excellent degree of privacy, while at the same time it was close enough to both it meant travelling to either was not onerous.

Of more importance was the obscure, small cove on the far edge of the property. Even his own slaves had no reason to go to it, making this the perfect location to maintain a spot to leave messages for Evan Ross. Access to the cove was via a steep path through heavy brush down to the water.

Some long forgotten owner of the property had built a small, long forgotten dock in the cove, tucked away in a spot that couldn't easily be seen from either the land or the water. Baptiste thought it likely whoever built it had used it for smuggling. Baptiste secretly repaired it and built a hidden cairn for messages to be left. Should Baptiste and Sylvie need to be extracted in a hurry, this was also where they would await rescue. Although message deliveries were the sole domain of Evan and James when they were nearby, a Royal Navy sloop based in Mole Saint Nicolas was tasked with doing a sail past the cove every night when they were not. If Baptiste were shining a light to sea, the sloop would instantly sail close to the shore and pick them up.

As Baptiste sipped his coffee and stared out at the sweeping blue vista of the ocean before him he turned his mind to the decision he had to make. The night before he slipped away to check the secret cairn and found the message he had left was gone and a new one was there in its place. Evan's message about the arrival of the two French spies was a concern, but whether it was enough of a risk to shine his light and escape was another matter.

Baptiste knew exactly who the two men were, having seen them on Julien Fedon's estate in Grenada on several occasions. Baptiste had not actually interacted with either of them, so whether they would even remember him was questionable. Even if they did, it was entirely possible the story Evan had concocted for Baptiste would allay any suspicion they had. The risk was one or both of them would somehow make a connection between Baptiste and James. Evan had given Baptiste free rein to decide whether to stay the course or run, which was yet another reason why Baptiste loved his commanding officer.

But Baptiste knew the decision, at least for the next few days, was already made, for he had no way he could leave without putting Sylvie at risk. If hard questions were being asked about why Baptiste had disappeared and she was to return in the middle of it, she could be in serious trouble. But even as the thought came Baptiste knew he had no intention of failing Evan regardless. Baptiste had faced risk before and would do so again. The problem was how to do it without putting Sylvie at risk too, something he discovered he was now loath to do.

As he finished the remnants of his breakfast and sipped at his second cup of coffee one of his slaves came forward bearing an envelope. Baptiste smiled as he finished reading the message it contained, for the solution he needed had appeared. Hedouville and his delegation had arrived and Toussaint was organizing a grand dinner reception for them in Fort Picolet the next night. The message was his invitation and Baptiste would attend without Sylvie, her absence justified by her mission to Santo Domingo. He would leave a note for her to be wary and escape at the first sign of trouble if matters went badly.

***

Fort Picolet was built on a rocky promontory on the western edge of the wide bay where Toussaint's headquarters was located in Le Cap Francois. Constructed over fifty years before its purpose was to defend French interests in the area from the marauding Spanish, ever seeking to control the entire island of Hispaniola. To date its many cannon had not been fired in anger, but with the Royal Navy on the prowl Toussaint had ensured the fort was well maintained and he liked using it as his base often, given the excellent security it afforded.

He also liked using it as a place to entertain and to do it with style. The grand dining hall held a table at which fifty people could be seated and Toussaint had invited enough guests to fill every chair. Baptiste was impressed when he arrived the next night, for although he had enjoyed several dinners in the hall before it was clear Toussaint was sparing nothing in his effort to impress the new arrivals. Whether his effort to appear as the statesman he wanted to be would succeed was another matter. But in the meantime Baptiste would learn whether he was recognized or not and hopefully enjoy himself while he was about it.

Baptiste expected the latter wouldn't be a problem, as Toussaint had from the outset forbidden all talk of politics, claiming the night was for celebration and nothing more. He had followed this with an endless display of culinary extravagance, which made Baptiste wonder how the table could continue to bear the weight of all the food before them. Slaves ladled out a variety of spicy soups to begin, followed by an endless, savory array of fish and meat dishes accompanied by a wide range of vegetables that grew on the island. Food shortages were a reality in most of the island, but not on this night at Toussaint's table. Numerous bottles of excellent French wines kept appearing on the table and as the night wore on the crowd became more and more raucous.

Prior to being seated Baptiste had inserted himself into a small group of men conversing with the spy Montdenoix and Baptiste was relieved to see the man gave no sign of recognition whatsoever. With this success behind him Baptiste relaxed and began to enjoy himself, although out of habit he kept his alcohol consumption minimal, unlike the rest of the crowd around him. When brandy, cognac, and coffee began to be served at the end of the meal several people rose and went to find relief from all the wine they had consumed. Several others decided to step outside into the fresh air of the night and stroll on the broad ramparts of the fort.

Baptiste rose from his seat and took his brandy glass to go outside. Having had enough of the crowds of people he made his way to the far end of the ramparts where they curved around the point and he found himself alone with his thoughts. He was staring out to sea when a drunken, slurred voice behind him intruded.

"I know you from somewhere. I haven't been able to place it, but I'm sure I've seen you before."

Baptiste turned slowly, setting his glass down on the rampart beside him, and found Fleming Linger standing before him. The two men were alone on this end of the ramparts. Although there were no lights on the ramparts, the moon was half full and it shone enough light they could see each other clearly enough. Before Baptiste could speak a flash of understanding came over Linger's face and he waved a finger drunkenly toward Baptiste.

"Ah, I have it finally! You were on Grenada, weren't you? Yes, you were one of that fool Fedon's servants."

Baptiste nodded to acknowledge the truth of this and told him his cover story. He hoped he was convincing enough, but as he finished he could see Linger was beginning to frown. Baptiste tried to steer the conversation away from his past by asking about his thoughts on the situation in Saint Domingue, but Linger interrupted him.

"No, wait, damn it. I remember. I remember seeing you talk to that English bastard who was spying on Fedon. You did so on more than a few occasions. It didn't occur to me how odd it was until well afterwards. And now, here you are in Saint Domingue."

Baptiste risked a quick look behind the French spy to assure himself they were still both alone, passing the move off as a shrug of puzzlement.

"I have no idea who or what you are talking about. I joined Fedon because I wanted to help and this is the same reason I am here."

"No, damn you, I think—"

Linger never finished his sentence as Baptiste wrapped his hands around the man's throat in an iron grip, borne of constant daily workouts to stay fit. The French spy writhed like a fish with a hook deep in its gullet, but was unable to free himself from Baptiste's grasp. Baptiste worked his way around behind the man and with a sudden, hard wrench he threw his foe headfirst into the walls of the rampart. The spy slammed into the wall and slumped against it in a crumpled heap. With a quick look behind him Baptiste saw no one was in sight. He looked at the man's skull and saw it was badly crushed at the point of impact from the force of being thrown into the rock of the wall. A steady trickle of blood was already oozing out of the wound.

Without hesitation Baptiste doused the man's face with the remnants of his glass of brandy. After one more glance to ensure no one was watching he lifted the spy and flung him over the wall, knowing the drop to the rocky beach below was close to a hundred feet. The dull thud of the body hitting the rocks was masked by the sound of the waves hitting the beach and Baptiste was certain no one would have heard it. Baptiste scuffed enough dirt and sand around to sop up and disguise the small amount of blood the man had left. With a last quick inspection of his clothes to ensure he had no blood on them, Baptiste took his now empty glass and made his way warily back along the ramparts.

With an abundance of caution he peered carefully around the corner, but he needn't have worried. The crowd on the ramparts had thinned and those who remained were deep in drunken conversation, paying no attention to their surroundings. Baptiste slipped back inside, making certain no one in the banquet hall was watching him either, and was gratified to see the people inside were as inebriated as those on the ramparts.

Baptiste smiled, as he was already composing a report to Evan in his mind. Being able to report success in disposing of one of the two spies bedeviling Evan for so long would make his commander a happy man. Not being caught in the act was even better.

***

Montdenoix had Linger's quarters searched after lunch when the spy still had not appeared. The fact he had not slept in his bed led to a more thorough search. They had still not found him by dinnertime, but one of Toussaint's soldiers finally thought to look over the rampart wall and saw the body wedged further up the rocky beach by the waves of the high tide the night before. Montdenoix personally inspected the mangled body when it was retrieved. The faint scent of brandy still lingered, detectable even through the smell of the ocean and the stench of decomposition growing ever stronger.

They agreed to discuss the matter over dinner with Toussaint and his key advisors. Montdenoix was incensed by what happened to his colleague and was suspicious enough he wanted to personally question everyone who was present the night before, even going as far as to express suspicion it was too much of a coincidence this had happened so soon after their arrival. Baptiste was careful to let others do the talking about the situation, but was gratified to see Montdenoix still gave no sign of recognizing him even in the cold light of another day when the spy hadn't been drinking. Hedouville was of two minds about the need to press the matter, but it was Toussaint who finally put an end to talk of questioning everyone.

"I don't understand your suspicions. You said yourself you could smell brandy on the man. Isn't it obvious what happened? The drunken fool decided to get up on the wall for a better view and fell off. Maybe he needed to piss. Or maybe he just had enough of life and decided to end it? The guests who were here last night will be insulted if you start questioning them. Unless you have something better to justify annoying my guests, I think you should just go make arrangements to bury him and be done with it."

Baptiste could see Montdenoix was gritting his teeth and holding back the retort he wanted to make. Baptiste was amused by the irony, for the only way Montdenoix could defend his suspicions and question everyone was to confess his true role as a spy. Montdenoix turned to Hedouville and shrugged, and Hedouville simply nodded his agreement.

With this out of the way the real business of the day got underway, while the various courses of the meal were served. As the meal progressed it became clear Hedouville's strategy was exactly what Baptiste had anticipated it would be. Every opportunity to flatter Toussaint was seized, while at the same time emphasizing his patriotism and loyalty to France, represented by the person of Hedouville. The two men dominated the conversation as the courses of the dinner came and went. Hedouville tried everything he could to wring an admission from Toussaint he would follow Hedouville's lead, but Toussaint put on a masterful display of saying plenty of benign, fine words while committing to absolutely nothing.

By the end of the meal Baptiste could sense a gradual shift in Hedouville's demeanor. At the start of the meal he seemed gregarious and was making an effort to cultivate an air of comradeship. As it became clear what Toussaint was doing Hedouville withdrew more into himself, letting others talk as he glared at Toussaint. His tone was clipped and cold at the end of the meal as he passed on the cognac Toussaint offered and rose from his seat, making arrangements for their next meeting before stalking out.

Toussaint waited until all of Hedouville's little delegation was gone and he was certain they were out of earshot before grinning from ear to ear and letting out a booming laugh. Baptiste laughed along with the rest of Toussaint's advisors.

"Well done, my General. He looked like he had a poker shoved up his ass by the time he left."

"He did, didn't he?" said Toussaint, laughing again. "Well, I'll just have to make sure it stays there."

"I think your next meeting with him will be less pleasant, Toussaint," said Raimond. "He tried flattery, next it will be threats."

Toussaint shrugged. "I've been threatened by everyone before and I'm still here. Besides, I know how to make threats, too. And the best part is he doesn't know matters are going my way, not his. I didn't have time to tell any of you the good news before dinner started. A messenger came in with a reply from General Maitland. He is willing to enter into talks directly with us without any preconditions."

A few of the men pounded the table in glee while others began applauding and calling out congratulations to Toussaint, who smiled grimly as he soaked in their praise. When they finally settled down again Baptiste spoke.

"Toussaint? You don't intend to tell Hedouville you will be negotiating with Maitland, do you?"

Toussaint shrugged and grinned again. "I thought about it, but why? Since I am in charge here and not Hedouville, what right does he have to

expect me to tell him anything? I imagine at some point he may learn of it and, if he does, too bad. We will deal with him if and when it happens."
***

Julien Raimond was proved right, as the next meeting held two days later with Toussaint, his advisors, and Hedouville was far less cordial. This time the Frenchman opened the meeting by offering a blunt assessment a reckoning would be coming for those who failed to understand the realities of what the situation could become. Dark hints at what might happen once significantly greater resources came from France, in addition to the more immediate possibility of direct support coming from the Spanish side of the island were made. Hedouville assured them all he had to do was ask and what he wanted would be granted. Having made himself clear, Hedouville demanded overall control of all of Toussaint's forces.

Toussaint maintained an obstinate, self-assured demeanor throughout the entire meeting, deflecting any possibility of acquiescence to what Hedouville wanted while continuing to profess his allegiance to France. Hedouville's eyes bulged wide when Toussaint insinuated the Frenchman did not understand local realities and the military situation, and would be best served by confining himself to broader diplomatic issues between France and other nations. Baptiste was amazed the Frenchman somehow mastered himself and did not explode at the insult. As it became clear Toussaint was not going to give Hedouville what he wanted the Frenchman made a visible shift in his approach, abruptly announcing he needed to contemplate his next steps further. The dark anger boiling beneath the surface was both obvious on his face and deliberate.

After arranging for yet another meeting in two days time the Frenchman once again stalked out. This time no laughter came from Toussaint and his men, although Julien Raimond attempted to lighten the mood.

"Remember the poker up his ass, Toussaint? Looks to me like its been replaced with a tree trunk and he doesn't like it."

Toussaint allowed a brief, small smile to play across his face, but he turned to face Baptiste.

"I wish your woman had brought more certainty, Baptiste. It is good there is unrest in Santo Domingo, but it must be more than this. We do not want a fight on three fronts and I do not want to give this man Hedouville what he wants."

Baptiste nodded his understanding. The timing of this meeting was good, for another message from Evan Ross had appeared beforehand at almost the same time as Sylvie returned from Santo Domingo. Evan's guidance was for Baptiste to present the situation on the other side of the island as volatile to a degree, but under control, in an overall desire to have Toussaint keeping an uncomfortable, wary eye behind him during the looming negotiations with the British. But Baptiste was also authorized to make Toussaint an offer, if the situation warranted it.

"Toussaint? I will talk with her more, but I think if we put a little effort along with some resources into it we could help matters along. Give our friends on the other side of the island a little money and maybe some weapons along with vague promises of support, too. Maybe we could even stage a few situations where we make it look like French sailors are behaving badly toward the Spanish women? If it ties down even some of the Spanish soldiers which might come here it could help."

Toussaint rubbed his chin and gave Baptiste a speculative look.

"You are devious, aren't you? But I like your thinking."

Baptiste shrugged. "Just trying to help. I am willing to dedicate some of my own resources to this effort, if you want me to try."

Toussaint waved a hand in agreement. "Yes, I do. It will give me more free time to find a way to deal with this bastard Rigaud."

Baptiste nodded, allowing himself an inward smile. Toussaint's rival, Andre Rigaud, had somehow learned of Hedouville's presence and had already threatened Toussaint with an all out attack if he wasn't included in any negotiations or agreements made with the new French administrator.

And having Toussaint, the most powerful leader of black forces on Saint Domingue, sensing threats in every direction he looked was exactly what Evan Ross wanted.

***

Evan rose from his seat to greet General Maitland as he came into the meeting room at his

Army headquarters alone and took a chair. Evan knew they would have much to discuss, given the General had been gone for over a week and it was now mid April. The General appeared tired, radiating an overall sense of preoccupation with the weight of the responsibility on his shoulders. Evan offered the General a glass of wine and, uncharacteristically, the General grasped at it as if it was a lifeline saving him from drowning. He downed half of the contents in one gulp before composing himself and looking at Evan.

"Let's be about it, then. What have you got for me?"

"General, negotiations with Toussaint's representatives have begun. It has all been kept rather broad, awaiting your return and whatever insights you have from your inspection tour. My spy assures me Toussaint is wary of what may come his way from both Santo Domingo and his rival Andre Rigaud. Unfortunately, making Toussaint wary has also meant a redoubling of the security around him. Assassinating him, at least for now, is virtually impossible. On the positive side, my man has found a way to eliminate one of the two French spies we are fighting, which may throw the French into some disarray."

"Excellent. And the Spanish on the other side? Any word of help to the French from them or any word of more French soldiers on the horizon?"

"Sir, nothing is impossible, but we have no indication of anything imminent. On this note Commander Wilton will be leaving tomorrow for Santo Domingo, where I expect he will be stationed for some time. His orders are to stir up as much trouble as possible for the administration there and I have every confidence he will succeed. Trust me, he has plenty of experience with this. The Spanish will be far too busy fighting the two fires springing up for every one they succeed in putting out. The only thing to prevent success would be the appearance of yet more French warships and troops. But even this will be problematic for them, because I have requested and gained approval to increase Royal Navy patrols and resources around the entire island. If more frogs show up they may still get past us, but they will have a hot time doing it."

The General nodded and downed the rest of his glass of wine. He sighed as Evan reached for the bottle and poured a refill.

"Thank you. Your wine is welcome, as is some positive news for a change."

"General, if I may? I get an impression the news is not so good elsewhere?"

The General shook his head. "I am glad I made the effort to tour our emplacements around the island, although I confess it has been tiring, discouraging, and enlightening all at the same time. It is a good thing the blacks did not press their advantage, for I think we would have been annihilated. The men overall have poor morale and need more respite. They needed to see me and I did the best I could to boost their spirits. But our positions are untenable in many places. Something must change, Captain Ross."

"What will you do, sir?"

"My officers want me to stay the course. Use

the respite of the negotiations to find a way to retake the initiate and push our foes back. I know our political masters want this, too. I appreciate their courage and willingness to try, but I just cannot see how to do it without consolidating our position. We simply cannot continue to hold the coastal areas, let alone Port-au-Prince."

"Are you proposing a full withdrawal, General? We will have to consider our wider interests and perhaps take further steps or a different approach if so."

"No, we are not there yet. I am not giving up, Mr. Ross. We must find some way to maintain a presence and influence on this island or no one will be satisfied with the outcome. No, at the moment my only real concern is now who we are dealing with. Are you certain continuing negotiations with this man L'Ouverture is our best option?"

"General, I am. He is the most powerful of the black leaders, although at some point I think there will be a reckoning between him and this man Rigaud. He controls the largest army on this island. I haven't been as successful in finding assets within Rigaud's camp as I have his rival, but I'm working on it. And this Frenchman Hedouville? Unless he finds some way to make a lot more French soldiers appear or to get some Spanish aid from the other side of the island, he does not have the power to enforce his will. Certainly he has some army units to command and the influence it brings, and he does hold sway over people because of who he represents, but negotiating with him would bolster his own efforts to appear to be in charge. Besides, I am absolutely certain he will consider our negotiating directly with Toussaint a major insult, probably enough to make his blood boil. I don't know about you, but I like this thought."

For the first time since he walked in the door the General smiled.

"You know what, Mr. Ross? I like this thought, too."

***

After several more strategy sessions with Evan over the next two days the General agreed to an overall approach and gave his lead negotiator approval to proceed. Evan was tasked with continuing to serve as an observer to the negotiations, watching the key opposition member's reactions as points were discussed and looking for clues as to what their real thoughts might be.

The General's chief negotiator was a British diplomat named Lord Alan Harcourt seconded to him from Jamaica. Evan had never met him, but knew of his reputation of having extensive experience in such discussions.

Evan was impressed as the man pushed Toussaint's representatives on several fronts. His first effort was to question whether Toussaint had authority over anything, followed by a long harangue about exactly how Rigaud might fit into the discussions. By the time he was finished even Evan was running doubts through his mind, but with effort Toussaint's men pushed back. Once they got past this the diplomat introduced the point the British were now aware of the presence of Hedouville and he demanded to know how the

French administrator fit in. Toussaint's representatives once again fought back with dark threats about the consequences of British intransigence.

By the third week of April the agreement both sides sought was finally reached. The British would withdraw their forces from all areas of the island with the exception of Mole St. Nicholas in the north and the town of Jeremie in the south.

Evan understood the logic of the General's choices. Mole St. Nicholas had strong fortifications and, even more important, an excellent deep water port the Royal Navy could continue to use. Jeremie was a good choice to retain also, as it was the largest town with fortifications in this area of Saint Domingue. Being situated on tip of the long peninsula of south province it could be easily supplied and defended by British warships off the coast in the event of attack.

Evan was amused at the cynical ease with which Toussaint's negotiator generously gave away something which was not his to give, for south province was the domain of Andre Rigaud and his men. But he was certain Rigaud would grudgingly agree to the deal, because he too was gaining access to British held areas and fortifications. Toussaint's representatives were pleased to gain British assurances all fortifications they were to withdraw from would be left intact, as they might well be useful should civil war with the forces of Andre Rigaud break out in earnest in future. Evan knew Rigaud would likely feel the same.

In return for it all General Maitland was given

assurances the property and safety of those choosing not to withdraw with the British would be respected and they would be left alone. What was noticeably absent from the agreement was any hint of ceasing hostilities. The General would be free to use both Mole St. Nicholas and Jeremie as bases from which to attempt expanding the British presence in Saint Domingue once again. Everyone knew the withdrawal would take time, so general agreement was reached the goal would be to have it complete by the end of May.

Evan knew he was going to be busy as a result.
***

Hubert Montdenoix wasn't used to being dressed down like this. He had served many diplomats over the years and each of them had their own style and way of approaching challenges, particularly when matters weren't going their way.

As he was now learning, Theodore Hedouville liked to throw things when he was blazing with anger. Two wine glasses already lay in shattered ruins from being smashed against the hard stone of the walls of the room in the fort they were meeting in. Montdenoix was careful to remain seated as he watched Hedouville pace with restless energy back and forth around the room, hoping the next item Hedouville threw wouldn't be directly at him.

"I tell you, Hubert, you must do better, damn it! How can it be we did not know this pig L'Ouverture was negotiating behind our backs with the damned British?"

"Theodore," said Montdenoix, permitting what he hoped was a weary look of commiseration to cross his face. "We have only been here a matter of a few weeks. While I do have sources on this island and will be making every effort to find more, it all takes time to contact them. With my colleague Linger gone my workload has doubled. And speaking of this, I am more than ever convinced his death was no accident. This obstinate bastard L'Ouverture has obviously been playing us and I think we are now seeing the real man and his thinking behind all the bullshit he has been feeding us. I suspect he knows the role Linger and I came here to perform, and they may well have seized an opportunity to complicate our efforts while they continued their traitorous negotiations behind our backs."

"Are you certain you are just not seeing spies behind everything?"

"Theodore, I assure you, I worked with Flemming Linger for many years. He was not suicidal, as Toussaint suggested, nor was he stupid enough to climb up on a parapet wall to take a piss and fall off, even when he was drinking. Yes, he liked his wine, but he was always in control and never overdid it. I am positive someone at the dinner murdered him."

"What about the British? Is it possible they found a way to have someone there and this was done to drive an even bigger wedge between us and Toussaint?"

Montdenoix grimaced. "I suppose anything is possible, Theodore. I have known for a long time the British have men who serve in the same way as I opposing us and they are very good at it. I've had hints at who they are, but haven't been able to put a stop to them yet. But even so, I can't see this being a deliberate British attempt to do this. If they have a spy in Toussaint's camp, they likely already know what a deceitful shit he is and they would have known of the negotiations happening anyway. No, Toussaint is doing an excellent job all on his own of keeping a wedge between us."

"Bastard!" shouted Hedouville, snatching yet another glass from the table and flinging it hard against the wall to join the others in smashed bits on the floor. He stood staring at it for a long moment before stalking over to the table and finally slumping into the chair across from Montdenoix, giving him a grim look as he did.

"Hubert, tell me we will do better."

"Theodore, we will. I am as angry as you and we will find a way to deal with all of these pigs."

Chapter Five
May 1798
Saint Domingue

By the end of the first week in May the situation in Port-au-Prince was bordering on chaos. Once word of the agreement and its terms was made public a storm of anguished, desperate people descended on the General's headquarters and it seemed unlikely to end anytime soon. A sizeable portion of them also displayed blazing anger at what was seen as yet another British betrayal, forcing the Army into doubling of the already heavy guard around the headquarters.

Adding to the chaos were unsubstantiated rumors of what the future might hold for the French émigrés and royalist supporters in the population. Evan quickly learned of talk about the harsh treatment people were expecting for the sin of being found in former British controlled areas after the evacuation. Torture in a dungeon or the lash would be followed by a date with the guillotines, which rumor held would appear in every public square. Evan was suspicious right away these rumors were being spread by Hedouville and his men in an attempt to either sabotage Toussaint's agreement or, at the least, to make life for the British miserable. The problem was it was all too easy to believe the rumors.

Evan volunteered to help deal with the overwhelming numbers of people seeking help in fleeing, despite the massive workload he was at risk of being buried under. Despite what was happening it was vital James stay the course with his mission to destabilize Santo Domingo and not remain behind to help Evan. James had seemed torn, seeing the situation, but agreed it was the right course of action. He promised Evan he would return as soon as he could. Evan watched him sail out of harbor with mixed feelings, for Evan was already working steadily from dawn till dusk and well into the night.

But the General was grateful for Evan's help. Evan had quietly suggested ways to organize the chaos and the Army clerks and officers struggling to deal with it all slowly came on board with Evan's ideas. A series of tables and chairs were set up for Evan and other officers to interview people in the big hall of the General's headquarters. Soldiers organized the sweating crowds into lines long enough to snake outside into the heat of the courtyard. Several people had small, squalling children with them and the noise was overwhelming. More than a few fainted from standing so long.

But it worked. Every day brought new crowds of people needing help as they learned a process was in place for sorting out who needed help the most. The problem was there were so many with dire needs. The other problem was exactly how to help them, for the needs were so varied.

One such example was the white French businessman Evan had spoken to only moments before. The man ran a small tailor shop in Port-au-Prince, mending clothing for anyone with need and supplementing this income by both making and selling clothes. He was a well-known supporter of the royalist cause with his own slaves to help do the work. He knew he could not remain behind, for fear of the guillotine. But everything he owned was tied up in the business and it was a hard way to make a living. His meager savings were not enough to hire a spot on a merchant vessel to take him, his family, and the six slaves he employed away to one of the two British enclaves soon to be left on Saint Domingue. Taking passage to another island was even further beyond his means.

Evan had done what he could. With space at a ridiculous premium on merchant ships and so many in need, a decision was made to save space on the warships which could be spared for refugees in serious and clear danger only. Room for large numbers of slaves to follow their masters was not available. Despite the offer of space on the next available warship out the man was totally outraged, for to leave behind any of his valuable slaves meant losing everything. Evan had patiently told the man what he didn't want to hear, though. Evan emphasized the truth was his story was no different than the three other businessmen Evan had already seen earlier this morning and they had all received the same answer.

This man didn't like the answer any more than the others had, but he chose to vent his frustration on Evan. He rose from the chair and pounded the table hard, swearing in an angry mix of French and English about British cowards. In his frustration he tried throwing a punch, which missed as Evan saw it coming and ducked. He didn't get a chance for a second one as two British soldiers shoved their way through the lines of people and seized him roughly by the shoulders, dragging him away. Evan could still hear him screaming as the soldiers threw him outside the perimeter walls and into the street. Without looking Evan waved the next person forward while scratching the man's name off his list.

"Well, what can I do for you?" said Evan, finally looking up.

This time it was a young black woman sitting before him and the first thing he noticed were the tears already forming in the corner of one of her eyes. The second was her remarkable good looks and, without bidding, the thought appeared in his mind she seemed a younger version of his own wife Alice, with her light, coffee colored skin and long, flowing dark hair. Even her features bore a similarity. The tears began sliding down her cheeks as she spoke.

"Sir, I need your help. I beg you. I have no one to turn to. If I am here when the French come I fear they will kill me."

Evan offered her a handkerchief as he responded.

"What is your story, please?"

"I will be honest with you, sir. My name is Jeanne Boucher. My mother was a slave my father purchased and freed. She died when I was a child and now my father is dead, too. He was a French businessman and his business here failed. He was much older than my mother and became very sick two years ago. The only way we could support ourselves was for me to—for me to sell myself. I did not want to, but there was no choice. I tried to find work, but no one wants a black woman for anything except, well—you know. I can read and write and do sums, because my father educated me to help with the business. This is also why he made me learn English. But he has now died and I have no one."

She paused a moment and reached out a hand across the table in supplication.

"Please, sir. I beg for your help. You don't know how truly horrible it is living here. Our neighbors know what I had to do and many despise me for it. I am fearful they will denounce me to the French when they come, for being a whore to the British, and for the sin of my father being a royalist supporter. I don't want to die here in this hell on earth."

Evan sat silent for a long moment, staring down at the table while he thought it all through and made his decision. He finally looked up and spoke, being careful not to smile as he did.

"Would you like a job?"

A fresh flood of tears streaming down her face accompanied the stunned look of wide-eyed, sudden hope flaring on her face. She licked her trembling lips and brushed the tears away as she replied.

"Sir, I am at your mercy. I will do—anything you ask."

"The kind of 'anything' you may be thinking of won't be necessary," said Evan, holding up his hand. "I don't wear a wedding band when I am working for security reasons, but I assure you I am happily married and intend to stay this way. My name is Captain Evan Ross, British Royal Navy. I am offering you a job helping my associate and myself. He is not here at present, but I think he would agree we could use a little help around here. Can you cook?"

"Sir, I love cooking. You will not be disappointed."

"Excellent, your duties will be to cook and clean for the two of us. I will also assess your ability to serve as a clerk. As it happens my regular clerk became ill and passed away with the fever, and I have yet to replace him. If you meet my standards you can do this for me, too. Finding quarters for you here with us might be a challenge, but we will figure something out. You will evacuate with us when we leave here for good."

Evan paused for a second to emphasize his next point with a pointed look.

"Be aware the Army soldiers here may see you as—someone desirable. I will make it known you are with us, as Commander Wilton and I may not always be present. The soldiers should therefore assume you are my woman and leave you alone, but I recommend caution. This will be for a three-month term for now and at the end of this time you and I will talk about where we go from here. I may have a solution for beyond this point, but we need to get to know each other first. I will also pay you standard rates for a Navy clerk, although you will certainly not be joining the Royal Navy. Is all this acceptable to you?"

The brilliant smile lighting her face was once again an eerie reminder of his wife when she was fifteen years younger. And from his experience with his wife Evan knew exactly what Jeanne was about to do. He forestalled her as she was rising from her chair to come around the table and give him a hug by reaching out his hand and putting it on top of hers.

"I know you want to come and show me your gratitude, but please don't. A simple handshake will do to signify your agreement. There are too many people watching us at the moment and if they see you give me a hug they will all think they are going to get what they want from me when their turn comes, which is not likely to happen."

Jeanne sat back down and grasped his hand in a firm handshake, brushing yet more tears away from her face.

"Sir, I agree. I will not fail you and you will not regret this."

"Very good. You can use Commander Wilton's room for now. I am almost done my shift dealing with these people for today, so please take a chair over here and wait for a bit. I will do one or two more interviews and then we will make arrangements for you to collect your belongings and move in."

Jeanne squeezed his hand hard and moved to sit nearby in the chair he indicated. Ten minutes later an Army officer relieved him on schedule and he took Jeanne to the two small rooms he and James were allotted. They arrived at the same time as two of the sailors from his ship, bearing yet another large packet of correspondence for him which had come from a recently arrived mail packet ship. Evan seized the opportunity the two men presented.

"This is Jeanne Boucher. She will be joining Commander Wilton and I as a clerk and servant. Escort her to her home and then bring her back here. If she needs a hand with her belongings help her."

Evan turned to Jeanne. "Do you have much to bring with you?"

On seeing her shake her head he turned back to the sailors.

"Very good. Let no one stop you. Deal with them as you see fit if someone tries. Jeanne, you will have to find space for your belongings in Commander Wilton's room, although it might be a little cramped. I am not certain when he will return, but if he does I will figure something out. I suggest make certain you bring only the essentials to meet your needs."

This time Jeanne wasn't settling for a handshake. She wrapped herself around Evan in a long, crushing hug of gratitude which brought back memories of his experience with Alice so many years before when he told her she was freed from being a slave.

And behind their backs the two sailors were grinning from ear to ear.

***

Hedouville watched Montdenoix come into the room and collapse into the chair opposite Hedouville's desk. Montdenoix's clothes were stained with sweat and Hedouville could smell how badly the man needed to bathe. The spy looked as if he had slept in his clothes for more than a few days.

"Hubert, I know I gave orders for you to see me

as soon as possible upon your return, but whatever news you have can wait another hour while you clean up and get something to refresh yourself. You look like shit. Smell like it, too, if I may be honest."

"I feel like it, Theodore. Thank you for the offer, but I would prefer to just get this done. It has been long since I had a bath, some sleep, some food and drink, and a woman, but it can all wait just a little longer."

"Well, then, let me pour you a drink and you can tell me your news."

After downing fully half of the glass of brandy set before him Montdenoix sighed and spoke.

"We are making progress, Theodore, but it is slow. First, the rumors we spread of what we will certainly do to some of these royalist bastards when the time comes have succeeded to a point. They have not stopped this damned agreement with Toussaint from staying in place, but they have definitely made life difficult for the British. And even if the scum find a way to escape us I don't think it's bad. Less complications for us to deal with, eh?"

"I agree and yes, this is good news. What else?"

"I have several possibilities in the works to gain more inside information, but as I said it is slow. Everyone is treading very carefully because, regardless of who is spying on whom, they know if they are caught it will be their doom. I have been trying to work with people who were already helping us and to leverage whatever access they had. One of my contacts put me onto a clerk in this General Maitland's headquarters who I think I have successfully recruited."

"Excellent! I knew you could do it, Hubert."

"Don't be so happy just yet," cautioned Montdenoix. "The man is a secret homosexual. I caught him in the act with a man I paid to entrap him. The problem with black mailing someone is the question of just how trustworthy the information he brings me actually will be. Information offered under duress must always be viewed with skepticism. The other danger is he may report the situation to his superiors and, if he does, they may try to feed us a load of nonsense."

"Hmm, the British aren't very tolerant when it comes to this sort of thing, so I choose to be hopeful. Well, we shall see. It is still an achievement, Hubert."

"Ah, but I am also working on both L'Ouverture and Rigaud's followers. I have a strong possibility with one of L'Ouverture's advisors. He will cost us gold, lots of gold, but if he does agree I think his information will be worth every ounce. I will let you know. I have other small possibilities, but they are not worth mentioning at this point. Much of my time was spent just contacting the lesser sources we already had in various places. It was always Linger's job, you see? But I am making progress."

"Yes, you are. As for me, I have been corresponding with this dog Rigaud. I hadn't thought it possible, but he seems even more arrogant than Toussaint. Well, it is the poor soil I must work with. He has finally agreed to a meeting with me later this month. If he proves more pliable I will happily throw our lot in with him, because this fool Toussaint is as obstinate as ever."

Montdenoix grimaced and downed the remainder of his drink.

"I wouldn't be too optimistic about Rigaud. I've not met him, but everything I've heard up till now suggests he is exactly as arrogant as he appears to be. And now, with your blessing to leave, taking a bath is a really appealing thought right now."

"You deserve a reward, Hubert. I have a new, young servant girl I think you will find most enjoyable. I know I did. She will do a fine job of scrubbing your back, or whatever else you want scrubbed."

Both men laughed as they rose from their seats.
***

Evan and General Maitland held a series of regular meetings with each other to discuss intelligence matters over the next ten days. Each time Evan's main interest was to learn whether the General had made any major shifts in his strategy, but he had not. As they concluded the latest meeting and Evan rose to leave the General held him back.

"Captain Ross, I have one other matter, not related to intelligence. A woman who needs help has contacted me. I know, this isn't remarkable around here, but she is the widow of a man who was one of the leading supporters of the royalist cause here. Her husband had minor family connections with some of our lesser nobility back home, so needless to say I must do what I can for her. This also means it is one more burden on my time I can't afford right now. Can I ask you to meet with her, assess her situation, and do what you can to help? Be assured I will agree to anything reasonable, but you know I can not go promising her anything and everything. So can you make time to deal with this matter?"

Evan agreed and the General promised to have a message sent for her to come to his headquarters the next day. Because of her status she would be escorted directly to one of the General's private rooms for the meeting, away from the ongoing chaos of the great hall.

At the appointed time the next day Evan entered the room to find a well-dressed woman with straight, blonde hair of roughly his own age seated alone at the meeting table. Her fine features showed the signs of her age by way of a few lines on her face, but she was still a stunningly beautiful, mature woman. She watched him walk over to the other side of the table and sit down. Her eyes widened for a moment and one eyebrow ever so slightly raised betrayed the question in her mind. Evan smiled, knowing what it was.

"Good day, madam. You are Amelie Caron and you are, of course, wondering who I am and where General Maitland is. He is extremely busy, as I'm sure you understand, but he has asked me to help you if at all possible. My name is Captain Evan Ross, British Royal Navy, and your next thought is to wonder why I am in civilian clothes."

The woman's face remained bland, but she gave him a brief nod to signal her agreement. Evan smiled.

"My role is to assist the General with various

discreet activities here. As such, it is preferable I not advertise who I am. I trust you understand."

This time she sat forward, placing her hands folded on the table before her.

"Thank you for your explanation, Captain. I am well aware of the need for discretion in many things and I appreciate your help."

"So, I need to know more of your circumstances. All I was told by the General is you are a widow and you have some family connections to the nobility in England?"

"You are correct, Captain. My husband was killed in the fighting six months ago. I have been struggling ever since to keep our affairs in order, but it has been a huge challenge for someone not used to running a business. And yes, I do have some connections to people in England. I confess the truth is I have never met them and they would be surprised to see me were I to show up at their door. But if using such connections opens doors for me when in need, I will do what I must."

"Of course. And how can we help you?"

Amelie sighed. "I have a home here in Port-au-Prince, but my plantation is in south province. It is some distance from Jeremie. I came here when my husband was killed thinking I would be safer, but this has proved to be wrong as matters worsened. At a minimum I need help getting back to south province, but I am not certain how safe it will be there. And yes, I have some resources and could hire a merchant vessel to take me away, but I would prefer to be careful with what I have and what they want for the service is outrageous. Our resources have dwindled, Captain. I have another, smaller home in Jeremie itself, but our plantation will not be within your lines and I fear it is lost to me. If some day you withdraw completely from Saint Domingue I will be at your mercy to escape, for this is what my daughter and I will need. I have no doubt it will be the guillotine otherwise."

"I see. Well, yes, we can help to at least get you to Jeremie as a start. It has taken us a lot of effort, but we are almost ready to pull out. I personally will be sailing for Jeremie in three days time. How many are in your party and do you have much in the way of belongings?"

"Four people, Captain. My daughter and I, my best house slave, and my overseer, who has been my guardian, is everyone I have. We will have but a few trunks. We will happily leave this place with little notice."

"Excellent. I will make room for you on my own ship. Your quarters will be rougher than you are accustomed to, because this is a warship, but we will get you there. It will also be crowded, for we have many others to help. Fortunately the trip to Jeremie is not long. As for what the future holds once the withdrawal is complete the General will have to decide what to do, unless I can come up with a solution. But for now, if you can be ready within two days time I will send a party to your home here to provide protection and assistance with your belongings."

"Thank you Captain, I place myself in your capable hands."

As she finished speaking she put a hand to her

mouth and a look of horror came over her face. She glanced quickly at where his missing arm would have been and back at his face before speaking.

"Captain, I'm so sorry, I—"

Evan laughed and waved his one remaining hand.

"Don't worry, this is an old wound now and, I assure you, my one remaining hand has become capable enough to do the work of two."

***

Evan stepped out with his drink onto the broad verandah fronting the entire length of the mansion overlooking the town of Jeremie and the oceanfront beyond. The day was warm and Evan had dreaded putting on his dress uniform, expecting it would be uncomfortably hot. Fortunately, an offshore breeze had sprung up and once the sun went down it had become a pleasant evening. Over a dozen British warships and triple this number of merchant ships dotted the harbor, their night lanthorns twinkling to create a pleasing sight.

The verandah was packed with people. With the withdrawal to the two British enclaves finally complete as agreed, the General had imposed on one of the richest grand blancs plantation owners to organize a ball at his home in Jeremie, in the hope it would help morale. Army and Navy officers in full dress uniforms mingled with lavishly dressed men and women of all ages, while servants strolled through the crowd offering drinks and small appetizers. A buffet table groaning under the weight of a wide array of food was set up inside for anyone who wanted more to eat. The sound of music wafted from a room neighboring the buffet, where yet more people were dancing.

On the surface everyone appeared to be enjoying the evening, but Evan could sense an undercurrent of tension running through it all. He drifted over to a large crowd, sipping at his drink as he went. In the center of it all General Maitland was holding court, surrounded by a ring of well-dressed plantation owners all eager to make their opinions known. Evan listened long enough to find the General was doing everything he could to soothe their collective fears and assure them he had by no means given it all up for lost, but he was facing plenty of skepticism.

"What you must remember is all we agreed to was a strategic withdrawal," insisted the General, sounding a little exasperated as he spoke to one red faced owner. "We did not agree to a cessation of hostilities. Give us time and we will make our presence felt once again."

"Time may not be on our side, General," said the owner. "None of us have our incomes any more. If you do not act, and act fast, you may find no one is willing to return to resume business."

Evan drifted in and out of a few other, smaller conversations. The groups of plantation owners were all expressing much the same view as what the General was currently hearing, while the Army and Navy officers were, as usual, limiting their conversations to military matters. Evan was unsurprised to find the Army officers espousing a wide range of views as to what should be done next. Some wanted to avenge their losses with an all out attack, while others wondered why the General was even trying to hold anything at all. The majority of them were somewhere in between. Being this outspoken was unusual, but the General was a leader who actively solicited the thoughts of his men. Since Evan had already heard many of those thoughts directly from the General he drifted back inside to refresh his drink.

A soft hand on his shoulder made him turn to find Amelie Caron smiling at him.

"Good evening, Captain. I hoped I might find you here."

"Ah, madam," said Evan, putting his drink down and giving her a small bow of greeting. "I too was wondering if you would come tonight. Have you settled in well?"

The week since the *Alice* had left Port-au-Prince for Jeremie had been busy. The *Alice* was fully laden with as many refugees as could be stuffed on board without hampering the ability of the crew to sail the ship. Even the open decks were filled with small groups of people who found themselves forced to sleep on the same spot they occupied during the day. The winds had not been favorable and it had taken almost three full days for the journey.

Evan had partitioned his quarters with temporary wood screens to accommodate even more people. His new servant Jeanne along with Amelie Caron's party had moved in. With so many people on board Evan had little time to spend with any of them. Although the people were far less demanding than expected, their small problems combined with the need to be wary of unexpected enemies at sea meant little free time for him to socialize. Their arrival in Jeremie was a blur as he ensured an orderly offloading of the passengers and went about putting the ship to rights.

"I have, Captain Ross. You were so busy I did not have time to properly thank you for all your capable help. I don't know what we would have done without you. And I must say, I am so very impressed with you. I had no idea how complicated sailing a ship can be, yet you somehow handled both your ship and all those people with ease. And now here you are, in your dress uniform, managing to also be the most handsome man present tonight. You should know I am not easily impressed."

Evan laughed. "I appreciate your kind words, madam. If I may return the compliment, you are doing a fine job of being the most beautiful woman present. And I have no doubt your gown is making the other women here incredibly jealous even as we speak."

Amelie gave Evan a brief, pouting look. "Thank you, but please don't call me 'madam' anymore. It makes me sound—old. Call me Amelie."

"You are far from old, and I shall certainly oblige if you agree to be my friend and call me Evan."

"I will happily be your friend, Evan. I'll be even happier if you will dance with me. You are such a capable man, I am betting you can dance despite your injury."

Evan laughed again. "Well, I confess it took me

a while to master it, but yes, I can dance. The women I dance with find it a little unusual not to have the left hand of their partner on their shoulder, but they all seem to adapt fast. And besides, I like dancing."

Evan found himself spending most of the rest of the evening with Amelie. With the weight of their daily cares lifted for the evening they both relaxed, enjoying themselves dancing and talking, stopping only to enjoy the food periodically.

Evan realized as the hour grew late he had drunk more than usual and gauged she had done the same, as she stumbled a couple of times against him unexpectedly. The third time it happened she fell fully into him and because he had only one arm he had no choice but to pull her close to steady her. As he steadied her Evan realized he was enjoying the feel of her body close to his. For a brief moment she looked into his eyes and he knew she was enjoying it too, but she regained her composure and stepped back in embarrassment.

"I'm sorry, Evan. I think I've had quite enough to drink and others are beginning to leave. I should leave too, but I have to say I truly enjoyed this. It's the first time I've felt without a care in months."

As Evan helped her into her coach she stopped him mid way. She looked about to see if anyone was watching, before turning to look at him as he held her hand.

"Evan? Can I give you a ride to your quarters? You could even come back to my home for one last drink if you like. It is no trouble and there is no one watching us who might gossip."

"I—you are very kind to offer it, but my quarters are not far."

"I understand," said Amelie, biting her lip for a moment. "Would you do me the honor of joining me for tea or a drink one afternoon at my home? Please?"

Evan paused once again, but nodded his agreement and she left after they set a date and time. He stood staring after the coach as it departed for a long time, before hanging his head briefly and walking away.

***

At the appointed time Evan knocked on the door to Amelie's home and was soon ushered through the house to her sitting room. She came in as tea was being delivered and when they were alone both of them made to speak at the same time. Evan laughed and signaled she should speak first.

"Evan, I just want to apologize for my behavior the other night. I know I had a little too much to drink and I may have seemed much too forward. You must think poorly of me. I hope you can forgive me."

"I certainly do not think poorly of you and I shall forgive you if you will do the same for me, as I felt much the same. I guess we both drank more than we normally would and under the circumstances I suppose it is no surprise we needed some enjoyment for a change. So we forgive each other?"

"We do. I am so glad you came today, because I want your opinion on the future."

"Certainly, but if I may? There is something

else I want to apologize for. It dawned on me you may be thinking I am—available, as I do not wear a wedding band on my hand. However, I assure you I am happily married and have been for many years now. I used to wear a band, but stopped doing so for security reasons some time back. Some of the people I deal with would not hesitate to harm those I love if they knew I was married and the opportunity arose. I am so sorry if I led you to think otherwise. I suppose I should learn to wear it on occasions like the ball we were at. But all I was thinking of was enjoying an evening free of care and I truly did appreciate your company. Perhaps more than you know."

Amelie took a deep breath before she smiled ruefully.

"Thank you for telling me. I confess I was rather hoping this could be otherwise, but I understand. I have been—lonely since my husband was killed."

"I probably shouldn't say this, but I will anyway. Were I not married, be assured I would readily make myself available for you. You really are an attractive woman and a wonderful person, and I have no doubt someone out there will make himself a very happy man when he finds you."

They both smiled at each other in silence for a few long moments before she finally recovered herself and poured him some tea.

"Thank you. So, I really do want your opinion, Evan. I am not sure of the future here. I know, the General may yet turn this around and we will regain what we had, but in truth many others are not optimistic. I'm afraid I share this thinking. With my husband gone I have nothing to hold me here. I would like a better place to raise my daughter if nothing else."

"I assume France or any of its possessions are out of the question?"

"Yes. Maybe some day if the pigs who have taken power are turned out, but I am not optimistic about this either."

"Have you thought of England? As you say, your relatives there may not know you, but they would at least be a family connection and they might be inclined to help a little to get settled."

Amelie bit her lip. "I have and I am not sure about this possibility. You and others have shown me a degree of kindness I would not have thought possible, you understand. The problem is sometimes others have been—cold."

Evan nodded. "I do understand. Have you considered America? The Americans are a rather independent lot, but perhaps they would be more welcoming. They are still struggling to build their country, though. There is also the matter of money. I'm sorry to ask this, but do you have sufficient resources to build a new life there or somewhere else?"

Amelie shrugged. "My husband was careful to a degree. As the situation grew worse he began turning some of our assets into gold, but make no mistake, our fortune was mostly in our plantation. I have my jewels, too. So yes, I think I have enough, if I am careful. As for America, I don't know. The political situation between America and France is not good now, and I am uncertain how welcome I would be there, too. And, I would know no one. So you see my dilemma?"

Evan nodded and sat in thought for a moment before responding. He told her of two other possibilities occurring to him and she bit her lip, looking away as she mulled the ideas over. She finally turned back to him and spoke.

"I had not considered those possibilities. I will give them thought. In any case, there is no rush for we are safe here for now."

"Yes, you are. Well, we will see what the future holds. Lets hope it stays this way and matters improve.
***

The meetings with Andre Rigaud in south province were spread over a period of three days. Rigaud's mansion in Jacmel on the south coast offered a stunning view of the ocean from the windows of the room they were meeting in. Hedouville used the first two days to gain a sense of the man and what his interests might be. He also tried the same strategy of flattery at first, much as he did with Toussaint.

As the meetings progressed Hedouville came to understand that in many ways both leaders were similar. Both were mulattos and owned plantations with slaves. Both had proven successes on the battleground as leaders. And both had egos the size of Saint Domingue. Rigaud lapped up the praise as if it was no more than he was due.

By the third and final day it was clear Rigaud was looking for much more than praise. While professing a greater willingness than Toussaint to work with Hedouville on everything, the price in return was enormous. Hedouville had expected money and power would be at the heart of his demands, but not on the scale Rigaud was looking for.

While both black leaders bore many similarities, they had one major difference in their thinking. Toussaint continued to profess an ultimate desire to some day free all slaves in Saint Domingue and keep them free, including the large numbers of pure black slaves populating the lowest social strata of the country. His goal to achieve this was always a vague future date and in the meantime he and other leaders in his camp continued using slaves as before, which was a contradiction still unresolved.

Toussaint's rival Andre Rigaud had no similar problem. Rigaud's goal was to maintain the coexisting systems of slavery and the established social order exactly as they currently were. The vast majority of his followers were free colored mulattos like him. Rigaud even went as far on occasion as to wear a straight hair wig, to appear as close to a white man as possible. As members of the social strata right below the pure white population they held an enormous degree of power, because the white owners were too few to control it all. Filling the gap made them an essential part of the economy of Saint Domingue. Rigaud and his followers liked the taste of power and had no intention of losing their position by freeing slaves.

Sensing Rigaud's pliability and willingness to

work with the French lifted Hedouville's spirits, until the price tag became clear. Rigaud wanted money and lots of it, so much the sum he named was enough it made Hedouville's jaw drop. He had wanted to laugh, but it was clear from the look on Rigaud's face the man was serious. After protesting vigorously the impossibility of giving Rigaud such a sum, the black leader simply shrugged.

"The price is the price and you must pay it. Toussaint and his men are still too strong in the north. If you want me to carry the fight to him I will need resources and more men. I am perfectly willing to do this, but I am not foolish enough to do what you ask without help. Our defenses here in south province are too strong for Toussaint, but we are not strong enough to move beyond our border with him, so we have a stalemate just now."

"But France has need of your help! You must understand we face many pressures from foes everywhere. Saint Domingue was a major source of funds and we must restore the flow of money in order to continue the fight. When matters are in hand and times are better France will be generous to those who help."

Rigaud shrugged. "Talk is fine, money is what is better. While you figure out how to find the money, we can also talk about a new order in Saint Domingue once we have full control."

"New order?"

"Saint Domingue is a complex place. I really think France would be best served by placing local people in power who understand it. I am certain the funds France needs so desperately will flow once the proper order is established."

When Rigaud's thinking finally became clear Hedouville shifted his strategy to making veiled, subtle threats about what might happen to those who failed to support the French administration, much as he had with Toussaint. He also added vague hints of yet more French troops arriving along with help from the Spanish on the other side of the island. Rigaud reacted the same way Toussaint had with ambiguous, neutral responses. Both men knew each was calling the other's bluff and neither was succeeding. But the meetings ended on a positive note with promises to consider what they had heard and agreeing to meet again at some point.

Two days later Hedouville rode into Port-au-Prince to the new headquarters they had established in fortifications the British had vacated. He was pleased to find Montdenoix waiting for him. Without even cleansing the dirt from the roads off him, Hedouville met Montdenoix in a private room, despite seeing Montdenoix appeared as exhausted as he was. Rubbing his own tired eyes, Hedouville told the spy to proceed with his report. Hedouville poured the glass of wine he had been looking forward to for the entire two-day journey back as he listened, filling a second glass for Montdenoix as well.

"Theodore, there is much happening. Three of the contacts I had in Port-au-Prince were murdered. The murders coincided with the British withdrawal and this is no coincidence. As I've told you before I have sensed for a long time I have opponents on the

British side and, I have to say, they know their business. I think they were actually watching these men and maybe even feeding them misinformation. But this is all not your problem, it is mine and I will deal with the British when the time comes. The main thing I have to report is there are signs the British Army may be up to something."

"Go on," said Hedouville, a frown creasing his face.

"You recall we had hoped this General Maitland might simply use his remaining two enclaves as staging posts to depart Saint Domingue forever, correct? I have received reports painting a different picture. The British are offloading large amounts of supplies in Jeremie from their warships, which are numerous in the area. If they were getting ready for a full withdrawal, this would not be happening. The same is happening in Mole St. Nicholas in the north, except it is nowhere near on the scale of what is going on in the south. And the number of warships in the north is no more than usual."

Hedouville sighed and sipped at his wine. "Well, we cannot have everything go our way all the time, can we? It would have been nice to have the British out of our way for a change."

Hedouville took a few minutes to brief Montdenoix on the meetings he had held with Rigaud. When he finished the two men looked at each other in silence. Hedouville knew the look of tired frustration on Montdenoix's face was showing on his own face.

"Theodore, something has to change here. We

are both doing the best we can, but these obstinate bastards we are dealing with here need some prodding to get into line. This man Rigaud sounds like a challenge, but Toussaint is going to be even worse now his ego is twice the size it was before. You should have seen him preening as he rode into Port-au-Prince. You would have thought he was riding in on a road made of gold plate and, naturally, he thinks he owns all of it. So is it truly not possible for more troops from France?"

Hedouville sighed. "I will write and explain the situation, but I am not optimistic. I was told in clear terms more help wasn't coming and we must work with what we have. There are far too many other pressures. This may sound strange, but I agree with this man Rigaud. If France wants the resources from this island to fund the many battles we face, we must make the investment to achieve it. But we shall do what we can. I will write again to Roume in Santo Domingo."

"Do you really think he can help?"

"He must. I brought very clear orders for him from France. He was tasked with keeping Santo Domingo under control by any means and with providing resources to us. The paltry number of French soldiers we have stationed in Le Cap Francois is insufficient to do anything meaningful. So I agree with you something must change. We need more options available to us. Well, have you anything else to report? I need to clean up and get some sleep."

"Ah, there is one other more minor item to report, but it is one I am enjoying and I'm sure you will, too. Our men have been scouring the areas abandoned by the British for royalist and émigré traitors. While many have escaped, we have indeed managed to capture some. We emptied the big prison a few blocks from here of our friends the British were holding and are now filling it with new arrivals. We will have to do some public trials to help the people understand where their true interests should lie, of course. I'm sure the guillotine the men are setting up will drive the point home."

"Excellent," said Hedouville, as both men smiled and raised their glasses to down the remainder of their wine. "We will find a way through this mess, Hubert. I know we will."

Chapter Six
June 1798
Saint Domingue

Andre Rigaud's mansion in Jacmel was once again the location for a meeting, but this time it was with Evan and General Maitland's chief negotiator Lord Allan Harcourt. They sailed in on a British frigate under a flag of truce after exchanging messages seeking agreement to meet. Evan volunteered once again to be a silent observer to meet one of their potential enemies and take his measure on behalf of the General. His other reason for doing so was because to date Evan had not succeeded in establishing a source inside Rigaud's camp and he wanted to see the area to look for possibilities he may have missed.

    The General reasoned they had something to gain from trying to forge an alliance with Rigaud and nothing to lose if it failed. Preparations for a new push to rebuild British fortunes in Saint Domingue would meanwhile continue apace. Evan had doubts about either course of action succeeding, but could not fault the General's logic. Within thirty minutes of the meeting beginning Evan was almost certain his doubts of success were well founded. As the day wore on Rigaud was as arrogant as Evan had expected him to be and was openly skeptical. By the time late afternoon came around Rigaud became blunt.

    "Look, I agreed to meet with you as a courtesy, not because I think you actually have any power. You British must face the truth you are a spent force here in Saint Domingue. Yes, you still have your powerful Navy, but your Army has shown they can be tamed, just like other armies which have come here."

"You may be underestimating British resolve, Andre," said Lord Harcourt. "But I must emphasize we are here to talk to you about an alliance which could change everything. I really think there are ways your interests and ours can be made to overlap."

"I'll tell you how this can happen. It's very simple. Right now, this country is divided between my forces and those of Toussaint. You are no longer a factor, whether you believe it or not. We are in a stalemate. To change it I need resources and my price is one you may not want to pay. I also want agreement Toussaint will be subservient to me if for some reason he must be accommodated when I finally do gain the upper hand, which I will. Your Navy and Army will take my battle orders and provide support. I am prepared to be generous to my friends when I am finally in charge of all of Saint Domingue, of course."

"I see. And your price?"

Rigaud named a sum so high both Evan and the General's negotiator sat back in shock. As one they looked at each other in disbelief before Lord Harcourt regained his composure and responded.

"Andre, I don't need to consult anyone on this point. I already know the sum you ask is out of the question. I really think you should consider other options and ways we can work together toward common goals. After all, you seek to maintain the existing social order and we share this goal."

Rigaud shrugged. "I will consider your words, but I doubt my terms will change. Were I to join forces with you many would be unhappy, so I must have a way to change that and make them happy. I trust you understand. Good day, gentlemen."

Evan felt the effort wasn't a total loss as they returned to the docks when he made note of an area housing numerous taverns and inns. Such establishments had always served as prime sources of information and Evan knew one of his crew who spoke fluent French would soon be frequenting them.

***

Evan found a report from James waiting when they finally returned to Jeremie. Evan had long since sent word of the British withdrawal to him, but this was the first report he had received in return. The message was a simple, one page letter Evan was unsurprised at, for James was always sparing with words. But the message it contained was good news, for progress was being made.

A series of insults written in French questioning Spanish honor were scrawled on the walls of the local mayor's office one night, while two other incidents where French sailors allegedly assaulted Spanish ladies had helped finally stir up the population. The fact the author of the insults was James and the two ladies happened to be local whores dressed and paid well for the occasion was a detail the French authorities missed. The local Spanish population was seething with barely concealed anger as a result. Fights between French sailors and Spanish soldiers in the local taverns were now a nightly occurrence.

James wasn't ready to declare his mission accomplished, but he felt confident enough to suggest Evan send word to Baptiste of progress being made. Evan agreed and prepared his own message to Baptiste. He had barely finished when word came the General wanted to see him. Evan made arrangements to send the message and went to see the General. The General had just finished debriefing Lord Harcourt, but was pleased with word the Spanish were unlikely to be a factor any time soon.

"At least we have some positive news, although I confess I wish this man Rigaud wasn't so obstinate. Mr. Ross, if you have time please join me for my next meeting. Some of the owners who relocated here have been seeking reassurances and I want to brief them on our plans to take the fight beyond Jeremie."

"General, are you certain these men will keep their mouths shut? I have no doubt as to their merit, but I cannot guarantee there are no French spies about to overhear loose talk."

The General shrugged. "I know. The problem with my job is sometimes I must also be a politician. Reassuring these people we are not abandoning them is a necessity if we are to maintain order."

Evan nodded. "Of course, sir. Yes, I will attend. I think it safe to tell them we are fairly certain of no intervention coming from the other side of the island, although obviously no details can be given as to how we know."

The meeting went as Evan expected it would, with the General emphasizing they would be taking steps toward solidifying their foothold in south province. Evan sensed disappointment it would not be the major push they were hoping for and the skepticism about the chances of success from the men around the table was obvious, but to a man they seemed to make a collective decision to take a wait and see approach. But as he sat listening an undefined sense of concern stole over Evan. By the end of the meeting he had resolved to make extra efforts to root out French spies in Jeremie, for he felt no confidence whatsoever the men listening to the General divulge his plans would keep them secret.

***

Three days later Evan sent word he needed to see the General and at the appointed time the General's clerk gave him Evan presented himself. The General appeared harried and Evan knew Army officers seeking his attention more and more beset him on all sides. Evan felt sorry for him, knowing it was only going to get worse the closer they got to the date of the attack. He also felt sorry at the news he was about to give the General.

"Well, what is it, Captain?"

"I'm sorry to report your plans to attack and gain ground beyond Jeremie may have been compromised, sir."

"Compromised? How so?"

"Sir, I put my men on alert because of our impending attack. I asked them to be vigilant in case they saw or heard anything suspicious. I gave the same orders to a few local sources I have here. One of my men inadvertently discovered something of concern and reported it to me. Unfortunately, we have discovered a local pigeon breeder who was operating in secret."

"In secret, you say. I see."

"General, we both know there is only one reason to hide the fact you are breeding pigeons. I have questioned the man and I think it clear he is a paid conduit. There are likely other people here feeding him information and we are actively rooting them out as we speak. He is not willing to admit to his activities yet, but we continue to question him in the prison. I have always been skeptical of information obtained when under duress, so I cannot confirm if word of your attack is now in the hands of your enemies. I recommend you plan as if it is."

The General sighed. "I know what you are thinking, Captain Ross. You are thinking it was a bad idea to be so free with our plans. You may well be right. But there were reasons for doing so and I am confident that even if they know the general approach we will take, they do not know all of the details let alone the date we propose to make our move. I didn't share everything with those men, you know."

"Of course, General. I understand."

"Well, the die is cast, Captain Ross. I must show resolve to our masters back home and this means sending men into the fire once more. I could wish for better circumstances, but then no one ever told me this would be easy. Keep me informed, Captain."

Evan saluted and left, feeling grim about their prospects for the future. As a leader, Evan was well used to the burden of sending the relatively few men under his command into danger. Being a senior leader sending hundreds or thousands into battle was a weight to bear on an entirely different level. The General was doing his best not to show it, but it seemed to Evan the lines on his face were etched a little deeper than usual.

***

Montdenoix came into Hedouville's office and sat down in time to watch his political master fling the letter he was reading across the room, scattering the individual pages everywhere. Hedouville scowled and looked like he wanted to keep throwing whatever came to hand about, but he put his hands palm downwards on the desk in front of him and took a deep breath, his eyes closed as he mastered himself. By now Montdenoix knew better than to interrupt and sat silent, waiting for the storm to pass. When Hedouville finally opened his eyes he let out an exasperated sigh and glared at Montdenoix.

"Typical. God, I should have pressed him harder when we were there. In fact, I should have forced him to give me the men and ships I wanted on the spot. How am I to achieve anything if I can't rely on the people around me?"

Montdenoix remained silent for a moment before speaking.

"Theodore, I am doing my best—"

"Ah, I am sorry, Hubert. I am not talking about you. This incompetent Roume in Santo Domingo has just replied. He claims nothing can be done because unrest is building and his troops are busy quelling it. Useless fool."

"I see. Well, I also have news. You recall I was successful in getting an informant into General Maitland's camp and I mentioned there were signs the British are up to something? Well, they are. I have received confirmation of an attack coming in a little over a week in south province. It seems the General wants to expand his foothold beyond Jeremie and I am not surprised. With the province surrounded on three sides by ocean the geography lends itself to this kind of move. So now we know, the question becomes what do we do with the knowledge?"

Hedouville sat back in his chair, rubbing his chin in thought for several long moments.

"The only way I can see to turn this to our advantage would be to pass the information on to Rigaud. I don't know if our help will strengthen our hand with him or not, but it is worth a try. The alternative is to do nothing, but if the British are successful they will continue to be a thorn in our side. Do you see any other possibilities?"

Montdenoix shrugged. "If Toussaint was a reliable ally we could pass it to him. He would probably attack Rigaud at the same time, giving Rigaud a war on two fronts to fight. With any luck it would be a bloodbath all around and we could step in to clean up the mess. Even better, it could rid us of one or even two of the obstacles in our way."

Hedouville grimaced. "The problem with this is neither of these fools is reliable. And my lack of trust in Toussaint is even greater than my distrust of Rigaud. No, I will draft a message to Rigaud and present the information as a token of good will on our part. It will be a card I can play later if I must, although I doubt it will carry enough weight to serve as a trump card. And when I finish it I will draft another letter to this incompetent bastard Roume. He will give us what we want or face the consequences. In the meantime let us keep putting out rumors the Spanish will be here to help soon."

***

Baptiste and Julien Raimond made their way into Toussaint's meeting room, having responded to a summons and met at Fort Picolet at the same time. Toussaint was alone in the room, waiting for them. After a slave brought drinks and they were alone Toussaint spoke.

"Thank you for coming, I have need of counsel and you two were the closest available. I have received word from Rigaud the British plan to attack him soon and he seeks help. I am of two minds about whether to do so, for I have been told from a reliable source this bastard Hedouville has met with Rigaud and they plan to meet again. I also keep hearing the damned Spanish will arrive, although when who knows."

"Toussaint, Rigaud may be a major pain in your ass, but at least he is French at heart," said Raimond. "The British have been left with no more than a couple of toeholds on this island. If we can do something to rid ourselves of them once and for all it will make the situation here less complicated. Rigaud will still be a problem, but he could then be isolated and dealt with later. So I think we should support him, within reason."

"I can't argue with Julien's logic, Toussaint," said Baptiste. "How does he know of this attack, though? Can you be certain this is not a trap?"

"He claims it is the Frenchman Hedouville who sent word. Some source they have in the General's camp learned of the plans. And no, I do not as a rule trust Rigaud, but in this case I think I at least believe the report he says he got. The General made no promises to us other than to withdraw to Jeremie and Mole St. Nicholas. Trying to regain territory in south province makes sense. It's what I would do were I in his shoes. And what about the Spanish? Baptiste, what have you heard?"

"I was actually making ready to come and see you when your messenger arrived, as I have only just received an update. I don't know where these rumors of the imminent arrival of Spanish troops to bolster the French are coming from, but I don't believe them. As I promised, I have friends in Santo Domingo doing what they can to make life complicated for the Spanish. The Spanish have been forced to station army units on the street corners throughout Santo Domingo and to boost patrols. And I notice the French here in Cap Le Francois don't appear to be stirring themselves to do anything in anticipation of soon to arrive help. It all means I see no problem from that quarter."

"So the question, Toussaint, is whether you can trust Rigaud, at least for the purpose of this situation," said Raimond. "I think you can and you should send help. Make sure they are on the lookout for treachery, of course. Do you have any other concerns?"

Toussaint grimaced. "I am not certain of Dessalines. Were it up to him we would be pressing with our army without any let up to wipe all of our foes off the map. He fails to understand a leader must use the men wisely, especially when we are talking about their lives. And of course, I expect you know I have days where I think he wants to usurp me."

"Maybe he does," said Baptiste. "But this is a matter of keeping him busy and out of the way. It sounds to me like you think supporting Rigaud is the way to go. If so, why don't you send Dessalines with some men to do the job? If nothing else, he can scout Rigaud's defenses while he is at it. It could prove useful in the future."

Toussaint sat silent for several moments before he smiled at Baptiste.

"You are so devious. I'm glad you aren't thinking of usurping me, too. Yes, we will send some help to Rigaud, including Dessalines to lead them and keep him busy. I think it is time we put some pressure on Mole St. Nicholas, too. The fortifications there are much too strong and we will likely get nowhere, but we can't have the British sleeping well at night, can we?"

The three men laughed and finished their drinks. And once again, Baptiste was already drafting yet another report to Evan in his mind.

***

The empty wine bottle smashed into the wall and shattered into numerous tiny shards, followed by the paperweight which moments before was sitting on Hedouville's desk. Montdenoix had made a point of sitting well back in the knowledge the information he was delivering was not what Hedouville wanted to hear and his superior's reaction was all too predictable.

"What is it with these people, Hubert? Are they all morons? How is it this Rigaud claims to loathe Toussaint L'Ouverture and then turns around and seeks his help? And Toussaint, who allegedly feels the same about Rigaud, decides to send the help he wants. These people make no sense. How am I supposed to deal with inconsistent buffoons like this?"

"Theodore, I agree. I don't know what to tell you, but this is what my new informant in Toussaint's camp has reported took place."

"Can you trust this source? Is this some kind of pig shit Toussaint or the British are feeding us?"

Montdenoix sighed. "I trust this new source as much as one can in this situation. Inherently, anyone you are bribing is untrustworthy because they are betraying someone they in theory serve. This, of course, means they could be betraying us and simply taking our money. But this man is in Toussaint's inner circle of advisors and I am paying him a ridiculous amount of gold to give us what we need. If I told you what I am paying him you would start throwing things at the wall again. But in truth, if what a source tells you over time is proved correct, it is only then you can start to really trust them."

Hedouville shook his head in disgust, before reaching over to a side cabinet to pull out a bottle of brandy and two glasses. After filling both he handed one to Montdenoix and sighing.

"You must forgive me my moments of frustration, Hubert. It just galls me badly that, once again, we are being left out of decisions as if we are unimportant. And this means it is perhaps time to change it all."

"What do you have in mind, Theodore?"

"I think it is time I sent a message straight to this General Maitland telling him I want to negotiate directly with him. After all, I represent France here, not L'Ouverture or Rigaud, and perhaps it is time to remind him of who it is he should be dealing with. I am also going to send a message to both L'Ouverture and Rigaud telling them to expect from now on I will insist on being involved in any decisions involving the British and their future on this island. And I think I will make it clear to both of them our forces will not be sitting on the sidelines in future if this doesn't change."

"Have our men been trained enough we are able to make such a point, Theodore?"

Hedouville shrugged and waved a hand to dismiss the concern.

"I will ask for a report from our commanders once again, but the new recruits we brought have had the better part of two months of rest and time to be trained. We now have close to three thousand men at our disposal. It is enough to perhaps make our presence felt. If I can cajole Roume into getting off his backside and he were to give us a comparable number of Spanish regulars, we would be a force to reckon with."

"Is it worth a personal visit to Roume, do you think?"

Hedouville shook his head. "It might well be worth it, but matters seem to be moving faster here and I am loathe to lose the time it would take to get there and back. For now, at least, I will not risk it. And Hubert? Keep putting out those rumors about Spanish help coming our way at any time. Let's turn the heat up."

***

Colonel Warrington was given the task of pushing through Rigaud's lines surrounding Jeremie. When it began the attack came without warning at dawn. Despite being forewarned an attack was coming, Rigaud's mulatto forces were still unaware of the exact date and found themselves stunned by its ferocity. General Maitland had ordered preparations to be masked as much as possible and spread out over a period of several days to keep his foes guessing. Despite the size of the force surrounding Jeremie, Colonel Warrington's men had the initiative and kept it. Within a few short hours of fierce fighting a hole was finally punched through Rigaud's lines and those on either side of the gap began melting away into the forest to the south.

Evan and the General were watching it all from a vantage point on one of the fortifications surrounding Jeremie. The smell of spent gunpowder and smoke filled the air along with the din of weapons fire and the screams of dying men, making it difficult even from their location to determine exactly what was happening. The heavy forest the mulatto army was using as cover didn't help either, but the British field guns the General had surreptitiously moved into strategic locations ripped into the forest and their foes position with devastating hails of canister and grapeshot. Each blast of the small, grape sized shot would spread in an arc sweeping away anyone in its path. Despite the difficulty in determining exactly what was happening, it was the General who pinpointed when the breakthrough came.

"There, Captain Ross. To our right, you see it? Our men on the flank are moving forward in good order and en masse. We will carry the day, at least for the moment. Well, this will serve for now as my response to this arrogant frog Hedouville demanding I negotiate with him. Now we just need to see which direction they will retreat. If it is toward Tiburon, as I suspect, our next task will be to provide a pleasant welcome for them."

Evan smiled. "The Royal Navy stands ready to help, General. I will pass word to them and be on my way. Until we meet again, sir."

***

The stab of light flashing from the big guns of the frigate firing as one in the pre dawn gloom three days later was still enough to blind those foolish enough not to look away or close their eyes. But Evan had been through this many times before and was deliberately looking away, as he wasn't about to be temporarily blinded.

Around him the men of Royal Navy frigate *HMS Imperious* were going about their business with the cool precision of the well-trained professionals they were. Evan smiled, for it felt good to be on the deck of a heavy frigate once more.

While he was all too happy to be Captain of his own ship the *Alice*, the power he could bring to bear on an enemy was nothing compared to the devastating punch of a full broadside from a forty-four gun frigate. Although Evan knew he had little to complain of, a big part of him inside lusted to be Captain of a ship like this. The desire was shared by every officer in the fleet, even those whose seniority had long since taken them past being mere frigate Captains. The agility of these warships and the power they could bring to bear meant they were frequently used in independent missions and it was every officer's dream to be in command of one, free to make their own decisions without interference.

The initial broadside from the *Imperious* was the signal for the four other nearby warships to join in and Evan had known to cover his ears. The shock from four separate, full broadsides coming within seconds of each other was immense enough to be felt as blows to the body. With every second the light was growing stronger and the officers on the quarterdeck to a man were focusing telescopes on the distant fortifications in the harbor of Tiburon, trying to determine the impact. Evan felt no need to follow their lead, for he knew the defenses in the harbor were being swept away and men were dying. More would soon follow.

The General's plan was working, at least for now. His forces chased Rigaud's men steadily toward Tiburon, as he had anticipated. Any hope Rigaud's men may have had of finding respite or of escaping by sea was dashed by the appearance of the Royal Navy warships blockading the port, established the same day they began streaming into the town. Rigaud's already weary soldiers would find no rest from the battle they could not escape. A steady stream of civilian refugees made their way through the British lines wherever possible, knowing what was likely to come.

Evan had dined the night before on the *Imperious* with the other five Captains. The dinner seemed surreal for Evan, for although he had sat around the table with other Navy officers many times during his career, he had never done so as a post Captain himself.

He did not know any of the men personally, but they made him welcome, despite being curious about exactly what it was he had done to warrant becoming a Captain when his command consisted only of his small sloop *HMS Alice*, lying to seaward of the big warships blockading Tiburon. Evan kept his responses to their questions vague and emphasized his tasks generally involved an element of diplomatic work. Although a couple of them raised an eyebrow at the vague answers they knew better than to press the matter. As the conversation progressed Evan soon made it clear to them he was a professional seaman and knew his business when it came to his ship, which was good enough for him to be accepted into their ranks without further question.

The evening was a curious mix of camaraderie and pessimism. As the wine flowed they all relaxed in the enjoyment of each other's company, as men with similar experiences and passions for their profession. They were also to a man pessimistic about the future of the British presence in Saint Domingue. Privately, Evan wasn't about to disagree, for he was coming to feel the same way. He also knew they would do their job despite whatever misgivings they all might have. In the spirit of comradeship the Captain of the *Imperious* invited Evan to join them before dawn to watch the bombardment of the town from his own ship.

Evan and his ship were present for only one reason. The General desired another set of eyes he could trust on the unfolding events, as he could not be everywhere. He also wanted Evan's unbiased opinion on the situation regardless of how matters went, for the General would be beset by others opinions on all sides especially if the attack did not go well.

Three days later Evan was beginning to wonder if matters were indeed not going well, as the stubborn defense of Tiburon continued. But contact was made with British forces ringing the town and they expressed optimism of prevailing soon. The punishment of the Navy bombardment continued, but with focus now on targets the Army chose for them.

The problem was a total victory had yet to be achieved, which was due to the sizeable number of troops who had dug in to defend themselves, aided by the large numbers of soldiers retreating from Jeremie joining the men already holding Tiburon. Colonel Warrington was still in command of the forces that had chased his foes to Tiburon and word came from him of his surprise at the sheer numbers he now faced.

Evan wondered if this was the product of Rigaud having received advance word of the attack and surmised these extra men may have been in transit to bolster the forces at Jeremie. He went ashore and questioned several captured soldiers, returning convinced they were indeed given plenty of notice the British would be launching an attack. But the progress the Army was making must have been enough for the General, as word came the second phase of his push to expand his foothold in south province was beginning.

With the help of the Royal Navy once again British troops landed at Cap Irois, on the western end of south province and further west of Tiburon. Driving anyone who resisted before them they quickly passed the men still dealing with the stubborn, tenacious defense of Tiburon and headed for a rendezvous with yet more troops landed at Bay des Anglais to the east. At Bay des Anglais a large force of Navy warships pounded the defenses of the town without mercy before troop ships disgorged yet more British soldiers in a steady stream. This time Colonel Francis Bains led the men ashore. Evan and his crew watched the landings from the *Alice* once again, having joined the force to watch this attack too.

As before, the warship Captains gathered to

dine together the night before the attack and as a courtesy invited the Colonel and some of his officers to join them. This time the meal was more somber, for everyone knew some of the men present might well be dead within twenty-four hours or less. The Colonel was coolly optimistic, but Evan sensed the man was under no illusions about the possible success of the mission. Colonel Bains was well aware of what was happening in Tiburon and knew it was likely he could face far more opponents than anyone thought they might. But he and his men would deal with what lay before them, regardless of the outcome. The night ended with the Navy officers offering a subdued toast to their Army brothers in arms.

***

Evan made his way to the General's meeting room in Jeremie once again over a week later. Evan had long since returned as he had far too many demands on his time to be absent for too lengthy a spell, but the General was out in the field with his men and had only recently returned the day before. His return was not triumphant.

He found the General working from his meeting room that day. Neatly organized piles of correspondence were spread in a large semicircle in front of him. The General looked up as Evan came in and on seeing whom it was waved a hand at the clerk ushering Evan in, ordering him to bring drinks. The General asked Evan to wait and continued working in silence until two glasses of French brandy had appeared in front of them and the clerk closed the door behind him as he left. With a sigh, the General put down the letter he was reading and reached for his drink. Evan did the same as the General spoke.

"Well, Captain Ross, what do you think?"

Evan pressed his lips together before shrugging. The General looked weary and drained from his time in the field, but Evan knew he needed an honest opinion.

"Sir, I think your men gave it their best effort and this was an unfortunate, but necessary step. It is sad so many men lost their lives to prove what I think we both knew before this began, but the die was cast even when we sat together in London with our political masters. I am not completely up to date on the current situation, as I have been buried in dealing with paperwork and trying to maintain my contacts on this island. When I last saw a report our thrust had stalled and we were facing an incredible number of foes. It seems this man L'Ouverture did indeed send resources to help his foe Rigaud. As I think I told you back in London, this island is complex and alliances which seem strange or even bizarre to us continue to be forged, at least when it is expedient to do so. If as I suspect we are pulling back, the alliance against us will disappear like the morning mist."

The General remained silent, toying with his glass for a long time before finally responding.

"Well, this is what I like about you, Captain. You are an honest man and you speak your mind. You are also not Army and do not carry the same baggage as my officers. They would all have me continue this madness, but I cannot."

The General sighed and took a sip from his glass. "So yes, you are correct we are pulling back. We will not be trying to hold any of the positions we took in our advance. Well, we will expand our boundaries a little around Jeremie to improve our defensive positions, so on this small, positive note I can claim at least a bit of success in solidifying our position here. They won't be attacking us any time soon, but I think this is about the only good thing I can say. I suppose I could add we managed to push them back at Mole St. Nicholas too. They pushed us so hard there I was forced to divert some men to the Mole in support. But for all this, it is over, Captain. I must now give thought to where we go from here."

"General, your logic was sound. Jeremie and south province are the closest part of this island to Jamaica. This Frenchman Hedouville is a long way from making his dream of expansion a reality, but if he somehow prevails and the French were to attack Jamaica, this would be the obvious place to launch it from."

"This is all true, Captain, and the need to deal with those concerns have not changed. I'm just not sure what my options are. Please give it all some thought and let us discuss this again when I am not so tired. We must find a way to salvage something from this. If you have a course of action you think can help achieve our goals I am listening. In the meantime I have decisions to make regarding new deployments of our forces. Please convey my heartfelt appreciation to the Navy for all the support they have shown us."

"General, I think the key to this is Jamaica.

Above all else, we must find a way to keep it safe. I don't want to be premature here, but I think I have a strategy forming in the back of my mind, which may be worth your consideration. The problem is I have not fully thought through the ramifications or exactly how we might employ it. I shall give this more thought and, of course, I shall also pass word of your appreciation to my colleagues."
***

The mood in the town of Jeremie in the latter days of June was subdued and growing more morose with each passing day, as yet more British soldiers returned to where they had started weeks before. The knowledge many had fallen and would not return, along with the presence of several injured men, did not help morale. All thought of holding balls or society events of any sort disappeared.

The harbor was packed with ships. A large number of the ships at anchor were Royal Navy, but they were outnumbered by merchant vessels of all sizes. Word of the situation had spread far and wide, bringing opportunity with it. Most were British ships from various nearby islands, but well over a third were Americans. Regardless of what island or country they were from, they were diverting to Saint Domingue because of the scent of money to be made. The lure of realizing even more profit from a trading voyage by stuffing a few desperate, well paying refugees onto their ship was worth a few more days at sea as long as their cargo was not perishable.

The problem was the price they sought for their

services had grown exponentially, as the merchants were betting the British would not try a second time to reverse their fortunes on the island. Those who could afford it were selling what they could and making deals to leave. Those who could not were increasingly desperate, necessitating regular Army patrols of the streets to maintain order.

In the midst of this Evan received yet another invitation to tea at the residence of Amelie Caron. Evan sent word of his acceptance and at the appointed time two days later was ushered into her sitting room once again. Amelie was waiting for him. After a few moments of small talk and sipping at their tea Evan went straight to the point.

"Amelie, you are, of course, wondering about the future given recent events. The lack of success with our recent offensive is obvious. The real question is what the General will do next. I have my own thoughts about this and may have suggestions for him, but I cannot read his mind any more than you. What you really want to know is whether the time has come to leave and find a new home elsewhere, correct?"

Amelie put her tea down and looked back up at him, a frank look on her face. Evan could sense the tension behind it.

"Yes, Captain, I do. I value your thoughts. To be honest, there are many here who are very distressed and, if I may say, they are panicking. It is not helping matters the prices being asked to get us off this island are exorbitant."

"I don't like to say it, but I do believe the time has come for you to consider the thought of leaving outright. As I said, I do not know what the General will do. This is just my personal opinion for you alone. The military situation here is—difficult. Even if the General prolongs our presence, I do not see a positive resolution for a very long time. And if we pull out, it is not clear how people such as you will be treated by whoever assumes ultimate control, which is yet another very large question with no clear answer. But you need not panic and neither should the others here. We are not going anywhere soon. Our defenses here in Jeremie are strong and given our foes need to regroup, as much as we do, be assured there is no imminent attack on the horizon."

"I see. This is reassuring, Captain. I appreciate your candor with me."

"Amelie, have you given thought to the possibilities I mentioned the last time we spoke?"

Amelie bit her lip. "I have, and I confess I am still of two minds. I agree they are good choices, but my only concern is I will know no one and have no support to settle in."

"Ah, but perhaps I can help with this, for I know someone in one of the two locations who I'm sure will help you."

Amelie's face brightened as Evan told her what he had in mind and after a few long moments she nodded agreement.

"Excellent. I shall return to my office and send a letter immediately. We will know of the response in time. And as for finding transport for you, as long as you still have only four people in total in your party I should be able to get you off this island without difficulty. I believe I can make arrangements to send you to Antigua on a packet ship and my wife will care for you until preparations can be made for the longer journey. If you wait a bit and book passage from there it won't be as expensive as the outrageous prices they want here. I will need to look into all of this, of course, but I am confident."

Evan finished his tea and rose to leave. "And now, I must go as I have many pressing matters to address."

Amelie rose with him and put on a brave face before taking his hand.

"I don't know what would become of me without your help. I will be eternally in your debt."

Chapter Seven
July 1798
Saint Domingue

The sight of *HMS Penfold* sailing into Jeremie harbor was the best thing Evan had seen in weeks. Evan was taking a break from the usual mountain of paperwork, which seemed to be growing worse every day, and was up on the deck of *HMS Alice* to stretch and walk about. The General had long ago offered him quarters in Jeremie and a place to work, but Evan had declined, knowing space ashore was at a premium.

Evan knew James would have spotted the *Alice* right away, but wouldn't know if Evan was present had they not already made provision for this exact situation. The two men had long ago developed their own set of coded flags for this and other purposes, enabling them to communicate privately while maintaining the fiction they were merchant vessels and not Royal Navy. Evan ordered the signal for 'captain repair on board' to be flown and went back to his cabin to await James's arrival.

Thirty minutes later Evan bade James to enter when he heard the knock on his cabin door. Without a word Evan pointed at the wine cabinet beside the table he was working at. Moments later James slipped into another chair at the table as he put a half full glass for each of them down. Evan finally finished the letter he was writing and shoved it aside, rubbing his eyes.

"Well, thank God you are back. I can use some help. How have you fared in Santo Domingo?"

"It took a while, but I am confident we reached a tipping point from which there will be no turning back. It helps the Spanish were already predisposed to disliking the French and having to take orders from them now adds fuel to the fire. I had to use a little more of our gold than I thought to get them going, but it helped too. It usually does."

"So are you confident there will be no Spanish troops coming our way?"

"As much as I can be, Evan. It may be possible this man Roume will try to send some token force here to pacify Hedouville, because rumors continue the pressure to do so is becoming ever stronger. If we get word the Spanish are caving in and doing what Roume wants I can make another trip to Santo Domingo. But for now, unless you want me back there again for some reason, I am yours to command here."

"Excellent," said Evan, taking the next several minutes to brief James on the latest developments of the situation in Saint Domingue. Although Evan and James had exchanged letters all along, of necessity they were brief and contained little detail. When Evan finished his briefing James asked what Evan wanted him to focus on now he was back.

"This devious shit Montdenoix needs to be your focus. Somehow, he managed to get a source inside Jeremie, who got word out of the attack. I haven't been able to track whoever the bastard is yet, but I think he must be a low level source. Of course, the General told the world an attack was coming and gave out some idea of the details. I understand why he did and as usual I curse the political reality, which forced his hand on the matter. Anyway, the source appears not to have known he was going to land forces at Cap Irois or Cap Les Anglais, so I think we don't have real cause for future concern. But we cannot rest. We both know Montdenoix isn't sitting on his backside. So if you can focus on him and what he is doing it would help immensely. If you can figure out a way to get a source into Rigaud's camp it would be a major boost, too."

A knock on the door interrupted further conversation and Evan called for whomever it was to enter. Jeanne Boucher came in with a packet of correspondence and placed it on the desk.

"Sorry, Captain, I didn't know you had a guest. This correspondence just came in from Barbados. I will leave you to it."

"Thank you, but please don't leave just yet."

Evan took a couple of minutes to introduce Jeanne to James. Evan smiled inwardly as he watched the almost tangible, electric flash of interest both of them showed toward each other as James shook her hand while Evan explained whom she was. James raised an eyebrow when he learned her role, but said nothing.

"So Jeanne is not part of the crew and I don't know how I am going to wean them off of their desire to change this when the time comes, because as near as I can tell they have all fallen madly in love with her. She seems to have kept them all at bay, too, although how she manages it is a mystery. Her cooking is as good as Baptiste's was, which helps plenty. James, you must dine with me tonight and sample her wares."

Evan put his hand to his head even as he finished speaking, realizing what he had said. He gave them a sheepish look as he continued.

"Ah—to be clear this would be your cooking I'm talking about, of course."

Jeanne gave Evan what appeared on the surface to be an innocent smile, but teased him with the flash of her eyes.

"Any special requests for dinner, Captain?"

"Hmm. Why don't you just surprise us? Make whatever your favorite dish is. Bear in mind we both like spicy food."

"Spicy it is. The usual time, sir?"

Evan agreed and she left, permitting herself one last quick glance at James. As the door closed behind her James turned back to Evan.

"Well, damn. Can you recruit one like this for me, too?"

"I assure you it wasn't planned. She was in distress and I merely seized the opportunity to help. She actually has been most useful, but I have no plans to make this long term. I am happily married, remember?"

"Yes, but I'm not. Maybe I can make her a better offer."

Evan laughed.

***

Almost three weeks after the offensive collapsed the General and several of his junior officers began turning their minds to what they might do next, as the many details of entrenching themselves into Jeremie again had fully occupied their minds to this point. The problem was, as usual, everyone had an opinion and none of them matched each other. Evan sat through the meetings at the request of the General and, as tedious as it sometimes was, he had to admire the creativity on display.

The plans all had flaws too easily identified, though. Evan thought the best was to make another attempt to take Tiburon and this time to focus all of their efforts on this one spot. The mountainous geography of parts of the island was so demanding that trying to establish defensive lines across the entire breath of south province was not worth considering. The General himself asked the question to expose the flaw in the plan.

"And will doing so materially change this stalemate, gentlemen?" asked the General. "If we take Tiburon it just means we will now have two places we must defend against a siege when our foes get around to it. And make no mistake, sooner or later they will get to it."

The men around the table looked at each other to see if anyone had a response, but none did. The General let the silence stretch out a few moments longer before closing the meeting.

"Gentlemen, I appreciate your thoughts on this. I will consider all of your ideas. You are dismissed. Captain Ross, please be so good as to remain behind."

When the last of them were gone and the door closed the General sighed, getting up to pour them both a small glass of brandy each.

"Well, I had to ask them, but I am not surprised

they had nothing I have not already considered. Every path forward is fraught with risk and most, if not all, of it is unacceptable. Your thoughts, Captain?"

"I have never felt qualified to comment on Army plans, sir. Having said this, I have no better military solutions to offer and agree with your assessment."

"Any solutions not involving Army plans? Anything the Navy could do to change the dynamic?"

"General, you recall we discussed this some time back and I promised to give thought to it. I have a possible way forward that may work, if certain matters can be resolved. This solution may have some military action, depending on how matters unfold. I have consulted my colleague Commander Wilton on it and we are both in agreement it may have merit."

"I'm listening."

"As I thought about this I kept coming back to the objectives our masters in London wanted us to achieve. Deny money from this island to the French, check French ambition elsewhere in the Caribbean and in particular Jamaica, keep the Spanish on their side of the island, keep the Americans out of this as much as possible, and most of all find some way to recoup at least some of our investment here. I think if we maintain our focus on those we may succeed. And if you think about it, most of those goals are by and large either happening or are within reach, at least for now. We just have to find a way to keep it like this. But the goal we need to work on most is to find a way to recoup our investment, because it is the one objective where we have much more to do. I think our masters would be happy if we could achieve this at the least. Would you agree, General?"

The General smiled. "If there is one thing guaranteed to keep our masters happy it is money, and hopefully plenty of it. So what is your thinking, Captain?"

Evan spent the next five minutes outlining his strategic approach and the rationale behind it. The General sat in silence, toying with his glass of brandy as he considered what Evan was suggesting. After Evan finished the General remained silent for several long moments as he stared into the distance, before finally reaching a decision and turning to Evan.

"Well. I suppose I shouldn't be surprised you are proposing this as a solution given how much involvement you've had with our diplomats over the years. I confess this had not crossed my mind as a possibility, although I'm no diplomat. So, I have a couple of questions. Are you certain the Spanish aren't going to stir themselves and come to this man Hedouville's aid? If they do, your plan falls apart."

"General, as I reported to you a couple of weeks ago my colleague Commander Wilton made considerable effort to stir up the Spaniards in Santo Domingo against their French masters. We just received a report from one of his people there they have kept the fire hot and the rumor is the French Governor Roume has once again denied a request from Hedouville for help. Sir, I have absolute confidence in Commander Wilton and his work."

Evan paused a moment to see if the General would challenge the point, but when he remained silent Evan continued.

"So, although I cannot as yet confirm the rumor, I am optimistic this man Hedouville is most unhappy at the moment. Without Spanish troops to back up his threats, Hedouville is weak. And as for more help from France itself? I acknowledge we can't be absolutely certain they won't send more, but I believe the truth is they sent everything they absolutely could out with this man Hedouville, at least for the foreseeable future. This island is too important to fund their treasury to hold anything back at this stage."

"All right, I can accept the logic. What about this man Rigaud? Where does he fit in?"

Evan shrugged. "I'm not sure he does. There is no doubt he is weaker than L'Ouverture. But this shouldn't stop us from at least reaching out and trying to negotiate with him, too."

"So the plan boils down to negotiating directly with everyone to achieve our ends, at least for now, including this bloody frog Hedouville? And we work with whoever is willing to come closest to meeting our objectives. Hmm."

"General, we may not have much of a foothold on this island anymore, but we are still a presence to be reckoned with and no one really wants to have to deal with us the hard way. Don't forget, the Navy more or less has a stranglehold on this island. Yes, a few ships do sneak past our blockade here and there because we can't be everywhere, but it forces their hand. They will all negotiate with us, happy or not."

"Captain Ross, thank you once again for your sage advice. I need a day or two to contemplate this strategy. It has a couple of elements to it which are novel and I must think through the ramifications."

Evan rose from his chair to leave. "I am at your disposal, General."

***

The General wasted little time making his decision. Word soon came from his office requesting Evan's attendance for a meeting with the General and Lord Harcourt, who was once again tasked with serving as chief negotiator. As before, Evan's role was to be the silent eyes and ears for Lord Harcourt in the room. Two of Lord Harcourt's senior assistants were to be sent to Jacmel enter into negotiations with Rigaud, while Evan and Lord Harcourt with two other assistants would sail to Port-au-Prince under a flag of truce to deal with both the Frenchman Hedouville and Toussaint's representative. Messages had already been sent and all parties had agreed, as Evan had anticipated. Once again the frigate *HMS Imperious* was called into service to both carry them to Port-au-Prince and to serve as home for the British delegation for the duration of the talks.

Lord Harcourt had deliberately requested morning sessions to negotiate with Hedouville and afternoon sessions with Toussaint's men, without making specific reference to the fact negotiations were being conducted with both factions. He had no idea whether all parties knew of the duplicate negotiations, but they had all agreed to the British requests. If his foes were indeed in the dark about what was going on, Evan was looking forward to watching their reactions when it all inevitably would become clear.

Their first meetings with the French representatives went as Evan expected. Hedouville himself attended and led the discussions with Lord Harcourt. Little was accomplished during the first several days other than to exchange positions on a wide range of subjects. Little or no common ground was obvious, but this too was expected. Each side felt the other owed compensation for losses, each side wanted apologies from the other, and both wanted assurances of no further meddling in the other's affairs.

What interested Evan was the presence at every meeting of a mysterious figure accompanying Hedouville. Although the Frenchman had brought a couple of assistants with him, as had Lord Harcourt, this man was not introduced and never said anything during the meetings. Evan had never met Hubert Montdenoix, but James had described in detail what the man looked like and Evan soon became certain this was the shadowy foe he had been at war with for so many years. As the meetings went on Evan also felt certain Montdenoix was tasked with performing exactly the same role as he was. Every time Evan locked eyes with the man they engaged in a staring contest to see who would blink first. Unless they were interrupted by something happening at the negotiation table, it was always the mysterious Frenchman who blinked first.

What was not surprising at all to Evan from the

outset Evan was the French assertion they were in charge in Saint Domingue. Lord Harcourt and his aides questioned the French ability to deliver results on negotiating points numerous times, asking whether or not any of the black leaders first needed consultation. Each time the matter came up the French treated the notion as if it were an insult. As the talks wore on Evan asked Lord Harcourt about it one night at dinner.

"Oh, yes. Of course we keep making the point," said Lord Harcourt with a smile. "Why wouldn't we? I enjoy annoying these pompous arseholes as much as possible. Besides, correct me if I'm wrong here, but as you know the French probably *should* be consulting them given how weak their bargaining position really is."

When pressed on the subject of the black leaders Hedouville walked a fine diplomatic line. The picture he painted was of a balance of both subservience to the French cause and strength to defeat the British should yet more attempts be made to regain territory. Questions of disputes between L'Ouverture and Rigaud were dismissed out of hand. Evan had to admire Hedouville's effort, for if he was to be believed they were all part of a big, happy French family under his paternal, guiding hand. Evan was certain Hedouville was well aware the British knew it was all nonsense, but everyone present also knew posturing during negotiations was an art form unto itself.

As they progressed one theme in particular kept coming to the fore from the French, to a point where Evan realized the topic was an obsession on their part. On the surface of the negotiations the French were maintaining a hard line approach when it came to the status of French émigrés and royalists present on the island. Beneath the surface it was abundantly clear the French harbored serious ill will toward this part of the population. Evan was certain a bloodbath would ensue if the British pulled out completely and somehow a French administration run by Hedouville ended up in overall control.

The contrast between the daily talks with the French administrator and Toussaint's representatives couldn't have been starker. On several occasions the talks with Hedouville bordered on becoming open shouting matches. An outside observer with no knowledge of the history between the two sides would not have been shocked to find they had engaged in open warfare against each other for the last several years. While the tone of discussions with Hedouville was thus distinctly cold throughout, the talks with Toussaint's men were much warmer, with an overall facade of cordiality. By comparison Toussaint's representatives were far quicker to descend into open hostility and dire threats, while returning equally fast to a genial willingness to work together, as long as they were getting what they wanted.

As with any negotiation, once past the opening statements of position the different sides set to work on small items they could find common ground on before working on the much bigger issues at hand. As they progressed, Evan noticed Toussaint's men considered the issue of the French émigrés and royalists a minor item. But as he gave more thought to the difference between Toussaint and Hedouville's thinking he realized it wasn't minor at all and could in fact be used to further his plan.

Evan was about to send word to the General of a possible opportunity arising from this difference via the packet ships coming and going almost daily between the negotiators and the General when the tone of the negotiations with Toussaint's men changed for the worse. Word had somehow finally reached Toussaint the British were negotiating with the French at the same time.

Evan and Lord Harcourt had engaged in a friendly bet over who would be first to complain about the dual negotiations the British were conducting and Evan won, although he knew it in truth was a coin toss result and not anything he could have reasonably predicted. Lord Harcourt was gracious about the loss, which was another point of amusement between them, because the loser would be providing a bottle of their best wine to share with each other at the first opportunity to do so.

Lord Harcourt made a point of keeping his demeanor calm when the angry faces of Toussaint's negotiators confronted them at the negotiating table on the matter. He made a show of throwing his hands wide to emphasize the problem he faced and put on an air of frustration.

"Gentlemen, put yourself in our situation. We don't know who is really in charge on this island. Is it Toussaint or this man Hedouville? Or is it Andre Rigaud? Everyone keeps telling us they are in charge, but we have no way to be certain, so we talk to all of you. Are you really so surprised?"

By coincidence a packet ship had come in late in the day and was held from returning right away while Evan went into a hurried consultation with Lord Harcourt and his aides in the evening. Later the same night the packet ship departed for the General with a hastily prepared joint message from both Evan and Lord Harcourt.

Two days later it returned, delaying the British negotiators from attending the morning session with the French team, although they sent a message of regrets. Evan and Lord Harcourt had both grinned at each other when they read the General's response. The British not attending the meeting without explanation would be a serious affront to the French, but they were going to be even unhappier the next day, for the General had agreed to pull out of negotiations with Hedouville. As expected, the tone changed dramatically when Lord Harcourt told Toussaint's men of the decision taking immediate effect.

Toussaint's men were much happier, but still suspicious, as the question of whether or not the British were engaging in separate negotiations with Andre Rigaud too had finally crossed their minds. Lord Harcourt had practically beamed as he told them negotiations had indeed been underway, but as a courtesy and out of respect to Toussaint they had ceased talks with Rigaud as well. Word had come with the General's response the talks with Rigaud had fallen apart with no resolution a week ago, which was a detail left unmentioned by Lord Harcourt.

The next day's meeting with Hedouville and his

party was brief. Lord Harcourt somehow maintained a bland face as he delivered the news to the stunned French negotiating team, but Evan knew inwardly his colleague was enjoying every second of it. Predictably, the French team exploded with outrage, as all of them tried talking at the same time. A stream of dark, vague threats of possible dire outcomes resulting from the decision quickly followed, but Lord Harcourt didn't intend to sit around listening to them.

"Gentlemen, the decision has been made," he said, rising from his seat. "Good day."

Montdenoix and Evan had once again locked eyes as Lord Harcourt was delivering the news. They kept glaring at each other as Evan rose with the others to leave. Evan was the last to leave the room and it was only then they broke off. He felt a strong sense of unfinished business with his foe and Evan somehow knew with certainty a reckoning with the man was in his future. He hoped his foe was welcoming the possibility as much as he was.

As they made their way back to the ship Evan couldn't help smiling, for the plan to this point was unfolding as he expected. The centuries old strategy of dividing one's enemies in order to conquer them was proving its value once again. In their earlier meeting General Maitland had at first balked at the idea of throwing their lot solely in with Toussaint, but as Evan fleshed out the plan the General had actually grinned. As Evan pointed out, anything that angered and frustrated the French could only be a good thing.

With a firm wedge now driven between

Toussaint and Hedouville, Evan was hoping his message to Baptiste two days before would ultimately force the gap even wider. If Baptiste were successful, the French obsession with the fate of the émigrés and royalists on the island would be the flashpoint to achieve the goal. All in all, it was a pleasant day and Evan was looking forward to sharing Lord Harcourt's best bottle of wine with him in celebration.

***

Francois Pierrot was adamant that doing what Baptiste was suggesting would be a bad idea.

"Toussaint, this is madness. Hedouville will go berserk if we do this. Would it not be better to use them as a bargaining chip with him?"

"Bargain for what?" said Baptiste. "This man Hedouville has dismissed all attempts to have him understand the true leader of Saint Domingue is Toussaint. Do you seriously think Hedouville would be prepared to change his thinking? I don't."

"But you can see how important it is to him," said Pierrot, a look of frustration darkening his face. "The issue comes up every time we have met or he has corresponded with Toussaint. Is it not abundantly clear the fate of these émigrés is of major importance to him? And the fact he now wants Toussaint to continue favoring French businesses and their contracts in Saint Domingue is no surprise, either. We are French. Toussaint is French. I think we should pull together and find a way around the British."

"And I remain convinced of the opposite, Toussaint. Francois here suggests using the émigrés as a bargaining chip with Hedouville, but I think you are better served by using their fate in talks with the British. They maybe don't care about the low level fortune hunters who came here, but they do have interest in supporting the royalists. Many of these people have ties to royalty elsewhere in Europe and England. Abandoning them to Hedouville's guillotine or dungeon isn't really an option for the British. So it is indeed something you can use."

Toussaint grunted and chewed his lip in thought. "Go on."

"Of course we are all French and Hedouville wants us to keep dealing with French merchants," said Baptiste. "But the fact is getting past the Royal Navy blockade is nigh impossible and this means they cannot honor their contracts. This detail seems of little importance to Hedouville. Toussaint, your people need supplies to keep starvation at bay and the plantations running. Look, the British have not become toothless. Toussaint, it is you and your people who will bear the brunt of the Royal Navy's wrath if we don't find a way to make a deal with the British."

"So you really think these people will agree to support me?" said Toussaint, looking at Baptiste.

"Toussaint, I do. What choice do they have? I think all you need do is promise to let them keep their lands and their possessions. You could even bring some of these people into your army. Many of these people have skills you could use and, who knows, their help may even tip the balance enough to deal with Rigaud once and for all when the

British are out of the way. In contrast, what does Hedouville offer them? They have no choice but to support you."

"I still think this is a bad direction to go in, Toussaint," said Pierrot with a frown.

Baptiste ignored him and continued speaking.

"Toussaint, the British have offered you a clear token they are throwing their lot in with you. I just think it is an opportunity that must be seized. You will need negotiating points with them for give and take. This is something they will want to see happen and doing so could reap even more benefits to you. The only downside is Hedouville will be an obstinate fool about it all, but what else is new? He already is one and has been ever since he got here."

As the two advisors finally went silent Toussaint sat with folded arms, staring at the letter from Hedouville sitting on the table before him. After a long pause he finally spoke, gesturing at the letter.

"This man Hedouville gives me nothing but demands and orders me about. He tried fine words when he first came here, but his words have not matched his actions. The British, on the other hand, have at least begun to show me respect. They agreed to stop talking to Hedouville without precondition and, so they claim, they have done the same to Rigaud before I even asked about it. I find having a little respect refreshing, so let us see if this respect continues in our negotiations. Baptiste, for now I see merit in your logic and see no downside. I will instruct our negotiators to go slow, but to consider using your approach if the British continue to be honest with us. I must give more thought to this, though. If some flaw we have not seen becomes clear we will put a stop to it and try a different approach."

"Toussaint, I do not trust the British," said Pierrot, the heat in his voice obvious. "Let me join the negotiations. I will push to keep them from stabbing you in the back."

Toussaint nodded agreement. "All right. Well, let us have a drink. It is a small start, but I think matters may finally be going in the right direction."

Baptiste smiled as he poured a glass of brandy for them all from the decanter on the table in front of them. He was amazed at how once again his commanding officer's strategy was paying off. A report would be on its way to Evan confirming this soon enough.

***

Montdenoix gave a weary sigh when the summons to attend Hedouville in his office came, but he had no way to avoid it. The thought he was overworked appeared unbidden in his mind yet again, but he had nothing for this either. He had engaged the help of another clerk to help him with paperwork, but he had still not found a suitable replacement for Flemming Linger and the daily grind of reviewing reports and preparing replies continued unabated.

The second Montdenoix walked in he saw the opened letter sitting on the desk in front of Hedouville and he groaned inwardly. With a surreptitious glance around the room he confirmed nothing was smashed or displaced, so he permitted himself a small glimmer of hope the news in the letter was good. But the second he sat down the look of anger on Hedouville's face dashed the hope. At the same time as the realization came Hedouville slammed a fist hard onto the table before him.

"My God, what is it with this fool L'Ouverture? Does he not see how his obstinacy is jeopardizing the entire future of France?"

Montdenoix sighed and gestured at the letter on the table before them.

"Let me guess. This letter is telling you Toussaint will not offer guarantees of what he will do with anyone or anything. He offers vague assurances he will take your wishes into consideration. He probably adds the usual caution we do not understand Saint Domingue the way he does and would be well served to rely on him. Have I got it right?"

Hedouville crumpled the letter into a ball and threw it into a waste bin beside his desk.

"Of course you do. So I expect you have word from your spy. What is the news?"

"More or less what you already know, except there is a concern Toussaint is not just sitting on the fence here. One of his other advisors is actively pushing for a friendlier approach to the damned British. He has even suggested Toussaint offer protection to the émigrés and royalists in return for their loyalty and service in future."

Hedouville's eyes bulged wide and he groaned aloud, putting his face in his hands in dismay before responding.

"Please tell me Toussaint has not agreed to this

madness."

"It is not for certain, but he seems to be leaning this way."

"Hubert, who is this bastard advising Toussaint go in this direction? Can we not find a way to eliminate him?"

"The thought has already crossed my mind, Theodore. His name is Baptiste. Apparently he is a mulatto plantation owner on the north coast outside Cap Le Francois. Unfortunately, my source decided to act on the spur of the moment, seeing which way matters were going. He volunteered to help with the negotiations to look out for Toussaint's interests, so he is likely already on his way to Port-au-Prince to do so. If he had not done this I would have him find a way to deal with this bastard. On the positive side, though, our man will be questioning everything the British are doing and with any luck will find a hole in their defenses we can exploit to turn this around. So for now, at least, there is no possibility of doing as you suggest. Were Flemming here I could send him to Toussaint on some pretext while secretly exploring the possibility. In fact, if the circumstances were right I'm certain Flemming would have solved the problem by now."

"There must be someone, Hubert."

"There is a possibility, Theodore. I have written to the commander of our forces in Cap Le Francois in confidence. He has suggested a man who may have promise. Evidently he can be—unmanageable at times, but he is a born killer. The thinking is I could use him for a one-time purpose, but it may be risky. The problem, Theodore, is I must meet him and build a proper plan and create an opportunity for him to succeed. If we don't do it right and this soldier is caught trying to murder one of Toussaint's closest advisors, it will not go well for us."

"Hubert, we do what we must. I know you are extremely busy, but I am wondering if this man Baptiste is a British spy feeding Toussaint what the British want him to. Make the trip to Cap Le Francois. I will try to help you in your absence, if you give me some tasks. But you mentioned your man in Toussaint's camp would be joining the talks? Hubert, this is excellent news. Have you given him any guidance?"

"Not yet, Theodore. I only just found out, remember?"

"I will give this some thought. At a minimum I suggest he should question British motives at every opportunity. I also think he should keep hammering at the problem the Royal Navy poses. After all, what is to stop them from conducting constant raids on all of Toussaint's ports?"

"I welcome your thoughts and will pass them on. Theodore, there is one other matter I was going to talk to you about. You recall I had concerns about one of the men attending the negotiations on the British side?"

"I do."

"My suspicions have been confirmed. As I told you before I have known for many years Flemming and I faced unknown opponents on the British side engaged in the same kind of activity we are. I have heard rumors over the years of a mysterious man with one arm actively opposing us and there have been too many such rumors to discount. It is an odd coincidence a man with one arm would be at the talks, and the fact he never says a word is suspicious. But I no longer have just suspicions. My source inside the General's camp is not well placed, but I requested he pay attention to this man if he could. Theodore, my opponent is named Evan Ross. He pretends to be a merchant, but I think he may be British Royal Navy. He does not wear uniforms and he sails about in a merchant vessel. So if he is just a lowly British merchant, what is he doing as an observer in our talks?"

"But you cannot be certain?"

"Theodore, in my world nothing is ever certain about an opponent until he is dead. And I think the time has come to make some arrangements for this. If I am right, our lives will be far less complicated. If I am wrong, well, who will miss one more British merchant stealing our business?"

Chapter Eight
August 1798
Saint Domingue

Evan had to discipline himself to keep his focus, for the urge to simply get up and find a fresh breeze with some shady spot to cool off was tangible. The stifling, sticky heat of August in Saint Domingue seemed to be affecting everyone in the room with him and it was a welcome surprise Lord Harcourt suggested they adjourn early because of it. Toussaint's negotiators also quickly agreed and they all filed out of the room with almost unseemly haste. Even with two slaves waving large fans in the corners of the room to move the air about it was an unpleasant morning for everyone in the stuffy, hot room. With the need to conduct talks only with Toussaint now they had collectively decided to move their daily meetings to early in the mornings because of the heat.

The problem was the decision to change the timing of the meetings was virtually all they had agreed on and Evan was frustrated in the extreme. The talks had begun well, but rapidly slowed to a crawl and turned unproductive. Lord Harcourt's own irritation with the situation had grown exponentially with each passing day.

Evan was still mulling over the situation as the British negotiating team made their way with their guards back to the docks where they would be picked up and ferried out to *HMS Imperious*. Evan had been wracking his brains for answers about the situation for a while, but hadn't been able to put a finger on what the problem was. When the sudden realization of the truth behind what was happening came it struck Evan like a bolt. Without thinking he slapped his head in dismay it had taken him so long to understand, drawing the attention of Lord Harcourt.

The flash of understanding was that a subtle shift in tone had come about when a new addition to Toussaint's team arrived. The new negotiator Francois Pierrot was at first all smiles, but with a degree of subtlety Evan had to admire his quibbling over small details soon turned to a constant barrage of questions and nagging doubts. Matters which the other negotiators were taking as a given were questioned. After a full week of this even Toussaint's original negotiators were letting subtle hints of their frustration show on their faces. But the man was a close advisor to Toussaint and they had no choice but to deal with him. Evan saw the questioning look on Lord Harcourt's face and gave him a rueful half smile in response.

"Yes, Lord Harcourt, something has just occurred to me. Let us discuss it on the ship tonight when it is cooler. For now I'm going to get as much of my clothes off as possible, find some cool tea to drink, and sit somewhere in the shade. With luck there will be a breeze to help me think, for this is what I need to do."

Lord Harcourt simply smiled in response. By now both men had come to know each other well and Lord Harcourt had long since learned of Evan's predilection to sit alone and think when facing a problem. By dinnertime Evan had examined the issue and the possible solution from every angle he could.

The Captain of *HMS Imperious* was the only other diner at the table this night with Evan and Lord Harcourt. The meal consisted of cold meats, bread, and hard cheeses, along with some fresh local fruit the cook had found and a bread pudding for dessert. No one complained at the lack of hot food. As they finished Lord Harcourt toyed with his glass of cognac and looked at Evan.

"Well, Captain Ross?"

"Sir? Ah, you are referring to earlier today. Sorry, I was mulling over what is going on and have come to the conclusion this is no accident the negotiations have ground almost to a halt."

"It's the new man, this Pierrot, isn't it?" said Lord Harcourt, looking rueful in response to Evan's nod of agreement. "Your reaction as we were returning today led me to give more thought to this. Yes, at first I was thinking he was just being diligent, but I see now perhaps it is more than this. Is this what has crossed your mind?"

"Sir, it is. He has gone from being just diligent to being a major pain in the arse. The clear sign is the frustration Toussaint's other negotiators aren't even bothering to hide. I can't believe it has taken me so long to see this. So yes, I am wondering if this bastard is in reality a pawn of the French."

Lord Harcourt was silent for a long moment before nodding.

"I agree it is a strong possibility. But even if he is not, he is without doubt the pain you speak of. So what are we going to do about it?"

"This is what I have been mulling all afternoon, sir. I see no easy answers, but there is one course of action I think we can try. As you know, I have a man inside Toussaint's camp. I think I will send him a message and explain what is happening. At the least he may be able to plant the thought in Toussaint's head this man is an obstructive arsehole. Who knows, he may even find some way to have the man recalled or sent to do something else. In the meantime I will keep thinking about it. Were we to try and just eliminate him with a fake botched robbery or something it may appear far too suspicious. So until we can come up with some kind of solution to this, I suggest playing our hand close and taking our time. No need to give away all of our negotiating points to him if he really is a French spy."

"Hmm. Well, I agree with your thinking. It's worth a try."

"Listen," said the Captain of the *Imperious*. "If there is anything you two can do to speed this up so we can get out of this pestilential place and back to sea where we belong, I am all for it. My men couldn't be any more bored than they already are. You can only have them do drills for so long before matters get out of hand. Thank God this man Toussaint agreed to let parties of women from the brothels come aboard periodically. I'd have a bloody mutiny on my hands otherwise."

Both Evan and Lord Harcourt laughed.
"Sir," said Evan. "I shall do my best."
***

Baptiste was sitting on the verandah of his

plantation enjoying the view when Sylvie came out to join him. Instead of taking her own seat she slid onto his lap and sat to one side with her arm around his shoulders. Baptiste looked up at her and grinned.

"Well, hello. What's on your mind?"

"Not what you are thinking. You already had me this morning, remember?"

Baptiste shrugged and kept the grin on his face. "This morning seems like it was a long time ago."

Sylvie shook her head in mock disgust. "Men. But seriously, I just came out here to be with you. You've been sitting out here staring into the distance for almost an hour. You have another message?"

"Yes," said Baptiste, pointing to the opened letter on the table before him. "And I confess I'm not entirely sure what to do about it."

Sylvie raised an eyebrow in question, so Baptiste explained the problem Evan had outlined to him in the letter. When he finished Sylvie gave a haughty sniff of disapproval.

"It wouldn't surprise me if this man Pierrot is a French spy at all. He's a complete pig as far as I'm concerned. But come to think of it, I saw him in Cap Le Francois several weeks back with one of those white men. It was around the end of June, I think."

"What white men?"

Sylvie gave him a look of exasperation. "Who do you think? One of those Frenchmen you have been concerned about, of course. Not this man Hedouville, it was the other one. We met them at one of those banquets Toussaint held at Fort Picolet some time back. Remember? Ah, Montdenoix was his name, I think."

"And they were doing what, exactly?"

"Talking to each other. They were just coming out of one of the taverns in town as I went by. They paid no attention to me whatsoever. I confess I thought nothing of it at the time, but perhaps I should have. You did warn me this Montdenoix is a spy."

"I see. But you also said Pierrot is a pig a moment ago. What makes you say this?"

"Well, that's easy. The cowardly bastard beats his woman."

"Good God, why? And how do you know?"

"Baptiste, you tell me, because I have no idea why he would do it. Why does any man beat his woman? It makes no sense. But what I do know is any man who does it is not a man. He is—my God, don't get me started. But you ask how I know? It's obvious from the bruises on her face and, so you know, she has had fresh bruises more than once. I saw her a couple of days ago and the latest ones are still healing. I can't say I know her well, but I have talked with her a few times. Her name is Solange. We've run into each other in town. Cap Le Francois isn't a big place. I offered her help, but she refused. It's the strangest thing, you know. Some of the women are ashamed when this kind of thing happens, as if it is somehow their fault. Bastards."

"Hmm. Well, this may have possibilities. I wonder how loyal she is to him? She may have information we could use."

"Loyal to him? Are you kidding me? Whores

are loyal only as long as you keep paying them."

"She's a whore? Damn, if she is the woman I think I remember from the banquet, she is quite good looking. Why would she be a whore?"

"Baptiste, this is called life on these islands," said Sylvie, pulling him a little closer. "Sometimes you get lucky and find the right man who wants to be with you. Sometimes you don't. I thought life in St. Lucia was hard, but in Saint Domingue, you do what you must to survive if you don't have anyone to support you. I don't know all of her history, but simply being good looking doesn't necessarily get you far. And I do know she is a whore because she told me she is. She is simply hanging on with him because she has nowhere else to go and the next man she finds might be even worse."

Baptiste was silent for a moment, reaching up to caress the side of her face.

"Well, as you say, sometimes we all get lucky. And as for this Solange, we may have found some good fortune here, too. Pierrot is away at these negotiations right now. Do you know where they live?"

Sylvie smiled. "I do."

"Well, then, why don't we go pay her a friendly visit? This might be her lucky day."

***

When Pierrot's woman finally understood she was being offered a way out of her predicament she broke down and cried, with Sylvie's arm around her shoulder. At first she was frightened when Baptiste questioned her about Pierrot and his relationship with Montdenoix , but Baptiste knew he had hit the mark by the flash of instant understanding in her eyes. On seeing it Baptiste emphasized she could be rewarded for her help if she knew something, with a gentle warning she could suffer even more were she to decline. An offer to come and work on Baptiste's plantation as a free woman to serve Sylvie was the escape route she needed and it brought a flood of grateful tears to her eyes.

When she finally calmed down she led them to Pierrot's his bedroom. Moments later she emerged and handed Baptiste a key. Motioning for them to follow they made their way to Peirrot's study and pointed to a locked drawer in his desk.

"I have not looked in this drawer, but I know this is the key and I long since learned where he hid it. I also think what you will find in there are letters and perhaps even gold."

Baptiste opened the drawer and pulled out two letters. Stuffed into the far recesses of the drawer was a heavy leather bag. Baptiste knew before he opened it Solange was right. Solange explained she had seen the letters delivered to Pierrot and, even better, could attest to a meeting Pierrot had held at his home with Montdenoix. She had overheard some of their conversation through an open door and seen the bag sitting on the desk between them as she walked by.

Later the same afternoon Solange appeared frightened to be questioned personally by Toussaint, but with Sylvie at her side she held her ground and answered all of his questions. Sylvie asked to leave with her when the questions finally dried up, but Toussaint had waved them all away, claiming he needed time to think.

Baptiste came at once the next day in response to the summons from Toussaint. He found him in his office in Fort Picolet staring in silence at the two letters and the now opened bag of French gold coins sitting once again on the table before him. Toussaint finally looked up and spoke.

"Thank you for your help. I have only one question. What was it prompted you to confront this woman Solange?"

"Sylvie had seen Montdenoix and Pierrot talking in town. It was only recently when I mentioned Pierrot was being obstinate she told me what she had seen. I began to wonder more and more about why they were talking alone, for I could think of no good reason. It seemed suspicious to me. Sylvie also knows Solange, and when I learned from Sylvie what a brute Pierrot has been to her, I decided to push the matter. Pierrot does not like me anyway, so what did I have to lose?"

"I see. Well, I believe you, and I thank you once again."

"Toussaint, I am so sorry it has come to this. I can't believe this man Pierrot would betray you so easily."

"I am no longer surprised by anything, Baptiste. In all the years I have been leader the British have been false to me, the Spanish have been false, Rigaud has been false, and now Pierrot and the French are false to me. I have learned I must deal with facts and not words. It is what they all do which is important and not what they say."

"And what will you do now, Toussaint?"

"Do?" said Toussaint, a grim smile on his face. "Ah, I have already acted. Pierrot has been recalled from the talks. It all adds up now, you see. I had received letters from the other negotiators about his behavior at the talks and now I understand what was going on. Pierrot does not know why he has been recalled, but he will know soon enough. He will have a personal meeting with me and then he will find a new home in the dungeon here in Fort Picolet while I decide his ultimate fate. I think I shall take my time. And some day I shall have to find some suitable way to reward you for your service."

Baptiste nodded. "There is no need for that, Toussaint. My reward is to see you succeed where my friend Julien Fedon on Grenada did not."

Baptiste smiled, for the knowledge Evan Ross would once again be pleased at the outcome was the far better reward Baptiste wanted.

***

With Pierrot gone the change in tone at the negotiating table with Toussaint's men was like the difference between light and darkness. The progress was such the General himself was brought into Port-au-Prince harbor on another British warship to speed communication and help with decisions on any changes in position. By the time he arrived so much progress was being made his attendance had gone from optional to a critical necessity. Evan and Lord Harcourt met with the General at the first opportunity.

"Well, congratulations are in order, Captain Ross," said the General. "Rooting out this man who was sabotaging the talks on behalf of the French has certainly changed the dynamic."

"I wholeheartedly agree," said Lord Harcourt. "We were getting absolutely nowhere with Pierrot at the table. My God, we would still be there at Christmas were he still around."

"I appreciate your sentiments, gentlemen, but it is my man in Toussaint's camp who deserves the accolades. I merely told him of the situation and asked him to see if there was anything he could do. I was expecting him to try and influence Toussaint somehow. I had no idea he would be able to ferret out this disruptive influence for us."

"You must find a way to reward him, Captain. If a commendation letter from me would help just say the word and I will have one for you. So, Lord Harcourt, where do matters stand now at the table?"

"Well, virtually all of the small and easy to deal with matters on the table have been addressed. The last few days have been spent discussing the larger issues facing us."

Lord Harcourt paused as a servant entered the cabin with a pitcher of cool tea for them all to drink. The heat had moderated slightly, but an offshore breeze had sprung up. With the windows open in the Captain's cabin where they were meeting it was much more bearable than it had been. When the servant left Lord Harcourt resumed.

"We have established the basic principle of a full, orderly British withdrawal from the island and, now this troublemaker is gone, Toussaint's men are perfectly willing to accept on faith we will leave the military installations intact with the big guns serviceable. In return, we have gained at a minimum agreement there will be no invasion of Jamaica. They in turn are looking for assurances the Royal Navy will not be back to plague Toussaint's ports and disrupt the trade I think he seems to want. In fact, I think he wants it badly. So, based on how this is unfolding, it seems to me this approach we have taken to Toussaint is the correct one. I am fairly certain if we were to continue hanging on to our tiny foothold on this island it would anger Toussaint and maybe even drive him closer to Hedouville. Despite all that has happened, Toussaint still seems to see himself as a Frenchman at heart, but we are driving a wedge between them."

"Well, one of our objectives is to frustrate French ambition here, so this is all good. But what do they offer in return for our promise not to harass their shipping and their ports?"

"Ah, this is where it is getting interesting," said Lord Harcourt, with a huge grin appearing on his face. "As I said, it is becoming clear he wants trade with us, for they were the ones who hinted at some sort of trade agreement first. Naturally, we told them it was a brilliant idea and neglected to mention this was exactly what we were going to suggest. So on this point at least we could be making excellent progress were it not for one related issue holding matters up."

"And this is?"

"The Americans, General. Toussaint does not want to give us a totally exclusive right to trade. Captain Ross and his man have learned Toussaint has ties to the Americans, which may explain what is behind this. Apparently he even has a business he owns somewhere in America. If true then it is obvious why he wouldn't see the Americans as a threat. Add it all up and you may have the true reason for why he is not receptive to this Hedouville's arguments that Toussaint should help take France's fight beyond the borders of Saint Domingue as well. So we will need to know your thoughts on this point now we are aware of it, General."

Evan was amazed to see the General's face light up as Lord Harcourt finished speaking. Evidently unable to contain himself any longer, the General burst out laughing hard enough he had to brush away a tear from one eye. Evan and Lord Harcourt looked at each in puzzlement, each trying to understand what had provoked the General without success. The General finally gathered himself and took a moment to recover as he poured a second helping of the tea.

"I apologize for this, but I couldn't help myself. Yes, I can give you guidance on this, gentlemen. You know, I sometimes have to shake my head at how events conspire to either hinder or further our efforts. In this case, I can give you some good news. As you know, the Americans have been at odds with the French at sea for some time now. Well, I have just received word the United States Congress has passed a trade embargo against France in mid June and the talk is this will quickly be amended to permit the President to reopen trade with other areas under French control. Of course, Saint Domingue is figuring prominently in the decision. The word I received of this included a directive from London to welcome such activity as long as it doesn't materially hinder anything we are trying to accomplish. Anything which annoys and frustrates the French is to be welcomed, as it were."

"Brilliant!" said Lord Harcourt.

"My God, that's perfect!" said Evan.

"Quite," said the General, still smiling. "Given we already have many ties with owners here and given how massive the business opportunities could be if this place ever settles down, I think it a reasonable point you can concede to Toussaint, Lord Harcourt. The Americans will try catching up, but I should think we would have plenty of business to keep our merchants busy. I will leave it to you to concede the point for something reasonable in return, of course. So is there anything else I need consider?"

"Ah, yes, General," said Lord Harcourt. "There remain two major issues to consider. The first is that most of the hardened royalist owners have already packed up and left or are about to leave, but there are many here still who were always lukewarm and had no real political convictions. These people are still very much Frenchmen at heart. There are also many who simply don't have the resources to get off the island or, if they do, have no idea where they will go. What strikes fear into them is what this man Hedouville will do if he somehow finds a way to gain the upper hand. These people have all clung to us for support and the quandary is what we can reasonably do to help them. Let's face it, our ships can only take so many, and what do we do with them if we take them aboard?"

"I understand and agree, Lord Harcourt. So what do we do?"

"Gentlemen, if I may?" said Evan. "This turn of events involving the Americans gives us the sway we can use to effect an agreement here. I think we should propose to Toussaint he do the same thing he did when we originally pulled back to Mole St. Nicholas and Jeremie. We have him respect the property and businesses of those who remain behind. Even better, we hammer home the suggestion he join forces with these people. This is effectively what my man in his camp did before and Toussaint agreed. The bonus is Hedouville won't like it at all, but this is also the risk. Of course, Hedouville isn't going to like any part of it all, but he in particular won't like this point. Toussaint will definitely be placing himself at odds with the man if he agrees. But if you agree, I can order my man to make every effort to convince him. If Toussaint agrees, I think the vast majority of these people will elect to stay and we will have far fewer people to accommodate."

The General was silent for a few long moments as he thought it through, before nodding.

"I concur. But Toussaint must agree to this too. I will not abandon these people. And your remaining issue is the biggest of all, isn't it?"

"Correct, General," said Lord Harcourt. "Independence for Saint Domingue. To date we have only danced around the topic, we have not actually gone there in any detail. But I think Toussaint's men know we are going to table this and I have no idea how they will respond. Captain Ross, do you have anything on this point?"

"I am afraid not, sir. This has evolved so quickly I have not had time to ask my man to broach the topic with Toussaint. I'm not certain he would have had opportunity to do so, though. This is clearly a sensitive issue and I think Toussaint would keep his thoughts close."

"Well, we can but try if you agree, General," said Lord Harcourt. "The problem is all we can offer is the formal protection of the British Navy were he to do so. I can think of nothing else to put on the table and even then, I'm not certain our masters would be happy with us making such an offer."

This time the General remained silent and stood up to walk over and stare in thought out of the cabin window. Evan knew it was a difficult point and the General was facing an impossible situation. The truth was he could face severe criticism regardless of which direction he chose to go in. After almost two minutes he came back and sat down.

"Gentlemen, I will provide you both with written direction to proceed as we have discussed on all of these points. My direction will include authority to offer Royal Navy support if Toussaint is willing to enter into a formal, public alliance with us. The consequences will be on my head if this turns out to be a bad decision."

"Thank you General," said Lord Harcourt. "I am optimistic we can bring these talks to a speedy conclusion. Ah, there is one last small point, General."

"Yes?"

"The outcome of all this is a treaty, of course. I suspect Toussaint will want to meet you personally to sign it. It is your decision, but I think you should. It would fit with our approach of showing respect to the man."

"General, I support this thought," said Evan. "Toussaint will not be able to resist the thought of meeting with a real British field General to sign a formal document, even if we are doing it in secret."

After a moment the General nodded once again.

"We have come this far, gentlemen. I confess I had not thought it would come down to this, but here we are and I agree. I also think it is time for a little celebration, gentlemen. I'm sure the Captain of this fine frigate has something suitable for the occasion in his wine cabinet. Let us have him join us and I will compensate him accordingly. I am certain he will enjoy the thought a degree of success is possible and the end may finally be in sight for this mission. I sense it is there for us to grasp."

***

Dessalines, Julien Raimond, and Baptiste were all present once again in Fort Picolet, having been summoned to attend the return of the negotiators from the talks with the British. Baptiste tried to read the thoughts of the men around the table by their faces, but most of all he was desperate to know what Toussaint was thinking. A few questions were posed, but the negotiators were able to answer each one with ease. When the questions ended Toussaint wordlessly looked at his advisors. Dessalines was the first to speak and he quibbled about trading with the hated white men, but Toussaint grew a look of frustration on his face and cut Dessalines off in mid sentence.

"Jean, what would you have us do? White men who control everything which matters surround this island. We need what the Americans and the British offer in trade to survive. There is nothing here which stops France from trading with us, other than their own arrogance to think we should deal only with them and the British Royal Navy, so what is the problem?"

Dessalines looked as if he was about to speak again, but stopped himself and after hesitating a moment threw a hand up to signify he was conceding the point. When Toussaint saw he wasn't going to speak again he looked at the others for their thoughts. One by one the negotiators and Julien Raimond all spoke. The only point causing uncertainty and indecision was the issue of independence. Baptiste was the last to speak.

"Toussaint, I think all of this makes sense. In particular, as I think I've suggested before, I'd say you need the expertise of the émigrés and the royalists as much as they need you. Hedouville won't like it, but this is his problem. I agree with the others about independence, though. This is a difficult issue and needs much consideration. It is a measure of the regard the British seem to have found for you they would offer Royal Navy support and you should not discount it lightly. There is no doubt declaring independence will attract attention from others, though. It is a huge risk to take. If you insist I really must give you a recommendation, it is you should take their offer."

Baptiste held his breath as he finished speaking, on edge to see what Toussaint's reaction would be. Baptiste had no guidance from Evan on the point of what to say about independence, so all he could do was offer his real opinion on the matter and hope Evan would approve. Toussaint sat silent for a long time, though. No one spoke for fear of breaking his concentration. With a sigh he finally reached for his glass of brandy and dashed the remaining contents down before speaking.

"I must think about this further. I agree with all of you on the main points of the agreement. I agree with you too, Baptiste. The really difficult question is independence. It tears at my heart, for I know we could do this and succeed. But I am French and this tears me, too. I think it would be hard for the people to understand and to accept no longer being a part of France."

Toussaint paused and looked at the negotiators.

"I shall consider this and give you my answer tomorrow at the same time. You will then return to Port-au-Prince and give the British our response. And yes, I do want to meet this General Maitland to sign a treaty. I will leave it to you to organize the details."

***

To celebrate the conclusion of the negotiations Toussaint's men insisted on throwing a banquet for the British delegation. Despite the British desire to be away to sea, it was an offer that could not reasonably be refused. The invitation was also extended to the officers of the British warship Evan and Lord Harcourt were staying on. While the General had already left Port-au-Prince, it still meant a substantial number of people would be in attendance. The irony was the banquet was held in the main hall of the fortifications the British had so recently vacated and left for Toussaint's men.

Evan did his best to keep a low profile, dressing in his best civilian clothing for the occasion. In truth he had little choice, for he had not brought a dress uniform with him to Port-au-Prince. Evan was happy enough to wear his lighter civilian clothing anyway as the night was warm, with little or no cooling breezes making their way through the town to the fortifications.

News Toussaint was not prepared to take the great leap of declaring independence, at least for now, was tempered by word he would agree to everything else. A date had quickly been set for Toussaint and General Maitland to meet in Mole St. Nicholas at the end of August to sign a treaty. At Toussaint's request, the signing would remain a secret for the time being due to the sensitivity of it. Everyone knew Hedouville was the problem Toussaint would have to find an answer to.

No one was prepared to let the lack of success on the issue of independence mar the evening. To their credit Toussaint's negotiators had organized a splendid banquet. The dinner courses being served seemed endless, as did the fresh bottles of wine appearing while others were emptied. By the end of the evening virtually all of the participants were red faced from the alcohol and the heat.

Evan was the exception. He had relaxed and

enjoyed himself, but he was a veteran of too many such banquets to drink to excess. By the end of the night he was the most sober of them all. Evan was one of the last to leave as they all filed out to walk the short distance back to the ship in the harbor. A number of Royal Marines had accompanied the British delegates to the banquet to stand guard and two of them stepped in to walk at Evan's side and serve as the rear guard. With a moon almost full they had enough light to make their way with ease.

The attack came without warning as they passed a darkened alley leading off the main street they were on. The Marine on Evan's left saw the glint of moonlight on the raised blade coming at them and was fast enough to call a warning and step to the side. The warning was close to being too late, but Evan had instinctively changed course and the blade flashed past his shoulder. Evan had time to register a trio of attackers bursting from the alley as he drew his own blade and met the next attacker full on. The scene quickly became a confusing, chaotic mass of struggling men shouting incoherently. The ringing of steel on steel mingled with grunts of effort and a cry of pain came simultaneously with the sound of a blade cutting through cloth and striking flesh.

Evan soon realized the assailant targeting him was an excellent swordsman, but Evan had long since attained mastery of his own sword. Many opponents over the years had assumed because Evan had only one arm he would be an easy target, and this miscalculation had proved fatal to more than one enemy. Evan had long since overcome the problem of needing his missing his left arm to balance his sword arm with many long hours of practice. The two men engaged each other hard and fast, with neither backing away.

The attack ended as fast as it began. Shouts came from the direction of the head of the British column, sparked by the sound of the fight. Evan's foe barked a command in French and the attackers fled back into the darkness of the alley. One of the Marines made to go after them, but Evan shouted an order to desist, for beyond its main streets Port-au-Prince was a winding maze perfect for anyone who wanted to lose pursuers. The labyrinth would also serve attackers wily enough to set an even deadlier trap for anyone foolish enough to chase them.

Within moments some of the lead group of Marines had returned in support, but the fight was already over. One of the Marines with Evan had suffered a cut on his arm, but the wound was not major. A Lieutenant from the frigate had also come back with them and he quickly had the now fully alert British party back on its way again after conferring briefly with Evan.

Evan was furious as they marched at speed back to the ship. As they reached the safety of the dock where the ship's boats were waiting to return them to the frigate, Lord Harcourt saw the angry look on Evan's face and came over to speak to him.

"Captain Ross? What was this all about? I expect it was not a simple attempt to rob us."

"You are correct, sir. The local thieves aren't stupid enough to attack heavily armed men. No, it was a deliberate attempt to kill and, more specifically, the sole target was likely me."

"How do you know?"

Evan's eyes glinted hard in the moonlight as he responded.

"Because I recognized the bastard who came after me. It was this bloody frog Montdenoix. I must be succeeding in my efforts to thwart his plots, because I think he decided the most expedient way to resolve the problem I pose was to kill me. Well, he isn't going to be happy he failed, because sooner or later I will find an opportunity for pay back and, unlike him, I will succeed."

***

The sticky heat of August was finally beginning to moderate by the very last day of the month, making time spent in the meetings between General Maitland and Toussaint much more bearable. The actual meetings were held in the home of a local plantation owner in a small town not far from Mole St. Nicholas. The main elements of the draft agreement were reviewed in detail once again and formally agreed to by both men.

The only point not covered in the draft document was the issue of independence. Over the course of two days the two men and their aides went back and forth on it yet again. Evan was present for all of it and by the end of it he sensed Toussaint was convinced of British sincerity. But despite this, his misgivings at the consequences kept him from agreeing to this last point. General Maitland expressed his disappointment, but assured Toussaint if he changed his mind he had only to ask for

British help. In the meantime, British merchants would happily support Toussaint and his men in the process of bringing stability to Saint Domingue.

Evan knew everyone present felt and understood signing the treaty was a watershed moment in the history of British relations with Saint Domingue. The actual signing was handled with as much dignity and ceremony as could be mustered. A sense of accomplishment permeated the room, leaving smiles on everyone's faces. Toussaint was surprised when it was revealed a further token of British respect for Toussaint was being offered, although it was up to him whether or not he wanted it.

Evan was unsurprised to see the huge grin on Toussaint's face as the black leader quickly accepted the offer, for resisting the opportunity of a parade in his honor was impossible.

Chapter Nine
September 1798
Saint Domingue

Four days later the harbor of Mole St. Nicholas was filled with a host of ships. Six British warships and double this number of British merchant vessels were vying for space on the docks of the small town. *HMS Alice* had sailed to the Mole for the occasion when Evan sent word to do so, joining the crowd of merchant ships. Toussaint and a large number of his soldiers were camped outside the town perimeter. The inhabitants of the town seemed stunned by the sudden bustle of important people hurrying about, transforming the town with a sense of purpose and monumental occasion.

Security was heavy. Toussaint was angered when he heard of the attack on the British delegates in Port-au-Prince and made it clear he didn't want to hear of any more such events. Evan, the General, and Lord Harcourt had all agreed they saw little point in raising the issue of Montdenoix being involved in the attack. Other than Evan's word, they had no hard proof of French involvement and it was felt pushing the matter might jeopardize the gains they had made. Evan was content with the approach, knowing he would find his own form of retribution to deal with Montdenoix. Several files of British Marines from the warships and companies of Toussaint's army filled the streets of Mole St. Nicholas as a result.

As rumor of a major event involving the British and Toussaint spread many people travelled to Mole

St. Nicholas, bringing with them a tangible mix of anticipation and fear of the unknown. Yet more temporary camps appeared while nearby smaller towns were packed with unexpected visitors unable to find rooms anywhere else.

On the agreed day of the handover the bishop of the town cathedral met Toussaint and his party on the outskirts of Mole St. Nicholas. Evan was embedded with a group of British officers tasked with monitoring for any signs of trouble. The large crowd gathered in anticipation watched as the bishop presented him with a large wooden cross, which the black leader accepted with what appeared to Evan to be sincere humility. When Toussaint had learned of what the British planned he specifically requested the bishop do this for him. The British were surprised to learn how deeply religious Toussaint was, but quickly agreed.

By now word had leaked out and it was widely known the British were surrendering Mole St. Nicholas to Toussaint. The people lining the route of his procession into the heart of town cheered and hailed him as a conquering hero and their savior. Women rushed forward to give him flowers and touch him. Many brought their children for Toussaint and the bishop to bless. The closer they got to the center of town and the main square the more densely packed the streets were. The procession took over an hour to wind its way through the crowds.

When it finally reached the main square Toussaint and his party made their way to a raised platform built for the occasion. General Maitland

and his party waited in full dress uniform, sweltering in the warmth of early September despite the large awning hastily erected to provide shade. A large open space between the stage and the crowd left, stretching off to either side of the square. Numerous guards lining it held the crowd back. The two men met at the center of the stage and shook hands, earning them a roar of cheers and applause. Their meeting was the trigger for a signal hoist of a flag to the warships in the harbor to commence a gun salute the General had requested.

The General was the first to speak as the big guns finally went silent. In a long speech he announced an agreement was now in place to hand over Mole St. Nicholas and Jeremie to Toussaint. He praised Toussaint's cooperation and willingness to ensure a smooth transition. No mention was made of the details of the secret treaty. The General assured the people he was certain Toussaint's administration would be just and fair. No mention was made of French involvement.

When Toussaint finally took the stage to speak it took a full three minutes for the cheering and clapping crowd to finally settle down. Toussaint was clearly enjoying every second, walking from side to side of the stage to wave and shake hands with some of the guards standing nearby. When he finally regained center stage he signaled for silence and the crowd slowly obeyed.

In the beginning Toussaint's speech was almost a mirror of what the General said, with plenty of praise for the General and the British. The first surprise to many in the crowd was when he announced Andre Rigaud would be given the honor of occupying the town of Jeremie. Evan could see despite their surprise the decision was welcome and many were offering approving nods at Toussaint's magnanimous gesture. No mention was made of the fact the British would not be offering parades or fine speeches for Rigaud. But the applause and cheers for the gesture was nothing compared to what came next.

Toussaint teased the crowd for a few minutes, hinting he had a major announcement to make. When he finally told them he would pardon all French émigrés and royalists who had not served under him in the interests of reconciliation the overjoyed crowd erupted, unable to contain their delight at the decision. Many began dancing and hugging each other while others started chanting Toussaint's name. Toussaint needed almost five minutes to calm them down before he could add he would even welcome his former foes to serve in his army, up to and including the point of being officers, if they were qualified. Once again, the crowd exploded with such joy it took several minutes to subside.

The reason for the cleared space in front of the stage was revealed as yet another surprise. Toussaint and the General conducted a joint review of their troops in a march past which took almost an hour to complete, for units of both armies participated along with several British Marines from the warships. The grinning troops waved at the crowds after saluting the two commanders as they marched past.

When the last of them were past the General signaled for silence once again to make one more announcement. As a further token of reconciliation the British were hosting a banquet in nearby Fort Georges for Toussaint and his senior officers, but the people were not to be left out of the festivities. The Army and the Navy were combining to provide a feast of meat roasted on spits in the central square of the town, while casks of rum and ale would be opened for all to consume and wash down their food. No one was to go hungry or thirsty on this day of celebration. Evan had not thought it possible the crowd could be any happier or more raucous than they already were, but this announcement sent them to new heights of frenzy.

The finale of the ceremony was left to Toussaint. Evan had expected yet more platitudes and expressions of appreciation for the British, but Toussaint surprised everyone one last time. Toussaint made a blunt point of telling the crowd the King of England had on this day shown him more honor and respect than France ever had. Some in the crowd looked uneasy at the statement, but many cheered with the same vigor as they had shown all day. He emphasized one last time how deeply grateful he was and he raised his arms wide as he told them it was now time for celebration, earning yet another roar of appreciation.

Evan needed little time to digest the meaning of the statement. Although surprised Toussaint had taken the bold step of emphasizing how much better England was treating him, Evan knew exactly what was happening. The statement was both a blunt snub and a veiled warning to the French, for Toussaint was making it clear he would side with those who treated him well. Toussaint's words were an instant sign of success for the British and cause for Evan to celebrate.

But Evan's face bore no smile and had not for most of the ceremonies. His focus throughout was on the one face in the crowd that didn't belong, but was there anyway. Evan had not been surprised to find Montdenoix present and had actually been actively searching for him, for he knew it would be impossible to keep someone from Hedouville's camp from learning of what was happening and attending.

The two men had locked eyes from across the square and Evan had maintained a steadfast glare at his foe throughout. Once again it was Montdenoix who kept averting his eyes and every time he returned his gaze he found Evan continuing to hold his cold stare at him.

Evan hoped the Frenchman would be haunted by his stare and the simple, unspoken message he was conveying. Sooner or later, there would be a reckoning.

***

"Captain Ross, it is so very good to see you once again," said Amelie Caron. "Tea will be served in a moment. I was hoping you would be in contact with me again soon, so your note requesting a visit was most welcome. There have been many developments and I was hoping you had not forgotten me."

"Madam," said Evan, as he took a chair in her

sitting room. "It would be impossible to forget a beautiful woman such as yourself. And yes, there has been much to keep us busy."

"I confess the arrival of this man Rigaud and his men here in Jeremie has been cause for some— discomfort among people such as myself. They have made assurances everyone will be well treated and so far, at least, that has been true. I am concerned what will happen if the presence of the Royal Navy is diminished or disappears altogether, though."

"Hmm, I understand and share your concern to a degree, madam. Our relations with Toussaint L'Ouverture have been much more positive than those with Andre Rigaud. In truth I was not surprised Toussaint gave Jeremie to him, since the front lines between Toussaint and Rigaud are a very long ways from Jeremie. Toussaint does not have a navy with enough power to either support or hold Jeremie for very long, so that really wasn't an option for him."

"So please do not keep me in suspense, Captain. Have you news for me?"

"I do, madam. My sister in Montreal has written in response to my query. She has settled in well and she will be very happy to help you do the same in a new life in Lower Canada, if that is what you choose to do. As we discussed, life in Canada is not easy, for this is very much still a frontier post. The winters can be quite harsh and long, while summer is apparently the opposite, although they can get the same kind of hot, sticky heat that we get here in the Caribbean for short periods. But on the positive side there is a large French population in Montreal and the surrounding countryside. My sister writes of a very active social scene in the city. She believes you will find many kindred spirits in the same circumstances as yourself once you are established, if it is your choice to take this step. Apparently many wealthy royalist supporters now call Montreal home."

"I see. Well, Captain, I won't keep you in suspense. As much as I do not wish to leave Saint Domingue, I fear I must. It has been my home for many years, but it no longer feels the same and I am not optimistic that peace will return anytime soon to this island. I fear there will be war between these men Toussaint L'Ouverture and Andre Rigaud sooner or later. I also think France will not accept having no real involvement here. As a parent I cannot risk raising my daughter in an environment like this, so it is time to leave. But have you any word of travel arrangements, Captain? I thought the price to take ship and leave here was ridiculous before, but it is now beyond reason. I would have to sell virtually everything I have and that would barely be enough."

"Yes, I can offer help there, too. I have looked into this as promised. You can take ship to Antigua and transit from there to Montreal when matters settle down."

"Antigua?" said Amelie, a brilliant smile lighting her face. "Have I the privilege of sailing with you once again, Captain? I would like that."

"Unfortunately, no. Our work here is not over yet, but I am optimistic it will be soon. To be honest, I have spent enough time here to last me a lifetime and would much prefer to be home with my wife and children once again. The Captain of one of our frigates has kindly agreed to give you, your daughter, and your two servants passage. He is scheduled to depart to Antigua for a refit in the Navy Dockyard I command there on October first. Will that be acceptable to you?"

"That is plenty of time for us to wind up our affairs here and be ready, Captain. Where would you recommend we stay in Antigua while we await passage to Canada?"

"Ah, that is easily arranged too. I will write a letter to my wife on this. We have expanded our home near the Dockyard recently and could offer you lodgings with us if you wish, as long as you don't mind having a couple of small children around. Alternatively, my wife is part owner of The Dockyard Dog Inn, which is close by our home. The customers of the tavern can be a bit rough sometimes, given most of them are sailors, but the people running it are adept at keeping them in line. You will find it a pleasant place to stay as well."

"Pleasant, you say. Well, anywhere free of strife would be most welcome. How long do you think it would take to arrange passage to Montreal?"

Evan shrugged. "It may be a little while. Your route may end up being a little circuitous on a merchant vessel, since to my knowledge there aren't many merchantmen sailing direct to Canada. The other consideration is the onset of winter. I'm told the St. Lawrence River around Montreal doesn't freeze over much or even very often, but anything is possible and they will be wary of this. You may wish to stay the winter in Antigua and see how you like it."

"I am French, Captain. Do you really think society in Antigua will accept me, even for a while?"

"There is only one way to find out. And besides, when was the last time you saw snow?"

"When I was a teenager, Captain. My daughter has never seen it."

"Well, I was in London in February and the cold and snow was a shock to my system," said Evan, with a wry grin on his face. "I suggest you think about staying in Antigua for the winter. Winter in Canada might be worse than what you experienced in France."

***

Montdenoix could hear Hedouville cursing long before he got to the door of the office Hedouville had established in the main government administration offices in Cap Le Francois. He was about to knock and enter when the crunching sound of wood splintering came from inside, as something was slammed hard against the stone of one of the interior walls. Montdenoix sighed, for he knew it was going to be another difficult session with his master.

Inside Montdenoix found Hedouville red faced with anger, pacing back and forth and muttering to himself, with the remains of a demolished wooden chair lying against the wall. When Hedouville realized Montdenoix was there he pointed to another chair on the other side of his desk for the spy to sit in. Hedouville paced for another few moments while Montdenoix watched in silence before he finally followed suit. With visible effort he finally calmed himself enough and he looked at Montdenoix.

"Tell me what you saw."

Montdenoix sighed and spent the next ten minutes giving Hedouville a full briefing of everything that had happened in Mole St. Nicholas. When he was done Hedouville sat in silence for a moment before hammering a fist hard down onto his desk.

"We have been far too lenient! Damn the man, does he not understand how generous and patient we have been?"

Montdenoix was well aware he had no possible answer to the question, so he remained silent. Hedouville finally looked at Montdenoix again, his eyes glittering like ice.

"There is more to this than what they announced, isn't there? Something is going on, Hubert, and we need to know what it is. I think they have reached an agreement of some sort. The British would not simply pull out of Mole St. Nicholas and Jeremie without getting something in return. They don't give in that easily."

"I agree with you, Theodore. There are rumors Toussaint has agreed to wide open trade with the British. There is no indication it is exclusive, but I admit is could be possible. I doubt it, though, because Toussaint is not that stupid. He knows France would never, ever, accept such a situation."

"Is there more to it than this, do you think?"

"I am working as hard as I can to find out, Theodore. These things take time. I—"

"Damn the man!" cursed Hedouville once again, interrupting Montdenoix before slumping back into his chair and sighing. "Well, we cannot let this pass. We must respond, Hubert. And Hubert? I need information. You must not let me down."

"Theodore, I was about to say I have managed to arrange for another source within Toussaint's camp. He is a servant and not anywhere near as well placed as Pierrot was, but I hope to have answers from him soon. I also intend to use him to take care of our problem. You recall I mentioned this advisor of Toussaint who has consistently opposed us? I have learned it was this same man Baptiste I told you of who exposed Pierrot and brought the matter to Toussaint's attention. I don't know if he is a British agent or not, but it really doesn't matter. The soldier I was planning to use was too unstable and unsuitable for this purpose. However, my new source is quite willing to take care of this problem for a fee and I have confidence. With this Baptiste gone it may be easier to bring Toussaint back into line."

"Hmm, well, that is a start, Hubert. I am sorry, but you must forgive my outbursts. I just find this whole situation frustrating beyond belief. But we must do something to regain the initiative in a public way. Would you not agree?"

"Patience hasn't got us very far to this point, has it?"

"No, it hasn't. I am going to put out a public directive. It will spell out exactly what French law states and that I am invoking it to order all émigrés be expelled from Saint Domingue. In leaving the homeland they have sided with the royalists by default."

Hedouville paused to shrug and look at Montdenoix meaningfully.

"I know what you are thinking. Yes, some of them are mere fortune hunters who care nothing for politics, but it is impossible to distinguish between them, so it is their bad luck if they are caught in our net. The property of the traitors and the royalist planters must be confiscated. I will have to walk a very fine line with my message, but I have to make it clear Toussaint has crossed a line himself by pardoning these people. Yes, I will paint him as a wayward son of France who has failed to fully understand French laws. Even better, I will suggest he has succumbed to wily British spies clouding his eyes to the truth. Yes, I like this thought. I will make it clear he can come back into the fold if he recants and submits to the clear authority I hold. What do you think, Hubert?"

"Toussaint won't like it, but I think it has a chance. There are many patriotic Frenchmen still out there."

"Good. I think it is also time to flex our military muscle. We may not have as many men as Toussaint, but they are worth much. It is time we stopped all military cooperation with him until he submits. We will increase our patrols of Cap Le Francois and remove any and all of Toussaint's army from it as a start. Toussaint must understand we are in the ones in charge here and not him."

***

Baptiste had never seen Toussaint so furious.

"This Hedouville is a fool! He has no understanding of the realities of Saint Domingue. I have tried to help him understand I am a true son of France, but my words are wasted. We must let the past bury itself and build anew here, but he insists on making enemies of those we need to do our work."

Toussaint sighed and with obvious effort mastered himself before turning to the men around the table.

"Well? I need ideas and thoughts."

"This is difficult, Toussaint," said Julien Raimond. "There are many people in Saint Domingue whose loyalty to France is as strong as your own. Of course, there are many who are just as loyal to you. But I agree his behavior is disruptive. He seems to be moving beyond just words and taking active steps to thwart you. Our soldiers in Cap Le Francois here are resisting orders to leave and, at least so far, the French are not pushing the matter. They are making it difficult to continue, though. Who knows if they will move to active confrontation?"

"I think the announcements Hedouville has made are damaging, Toussaint," said Baptiste. "He has been very clever in how he has presented the situation."

"Yes, yes, but what do I do about it? If I directly confront him it will force many to take sides. I am confident of winning, but I am loathe to make loyal Frenchmen make this difficult choice."

"Well, perhaps the solution is for you not to confront him directly then," said Baptiste, rubbing his chin in thought as an idea came to him. "He has tried to put you in a bad light and sway opinions against you. We must therefore find a way to turn it around and sway opinions against him."

Toussaint and Julien Raimond both frowned, before Toussaint spoke.

"Well? How do we do that? You have something in mind, don't you?"

"Hmm, yes. An idea just occurred to me. It may well cost you a little money, but it could prove worth it. If we were to find some loyal supporters angry enough to show their frustrations in a direct way it could sway the larger population fully to your side. For example, everyone knows which local merchants are faithful to France and will follow Hedouville's direction regardless. So why not have your faithful supporters attack these warehouses to show their unhappiness? Perhaps a way could be found to reward a few of your true supporters to incite people to action."

Julien Raimond grinned as he digested what Baptiste said.

"Huh. I like this idea, Toussaint. I don't think it would take much to goad people into doing what he suggests. There are many out there who really are very unhappy with what Hedouville is doing. And meanwhile, you will take the high road here. Express public sorrow that this man does not understand the local situation. Tell everyone how hurt you are at suggestions you are wayward and not truly loyal to France, which is actually the truth.

Make it clear you will continue on the hard path you believe is right for both France and the people of Saint Domingue."

"Exactly," said Baptiste. "This man Hedouville is trying to take something away from people, which is never a popular thing to do. You are doing the opposite and trying to promote working together. Toussaint, I think this is a winning strategy."

This time Toussaint wasted no time in thought.

"I agree with you both. Let's do this. And as for the army, I will tell them they are not to take orders from the French. It is time for Hedouville to come to his senses."

***

Two nights later Baptiste made his way back to his plantation from Fort Picolet, declining the opportunity to stay and dine yet again with Toussaint and the others. He had remained there to help coordinate the effort to turn the tide of opinion against Hedouville. Word was sent everywhere in Saint Domingue under Toussaint's control of what was needed and it was not long before the people's response came. As Julien Raimond had anticipated, it took little effort to move the people to action. Reports of damaged, burning, and looted French businesses and warehouses all over Saint Domingue flowed in. The sheet scale of the response surprised even Toussaint. Toussaint's message was an even greater catalyst than the money that made its way into the hands of a few key, vocal supporters.

Baptiste rode back to his home with a firm sense of accomplishment. Toussaint smirked when

Baptiste told him truthfully he felt too long away from Sylvie. She was still dominating his thoughts as he rode into his stables and left his horse with his stable hand to be cared for. The attack came as he was making his way in the dark along the path to his mansion.

With only the dim light of a quarter moon to light his way he was moving with care in order not to stumble. The snap of a branch accompanied by rustling leaves warned him he was not alone and he turned in time to meet his attacker. The barest glint of moonlight on the knife stabbing at where his back would have been a millisecond before was enough to aid him in grabbing the assailant's knife arm in time. His attacker smashing into him was a heavy blow and the momentum made them both crash hard to the ground. Both fell on their sides and grunted as the air was driven from their lungs.

Baptiste quickly realized his assailant was male. The man was strong, but not enough to free his knife hand from Baptiste's grip. The two men rolled back and forth on the ground in desperation, each trying to gain advantage over the other in any way they could. His attacker tried to head butt Baptiste, but missed and smashed his head into the side of Baptiste's face instead. Baptiste tried to bite the man's hand holding the knife, but his assailant pulled away when he realized what was happening. Both of them tried to knee each other in the groin without success. With the two of them matched in strength, neither was able to gain traction as they continued rolling on the ground.

The struggle to find some advantage was

finally won by Baptiste, who knew the ground they were fighting on better than his opponent. Despite the dim light he was aware they were close to an old tree stump that had been cut down long ago to widen the path. Rolling his assailant as hard as he could in its direction Baptiste made certain it was his foe who struck the edge of the cut stump, with the hard edge of the stump hitting in the middle of his back. The man gasped out in pain and surprise as Baptiste had used all the force he could muster to ensure maximum impact.

Hitting the stump was enough for his foe to lose focus for a couple of seconds, which was plenty of time for Baptiste to use the advantage to drive his knee hard between the man's legs. This time his assailant screamed in pain and his grip on the knife loosened. Baptiste quickly grabbed it and drove the blade deep into the man's heart. Baptiste was still on his knees trying to catch his breath when the stable hand and two other servants came running up, drawn by the sound of the fight.

Baptiste got to his feet, breathing hard from his exertions and brushing the dirt off his clothes as his men asked what had happened. Baptiste explained and had them drag the body into the stables where a lantern could shed more light. He looked down at the man's face and frowned, before finally recognizing him and remembering he was a servant in Toussaint's household.

"What do you want us to do with him, master?" asked one of the men.

Baptiste took a moment give it thought before reaching a decision. Sylvie would have to wait a little longer for his attention, for Baptiste was going back to Fort Picolet.

"Throw him in the back of the cart and harness the horses. Toussaint will want to know what his servant has been up to. I'll bet we shall find yet more French gold in this man's quarters."

***

"I cannot believe this man," grumbled Toussaint under his breath as he and Baptiste made their way toward the room in Fort Picolet where they were to meet Theodore Hedouville and his entourage yet again. "He tries to undermine me and now he wants to talk more."

"I think this is a good sign, Toussaint," said Baptiste. "It probably means our tactic of turning the tables on him worked."

"Well, it hasn't worked to rid me of his presence once and for all. I wish I could find a way to get him off this island and sent back to France like we did with Sonthonax last year."

Baptiste sighed. "Unfortunately, that they sent someone else is a sign the Directory is not yet willing to work directly with you. But you are right, as it would be good to be rid of him. Who knows, maybe if we can find a way to do the same to Hedouville they will finally understand and do what they should be doing."

Baptiste was expecting a tense meeting and he wasn't disappointed. Although Hedouville was the one who had requested the meeting, he acted as if it were the other way around. The meeting soon descended into a predictable series of veiled threats and accusations. Hedouville accused Toussaint of making a secret agreement with the British while Toussaint argued Hedouville was jeopardizing any chance of peace for the island and putting loyal French citizens at odds with each other. Hedouville argued Toussaint had no understanding of French law, which Toussaint brushed aside and in turn accused Hedouville of hiring an assassin to murder his faithful advisor Baptiste. The meeting ended with no agreement on anything other than to meet again.

The two parties met again three times over the course of the next two days. Hedouville surprised Toussaint by once again bringing the larger picture of the situation in the wider Caribbean to the table. Hedouville pressed hard on the need to take the war to the British by invading Jamaica and to counter the designs of the Americans by attacking the disputed territories of the southern American continent. In the final meeting Toussaint lost patience with it all, unable to contain his frustration any longer.

"Theodore. I am a patriotic Frenchman. If you cannot see that, it is your problem. I am not willing to jeopardize what we have here in Saint Domingue by engaging in this foolishness. You are asking me to attack the British, who have treated me with respect, and antagonize the Americans, whom I regard as friends. Even if I had no respect or friendship with either of them, there is no way I can do as you ask. You want me to support engaging in a war on two fronts. Actually, it is three if you count Andre Rigaud in the south, because were I to be mad enough to agree to this he would invade my territory the second my armies left our shores. I suggest you go away and consider my words. I cannot say this any clearer than I have. As I said, if you cannot understand any of this it is not my problem."

Hedouville remained silent for several long moments, his face a frozen mask. He finally leaned forward to make one last attempt.

"Toussaint, you do realize Governor Roume in Santo Domingo has promised troops and is working on sending them here even as we speak, do you not?"

"Is that a threat?"

"No, it is merely a fact."

Toussaint shrugged and made a point of looking from side to side before speaking.

"You have been talking about Roume sending troops here for many weeks. I see no troops. In fact, I keep hearing he has problems in Santo Domingo and I don't think they will ever appear."

"Well, once again you are misinformed, Toussaint. I regret that is so. I see little point in continuing this for now. I will be in touch when we need to meet again."

Toussaint shrugged and watched as the French delegation got up and left the room. When the door had closed behind them Toussaint shook his head and turned to Baptiste.

"Please tell me one more time he will not get reinforcements from Santo Domingo."

"It would be news to me if he is. I am certain he is bluffing, Toussaint. As you say, he has been talking about the possibility for a long time, but nothing is happening. To be certain, I will get an update on the situation as fast as I can."

"Please do. We have come too far to let something stop us now."

Baptiste smiled. An urgent message would be left for Evan Ross that night.

***

After two days of hard riding Hedouville and Montdenoix found lodging at the fort in Jacmel and sent notice to Andre Rigaud of their arrival and desire to meet. An invitation to dine at his mansion the next night appeared swiftly. The two tired Frenchmen dined alone the night before, aware of how dire their situation was becoming.

"Are you certain of this, Theodore?" said Montdenoix, betraying the doubts he felt and swirling the wine in his glass distractedly as he spoke.

"You can read Roume's letter for yourself if you wish. He claims he has finally cajoled the lazy Spaniards into detaching three hundred and fifty men to help us. He further claims he is trying to have them double the number. A troop ship and escort is being readied, but it is all being done on Spanish time and nowhere near as fast as we want it. He has no firm date to offer, but promises to have them on their way on or before the end of September."

Montdenoix sighed and shook his head. "My God. And here I am, hoping he was sending ten times that number at least. This is but a drop in the ocean."

Hedouville shrugged. "It is a start, Hubert. I

don't like it any more than you, but I work with what I have. I can at least point to them when they do arrive and pretend this is just a first wave of thousands more. Maybe then this fool Toussaint will pay attention."

"But meanwhile, here we are about to propose throwing our lot in with Rigaud. Does this mean we should wait?"

Hedouville shook his head. "No. I am done with waiting. Toussaint is so obstinate it is clear to me our time is wasted talking to him further. If he approaches us it would be another matter."

"Theodore, there is one thing which concerns me in this approach to Rigaud. Don't get me wrong, you understand. I don't care who we work with as long as our ends are achieved. My concern is the troops themselves. We have somewhere over two thousand men, most of who are in and around Cap Le Francois. Add to that these Spaniards and we have a reasonable enough force to reckon with. But if we throw our lot in with Rigaud our men will be isolated in the north and our ally Rigaud is far to the south. Shifting their post to the south would make sense, but how we achieve it will be difficult. If we send them by ship the damned Royal Navy is sure to sit up and take notice. If we send them overland they in theory would be crossing hostile territory. Who knows what Toussaint will do if we go this route?"

"Hubert, you are too far ahead of the situation. I agree this is a problem, but lets face it. The troops we have are not making Toussaint lie awake in fear at night. We can certainly make his life a little more difficult than it is, but that is all. No, it is Rigaud who keeps Toussaint awake. So we leave our men where they are, as a thorn in Toussaint's backside. If this becomes all out war then our men's presence will draw valuable troops away from the fight with Rigaud."

Montdenoix shrugged to acknowledge the point and nodded. "I understand and I agree. Well, it is all coming down to Rigaud."

"It seems to be. I don't expect this to be easy, but we must find a way to convince him. If I must flatter this fool every day for a week I will do so. It is for the good of France and I do what I must. To tomorrow."

As Hedouville extended his glass in toast Montdenoix automatically touched his glass to Hedouville's.

"To tomorrow."
***

"Theodore," said Rigaud. "I understand why you have come and everything you are saying, but I must tell you I think this a waste of time. I hear Toussaint has complained of a lack of respect from France and the Directory. Well, I have the same concern. You were not here, of course, but your predecessor Sonthonax was abominable towards me. I was not complaining when Toussaint found a way to have him recalled. So I ask you, why should I suddenly be your friend? How exactly will you be any different? Has the Directory changed its thinking so much?"

Montdenoix sighed inwardly. He was wary of his superior's reaction to being turned down yet again, but to his surprise Hedouville maintained his composure. This was the third day in a row they had met to discuss the situation and to Montdenoix's eyes it was all moving much too slowly. But despite the rejection, Hedouville seemed energized and carried on as if Rigaud had said the exact opposite. Realizing this, Montdenoix began wondering if Hedouville had seen something he was missing. He refocused on the discussions and slowly Montdenoix began to see the subtle change Hedouville's diplomatic senses had picked up on long before he had. Rigaud was finally beginning to respond to the flattery and attention.

Three days later the tide had fully turned and Rigaud was theirs. Hedouville had shifted his position, emphasizing the need to eliminate Toussaint first. A secret, firm promise to restore slavery everywhere on the island went in hand with the elimination of Toussaint. On the sticking point of money Rigaud finally accepted a general commitment to send what resources they could to help build his strength. As the British represented the greatest external threat, an invasion of Jamaica would be the next step for the new alliance and once success was in hand an action to deal with the Americans would follow. Whether Rigaud was lying was irrelevant. Hedouville reasoned that although Rigaud had as big an ego as Toussaint and wanted to be in total charge when it was all over, it was a problem he could work on once Toussaint was eliminated.

Montdenoix smiled as they concluded the talks, for after many trials they were finally making progress. And succeeding with this meant the damned British spies dogging him would grit their teeth in frustration at the failure of their efforts.

Chapter Ten
September 1798
Saint Domingue

The sticky heat of the summer was finally beginning to abate as the month of September wore on. Even better, a steady breeze coming through the windows of his cabin meant it was actually pleasant to meet in Evan's cabin for a change. With the secret alliance to Toussaint, Mole St. Nicholas now became the de facto British headquarters for their remaining time in Saint Domingue. Everyone who wished to leave under British protection was told to travel and be present no later than early October in the Mole, Port-au-Prince, or Jeremie. Space remained at a premium on the merchant vessels available, while the Royal Navy ships were full with those who had enough sway to claim a spot.

The harbor of Mole St. Nicholas was still crowded with all manner of ships as a result. Evan and James anchored offshore near each other and a number of British warships, so the row over was not long. Evan and James had agreed Mole St. Nicholas would be their meeting place over two weeks before and James had only now returned from his ongoing efforts to find a source inside Hedouville's camp.

"Damn me, how certain are you of this?" said Evan, after listening to a quick summary of what James had learned.

"My new recruit Jeanne is serving us well, Evan. With Baptiste and Sylvie's help she was able to befriend a cleaning woman in Hedouville's headquarters. Sylvie was too well known around

Cap Le Francois to make the approach, but no one knew of Jeanne. Baptiste assured me he is confident of the information she has gained for us. And to be honest, it makes sense."

"You used Jeanne for this mission?"

"Why not? She seemed capable. She was also very willing."

"Willing, eh? You rogue. I confess I wasn't terribly surprised to return and find you had borrowed her services. But do go on."

James laughed, before turning serious once again.

"So Baptiste says what this woman overheard is corroborated by what he knows of the timing. Montdenoix and Hedouville were in fact gone from Cap Le Francois on the dates she claims they went to Jacmel, which was after a series of failed talks with Toussaint. And I think her claim to have overheard the two of them celebrating a successful alliance with Andre Rigaud fits. We all knew it was only a matter of time before they gave up on Toussaint and went elsewhere."

"I agree. And Baptiste is still under no suspicion?"

"He says he is fine, although he is wondering what the plan will be to extract himself and Sylvie. The time to do that is clearly coming soon. Of more concern is Toussaint remains worried about Spanish troops from the other side of the island. Hedouville claimed yet again a wave of troops would soon be on their way in the last meeting before calling off their talks. Toussaint called his bluff, but promptly asked Baptiste to look into it yet again."

"Hmm. Well, this is where I have news for you. A report came in while you were away from your source inside Governor Roume's headquarters. It seems this man Roume really has somehow managed to browbeat the Spanish into actually doing something. A number of soldiers are being readied, although she is vague as to how many. I don't think it is much, as she reports only two ships are being prepared. She overheard the target is to have them on their way by the end of September."

"Good God. He must have put a real fire under their backsides. Do you want me to go back to Santo Domingo?"

"Yes, I think we need to put the fire out before it takes hold. In fact, I don't know about you, but I am getting tired of these two goddamn frogs making problems for us. We have come too far to let them mess this up again."

"I'm with you there. But you have an idea, don't you?"

Evan smiled and explained what he had in mind. By the time he finished speaking a huge grin was on James's face.

"Evan, that's brilliant. Do you really think we could make it work? If it does I'm sure Baptiste will do his part. It may well be the tipping point."

"Well, if you have no further use for my clerk she can get started right now. It will take a while, because she will have to do it with care, but she seems quite meticulous. I'm sure there will be plenty of opportunities to reacquaint yourselves later."

James grinned again. "I confess I have rather

been enjoying her company. But duty calls."

"Yes, it does. And first, we must get the situation in Santo Domingo under control. I think you might need some help doing that."

"Help?"

Evan once again explained what he had in mind and James was unable to stop from laughing as he glanced out the window at the big frigate anchored nearby.

"Well, you're going to be popular. I'm quite sure our friends out there have been getting rather bored lately."

"Indeed. And while you are off doing this, I think I should pay this fool Rigaud a visit. Honestly, I don't know what Rigaud is thinking. I doubt very much this alliance with Hedouville will succeed, but if it does it will not be long before Rigaud himself is the target. The game is all about who is in charge on this island and I simply don't see him holding a winning hand. I think it prudent we point this out to him one last time, though. Toussaint may not want independence and he may not have the formal protection of the Royal Navy, but I'm quite sure we will not be shy about helping him where we can, especially if he is opposing the French."

James nodded. "Makes sense. I am to await orders to sail, I assume?"

"Please. I need to have a conversation with General Maitland and our colleagues in the Navy. Thank God they are all available and here right now, so this shouldn't take long. With any luck we can put this all in motion and be away from this infernal place soon. I miss my family and my home.

Never thought I'd say that about Antigua, but it's true."

James shrugged. "My home is my ship now. Of course, it would be even better if I had a clerk like the one you found to keep me company."

Evan laughed.

***

General Maitland and the other Royal Navy Captains were unsurprised when Evan told them of the new alliance Hedouville had forged with Rigaud.

"He wasn't left with much choice, was he?" said the General. "But you are proposing to talk to Rigaud about this? Why?"

Evan took a few moments to outline the gist of the negotiating points he intended to use with Rigaud. When the General nodded slowly after digesting this a moment Evan continued.

"If we can completely isolate this Hedouville and he is left with no allies here, he becomes toothless. Those with deep loyalties to France may secretly want to support him, but if the people with real power are not doing so, then the masses will follow the power. We have something to gain and nothing to lose. I intend to be polite, but blunt, and will not offer him the crown jewels, General. He needs to make an accommodation with us and not Hedouville. I am working on an alternative plan if this doesn't get us anywhere. There are details to take care of before I can say with confidence it will help."

"I see. And meanwhile, your colleagues here have found your plan to deal with the Spanish passes muster?"

"Absolutely, General," said the senior frigate Captain on station, a wolfish grin on his face. "We all volunteered for the mission. The winners had to use their seniority to sort out which ships get to go. Right now we'd all sail from here to the moon if it meant we were going to see some action."

The General smiled. "Well, then. I guess you should all be about it."

***

Rigaud received Evan in the same meeting room they had met in before during their earlier talks. Rigaud was slow to accept the request to talk and Evan had to sit at anchor waiting for almost two days before being given approval to see the black leader. Rigaud gave him a stony look as Evan took a seat across the table and thanked him for seeing him.

"It took me a while to remember you," said Rigaud. "You were not the one doing the talking when you were here before. What exactly is your role, sir?"

"Ah, you should think of me as a diplomat, sir."

"A diplomat. You know, I've been told there are British spies about. Is diplomat a fancy word in your language that also means spy?"

"No, I am a diplomat at the moment and I have come with both a message and a suggestion."

"A message. I see. Well, out with it."

"The message is we are aware you have entered into agreement with this French administrator Hedouville. While we fully understand why you may wish to do this, we do not believe this is a sound course of action. There are two possible outcomes as a result, of course. One is Toussaint will eventually attack and defeat you both. Our expectation is Hedouville's help will not be enough to turn the tide for you, especially as the additional troops he thinks he will be getting soon from Santo Domingo will not arrive."

"Won't arrive, you say. You seem certain of it."

"Trust me, it is not going to happen. The second possibility is you will somehow overcome Toussaint. You will thus become the sole focus of French efforts to remove you and we are certain they will succeed. It is obvious to us the Directory has no interest in having either you or Toussaint in charge here in Saint Domingue, which is abundantly clear if you look at French actions and stop paying attention to their words. We, of course, will meanwhile no longer have a presence on this island, but the fight with these madmen in France will continue. The Royal Navy will continue to be a force to be reckoned with regardless of which scenario plays out."

"I see. You know, I find you the most direct diplomat I have ever met. Are you sure you aren't a spy?"

Evan shrugged. "Think what you will."

"You said you have a suggestion."

"I did. We do not believe it has to be this way. There is a third option and this is our suggestion. Renounce your alliance with Hedouville and reach an accommodation with us, as we obviously have done with Toussaint. Reach another agreement with Toussaint as well. Agree that Hedouville must be sent back to France, as he does not understand the needs of Saint Domingue. Take steps to eject him, forcefully if need be, in concert with Toussaint. Once this is done you and Toussaint will be free to deal with each other once and for all, in whatever way you see fit. We will not interfere. The victor will then inevitably have to deal with the Directory once they stir themselves. Of course, the Royal Navy will still be a factor and we could perhaps be of assistance to whoever the victor is. The choice is yours."

Rigaud was silent for a long time before he stood up and went over to stare out the window at the horizon. After almost two minutes he turned and came back to sit down. His face was still the same frozen mask it was when Evan had first entered the room.

"You British are so very clever, aren't you? You seize even the tiniest opportunities and try to twist them to your advantage. I do give you credit for it. But there is one thing you have not understood from the beginning and, from what I can see, you still don't understand. You treat Saint Domingue as if it is a separate country on its own, but it is not. This *is* France. I cannot say it any clearer than this. Toussaint understands this, but somehow you do not. So when you ask me to betray France you are talking nonsense. Why would I look for someone else when the most beautiful woman in the world is already in my arms?"

"And this is your answer?"

"It is my answer. Be grateful I have not simply thrown you in my dungeon, which is usually what I would do with a spy. Now please leave and never come back."

Evan rose and gave him a brief bow. "I appreciate your time. Good day, sir."

***

The Rio Ozama was filled with the usual small fishing boats and merchant vessels, but they weren't the focus of interest for James as he sat in a waterfront tavern near the mouth of the river in Santo Domingo. The only purpose of the almost untouched mug of ale on the table before him was to provide a reason to sit and watch the big ships slowly being loaded further down the docks in the center of the harbor front.

James had already made contact with Monique and delivered yet another payment to her for her efforts. She was overjoyed at the amount, for she now had more than what she felt she needed to escape. James made her aware of the situation on the other side of the island and the likelihood he may not be back in future. Monique was both sad and pleased at the same time as a result, and gave him a big, long hug before they parted.

In fact there were three ships being readied for sea, although James couldn't see any sense of urgency to the work being done. Several large casks of water and other supplies were stacked beside each of the ships waiting to be loaded. The explanation for how slow the work was proceeding was likely the two yards that were down on one of the ships, although they appeared to be readying them to be remounted. Two of the ships were Spanish frigates while a third was a large merchant vessel James was certain they were converting to serve as a troop ship.

The workers put their tools down and went home long before the sun was ready to go down. James had long since paid for and ordered a second drink, which was now almost gone. He didn't need a third, as he had seen everything he needed to see. Most important was the number of guards posted, which appeared to be minimal on all of the ships. This tallied with what James had seen earlier in the day, as it seemed a large number of Spanish sailors were off ship and more than likely already making ready to settle into their favorite tavern for the night. Spanish coast guard ships were patrolling the harbor, but there were only two and they were quite small, with a large area to cover.

Two hours later James was far offshore, having sailed the *Penfold* out to sea before the sun went down. Although the half moon gave some light, the high hazy cloud that was covering most of the sky kept dimming it. The British warships were waiting at the rendezvous as expected and James had himself rowed over to *HMS Imperious*, the frigate serving as the gathering place for their conference. On seeing the *Penfold* appear the senior officers from the other warships did the same. When they were all together James briefed the officers in detail on what he had seen. Looks of disbelief began appearing one by one on the faces of the officers crowded into the Captain's cabin.

"My God," said the Captain of the *Imperious*. "Are they mad? They do know we patrol out here, don't they?"

"Why would they not be loading these ships up the river where the fort can protect them better?" asked another officer.

James grinned. "Too lazy to move the supplies up river to the ships? Too stupid? I have no idea, but I'm not complaining."

"And the fort at the mouth of the river?" asked one of the Lieutenants.

This time James shrugged. "From what I could see the taverns in town were full. They are likely all making time for their favorite whores before they ship out. Who knows whether their friends in the fort are doing the same?"

By the time he had answered their remaining questions it was clear the mission would proceed. Having done his part James was rowed back to *HMS Penfold* to watch the show. Three hours later the British frigates closed the shore in a line with their lights doused. James knew they were far enough outside the patrol routes of the Spanish coast guard ships to remain undetected, yet close enough to keep the row to shore manageable. As it was now well after midnight James knew their timing was perfect.

With the *Penfold* a short distance away and out of the line of fire James had a commanding view of the scene. The hazy cloud cover continued to serve them well and James knew the Spanish coast guard would have difficulty seeing what was happening until it was far too late. His master's mate was standing beside him with a night glass watching the scene and he pointed toward the British frigates.

"The first boats are away, sir. More following."

The other bit of fortune that night was the men had only light swells to cope with as they rowed in silence to the shore. But James knew it wouldn't be long and soon enough the need for secrecy was over.

The lights of Santo Domingo in the distance made it hard to see anything, but the first sporadic crackle of small arms fire finally drifted out over the water. James wished he could be a part of the attack, but he knew his duty was already done for the day. A moment later the deeper bark of swivels mounted on the cutters which had gone in came and James knew the grapeshot they were loaded with would be cutting down anyone foolish enough to be in the line of fire. Despite being out to sea James could make out the pinprick flashes of the swivels as they continued firing.

After twenty minutes of steady firing the sound of weapons fire finally diminished, but another twinkle of light appeared in first one spot, followed close by a second nearby. James gave a grim smile to his master's mate at the sight.

"Two fire ships only. Hmm, I wonder if this means they managed to cut one of the frigates out? We will soon find out."

As the minutes went by the distant flames grew ever larger. The swivel guns resumed firing at a steady pace and continued for a few more minutes, but James knew it would end soon enough.

"Sir, they are coming out and they have a frigate. I just saw the shadow in the moonlight."

The Spanish fort guarding the harbor finally made its presence felt as several of its heavy guns spoke for the first time. The British warships were waiting for this and targeted the flash of their guns, returning the fort's fire almost as one. James couldn't see the fall of shot, but he knew what fearsome damage a broadside from even one frigate could do. Three minutes later the fort managed a second round, but there were far fewer shots than before. The British warships were already waiting once again and another round of broadsides roared out. This time the fort remained silent in response.

When it came the flash of a much larger explosion seared the outline into his brain of the frigate sailing out between him and the harbor front and it was some time before his vision cleared. James couldn't see it, but he knew the magazine of the second frigate had blown up and debris would be raining everywhere.

As dawn finally broke a few hours later James saw a new frigate had indeed joined the British warships and was flying with a British flag over the Spanish one to signify her capture. James was close enough he could see she had suffered minimal damage in the raid, but some of the rigging and areas of the deck he could see were still a mess. Dark stains of blood ran down the sides of the ship in a few spots. A signal flag was sent up from the *Imperious* requesting captains repair on board so once again James was rowed over. The crowded captain's cabin was now filled with smiling officers all excitedly talking about the night's action.

James quickly learned the mission was a total success. The raiders had lashed the small fire ships to the troop vessel and one of the two frigates. To the dismay of the raiders the latter was too well defended to cut out, leaving them no choice but to fire it too. Once they were alight the Spanish had no way to stop them, for the fire quickly took hold in the dry wood and the sails. Repairing the ships would be a huge task, if they were even repairable at all. The mission had cost five British Marines their lives when the Spanish opened fire from hiding and a similar number of men had various small hurts, but these were deemed reasonable losses for a raid of this nature. Shots of French brandy were passed around and the Captain of the *Imperious* toasted their success when the debriefing was complete. After they drank the toast he turned to James with his glass raised once again.

"And here is to you and your colleagues, sir. If you could dream up a few more missions like this we will all be in your debt."

James grinned. "We shall do our best, sir. Next time we will try hard to think of one where I can join the fun, too."

***

The invitation to dine with the General ashore that evening in Mole St. Nicholas appeared within an hour of Evan's return. When he arrived at the fort he found one other person would be attending with them. The man was in civilian clothing like Evan.

"Ah, Captain Ross, thank you for coming. Allow me to introduce Sir Sidney Davis. He is joining us for dinner tonight. So you know, you may speak freely in front of him on any topic."

Evan did his best to hide his sense of alarm about the notion, but didn't succeed as well as he thought. The General gave him a small smile as he poured a small brandy for them both to enjoy before the meal started.

"Sir Sidney is well aware of our strategies here in Saint Domingue, Captain. He is a very good friend of our Prime Minister and he also happens to be my brother-in-law. I've known him for many years."

"I am in the business of trade, Captain Ross," said Sir Sidney with a smile. "To be more precise, I serve in a capacity similar to what I understand you do. I am an advisor specializing in the background details affecting British trade, wherever we may be operating."

"I see," said Evan. "And you work for whom?"

Sir Sidney laughed. "Anyone who will pay me, of course. Think of me as an independent specialist providing risk analysis of situations from a business perspective. For example, much of my work is done for the British government or Lloyd's, but they are not my sole customers. In other words, I trawl for information much as I gather you do. This sometimes involves going to places and doing things others would rather not. I do what I must. Once I have a grasp on matters I prepare a report with thoughts on what might come next. Businesses don't like the risk of big losses that could arise in volatile situations."

"Quite," said the General. "Which is why he is here. Sir Sidney came out to assess the situation with these infernal American traders, who seem to be breeding throughout the Caribbean faster than the mosquitos. Since he was here, some of our local traders asked him to have a conversation with us about Toussaint."

"Yes. They have mixed feelings about the current situation. On one hand the allure of finally being able to trade safely here is incredibly tempting and they are most pleased at the thought. The problem is the risk still seems high. Yes, they have been active here in Mole St. Nicholas and Jeremie, but this is because the Royal Navy and the Army both have a presence still. The concern is what will happen when the Army is finally gone once and for all. No one has dared risk cargo for fear of the cost if Toussaint fails to hold up his end of the bargain. The General and I were discussing this problem when you conveniently appeared. He tells me you are a rather creative fellow, so we decided to wait and see what your thoughts might be on how to resolve this."

As the first course of their dinner appeared the General ordered wine for them all and turned to Evan after the server had left.

"We do not need your thoughts right away, Captain. Enjoy your dinner. Meanwhile, you can tell me the outcome of your visit to Rigaud."

Evan explained what happened as the meal progressed. The General nodded in response.

"I am not terribly surprised, given the reception Lord Harcourt got earlier. But it was worth a try. I wish I knew how the mission to Santo Domingo fared, though. It is the wild card in the situation right now."

"I expect you shall know soon enough, General. I have every confidence you won't be seeing any Spanish warships around here anytime soon. But meanwhile, I believe I do have a suggestion for you and Sir Sidney."

A server appeared with wine and poured glasses all around for them. The General waited until the server removed their first course plates and left before raising an eyebrow in question to Evan.

"Well?"

"Sir Sidney," said Evan with a smile. "If General Maitland is willing to provide some surety, I think a test is in order. How would you like to take a little trip with me?"

***

Four days later Evan was on the deck of *HMS Alice* as she sailed into Cap Le Francois. Standing beside him was Sir Sidney, who was dressed in civilian clothing similar to what Evan was wearing. For the purpose of their visit to Toussaint's home base Sir Sidney would pretend to be exactly what he was, a representative of other British merchants looking for opportunities.

The trip was made possible by the General's willingness to have the government stand surety for a cargo in case it all went wrong. In the end he had to buy a cargo from a trader and he had grumbled about Evan's willingness to be free with the government's money, but by now Evan knew the man's sense of humor well and was aware the General was having him on. Cap Le Francois was the ideal location to test whether the cargo could be sold with ease because of the presence of Hedouville's French troops. Both the General and Sir Sidney had seen the logic that if trading could be done with success in Cap Le Francois, it could be done anywhere.

Going to Cap Le Francois served two other purposes. The first was Sir Sidney would be free to take whatever time he needed to connect with local buyers and even make tentative deals on behalf of the traders with cargos already sitting in the harbor of Mole St. Nicholas. The second was Evan could visit Baptiste.

Their meeting the night before had not lasted long. Evan was forced to leave a message requesting a meeting for the next night at the drop location and sail out to sea again before returning the next night. Fortunately, Baptiste picked up the message and was waiting for Evan when he was rowed ashore.

Evan had used the time on the journey to Cap Le Francois to think through more of the details of his alternative plan now he knew Rigaud would not budge. By the time he met Baptiste he was ready with his instructions for what was needed when the time came to implement it. The grin on Baptiste's face had stretched wide across his face when Evan explained his intent.

"Sir, that is brilliant," said Baptiste. "The sentiments here are very raw at the moment. The blacks do not understand why France is not supporting Toussaint. I think this will push them over the edge."

"Which is exactly what I am hoping for."

After discussing further arrangements for extracting Baptiste when the time came the two men parted, but not before Baptiste stood to attention and saluted.

"Sir? Permit me to congratulate you on your promotion. Commander Wilton told me of it when he was here. I cannot think of anyone more deserving."

Evan paused a moment. "Thank you. When this is over you and I will have to find a way to reward you, too."

The next day when they finally docked Evan was surprised at how smoothly it all went. The guards posted everywhere Evan looked were obviously Toussaint's men, but frowning French soldiers could be seen passing nearby. Evan was wary of what they might do, but every time they came close Toussaint's men did too, glaring at the soldiers with hard eyes. Each time the soldiers did a quick about face and left.

The harbormasters seemed a little surprised to find a British trading vessel coming into port, but word soon spread of their presence and Sir Sidney quickly became the most popular man on the docks. With all the disruptions to French trade by the British, the area was for a time left solely to the Americans and they had not been able to keep up with the needs of plantation owners and businesses. A purchase of the goods Evan had brought was quickly arranged and Evan had his men offloading the cargo as fast as possible. By the end of the day the job was done and Sir Sidney had a handful of contacts for the traders waiting in Mole St. Nicholas to sell their wares to.

"Well?" said Evan, as Sir Sidney finally made his way back to the ship and they made to free the

Alice from its mooring. "You look thirsty. The crew knows what they are doing. Let's go have a drink in my cabin."

"Excellent idea, Captain. I am simply parched and I'm tired, too."

When they were finally seated with drinks in hand Sir Sidney told Evan of his success.

"This was an excellent idea, Captain. It appears Toussaint put the word out to expect British traders and to treat us well. There are shortages of many essential supplies. We sold the cargo for a lovely profit. The man we bought it from in Mole St. Nicholas will be cursing himself for not taking at least some of the risk. But no matter, for everything I saw leads me to believe there will be no problems."

Evan smiled.

***

By the time Evan and Sir Sidney returned to Mole St. Nicholas the warships were back in harbor with their capture. James had returned with them and had gleefully reported their success already to the General. When Evan and Sir Sidney in turn told him of their success at Cap Le Francois the General had beamed with pleasure and insisted on offering them a drink.

"I must confess, Sir Sidney, I was having doubts about how all this was going to work, but we are meeting with success at every turn. And with the Spanish not coming to plague us it is even better. Now if we only had a way to rid the island of this meddling Frenchman Hedouville I would be a truly happy man."

Evan cleared his throat to catch the General's attention.

"Well, actually, I may be able to help with this, sir. I can't guarantee anything, but you may recall I mentioned some time back I was working on a fallback plan? The preparations I put in motion before we left are now complete and, combined with what my man in Cap Le Francois can potentially do for us, I think it could work."

The General and Sir Sidney looked at each other before turning back to Evan.

"Don't keep us in suspense, Captain."

Evan unrolled a piece of paper he had brought with him and passed it over to the two men. The document was in French and Evan translated what it said for the benefit of the General, who didn't speak the language. As he finished both men looked at him.

"Where did you get this, Captain Ross?" asked Sir Sidney.

"From my new clerk, sir," said Evan, unable to keep a grin off his face. "She has a very good hand and eye for copying. I've had her preparing several of these for use."

Understanding dawned at the same time on the faces of the two men and they both grinned too.

"And your plan?" said the General.

Evan sketched out the details and answered each of their questions, although the two men had relatively few. When the questions dried up Sir Sidney finally turned to the General.

"Well, damn me, but I think Captain Ross is right. This might just work. Our traders will be even happier if the French are finally no longer around to annoy us on this island."

"I agree. Captain Ross, your reputation is well deserved. Yes, please do make your plan a reality. What about timing?"

"I suggest we time this to coincide with our departure in early October. It may not work, but I think if we no longer have a presence on the island it will be much easier to protest our innocence in case someone tries to pin it on us."

"Well," said the General. "With any luck we will all be away from this infernal place a lot sooner than I thought we would be."

Chapter Eleven
October 1798
Saint Domingue and Antigua

Even sitting inside Evan's cabin on *HMS Alice* was no escape from the noise and bustle of Mole St. Nicholas harbor. The early October weather was still hot enough any thought of closing the windows of his cabin was impossible. But with the deadline to leave rapidly nearing the efforts to get people and their belongings away had kicked into high gear, making the port a hive of noisy activity. Despite it all Evan had found a spot to moor the Alice on the docks for the convenience, although he was now regretting the decision. Evan and James did their best to ignore it as they sat in conference discussing making the details of Evan's plan and timing work when a knock came at the door.

Evan sighed and called an order for whomever it was to enter. To his surprise Amelie Caron and her daughter came into his cabin. Both men stood to greet them and Evan came around his desk to take the hand Amelie offered him.

"Madam Caron, it is wonderful to see you again, although I confess I am surprised. I thought you were on your way to Antigua."

"I am, Captain, and please call me Amelie. Have we stopped being friends and you no longer want to call me by my name?"

She laughed to see Evan's consternation and she continued before he could respond.

"The frigate taking us to Antigua was delayed and then given orders to stop here briefly for mail before continuing onward. When my daughter saw your vessel she imposed on our Captain to give us just a little time to come by and give you our thanks one last time. I agreed, for I don't know how long we will be in Antigua or if we will even be there when you return. Are you still unsure of when you can leave here?"

"I'm afraid so, Amelie. I don't expect it will be long, but how matters unfold will determine this. Please reassure my wife when you see her it won't be any longer than it absolutely has to be. She knows you are coming and is making room for the two of you in our home. But forgive me, for I must introduce my colleague here. This is Commander James Wilton. James, this is the lady I told you about, Amelie Caron and her daughter Cecile."

"I am enchanted, madam," said James, sketching a brief bow.

"Ah, the courageous Commander Wilton. Your Captain told us a few stories about you when we sailed with him. You both lead such exciting lives it sometimes make me wish I were a man. Well, Captain, we were warned not to stay long and you are undoubtedly busy, so we will take our leave."

Amelie reached out and took Evan's hand once more.

"You have been so very kind to us. I wish I had some way to repay you. But this will have to do."

Stepping close she gave Evan a kiss on both cheeks of his face. As she stepped back again her daughter came forward and did the same.

"You are our hero, Captain Ross," said Cecile.

"I hope your travels are safe," said Evan as the

two women turned and left, waving goodbye before closing the door behind them.

Evan took a deep breath of the faint hint of perfume remaining in the air as he stood absentmindedly staring at the door. A moment later he realized James was looking at him and he went back to the other side of his desk to sit down again. James spoke as he followed suit.

"Telling stories about me, were you?"

"Ah, they wanted to know more about me and what I do," said Evan with a grin. "I had to edit a lot because you were part of some of the stories and, of course, some of your exploits aren't for delicate ears, now are they?

"Of course. But I confess I am once again amazed at your bravery."

"Eh? My bravery?"

"Did you not notice the way this Amelie looks at you? If she isn't madly in love with you then I'm a Frenchman. So let me see, you find a way to rescue an extremely good looking woman, make her fall in love with you, and then send her off to stay with Alice? Evan, you are a braver man than I."

"I don't—oh," said Evan as understanding finally dawned. He gave James a sidelong glance.

"You think Alice is going to be jealous, don't you? Damn me, I confess I hadn't thought of that."

James laughed. "Well, you may want to put some thought into it and make sure you have whatever your story is going to be straight when you get home. Maybe some consideration as to how you will reassure her she is still the best looking woman on the island of Antigua and the only one you are interested in? The good news is you still have time to figure it out."

***

The ceremony was set for mid morning four days later at the request of the British, as standing around in a heavy uniform in the afternoon sun was never a good idea. This time no stages were built or march past of troops to review was organized, but effort was made to ensure it would be no less of a momentous occasion nonetheless. An area along the waterfront docks was reserved for a large file of Marines from *HMS Imperious* in their dress red coat uniforms to stand at attention with their backs to the water and their ship, tethered by lines to the dock for the occasion. To their front a small table was set up on which rested two glasses and a decanter of brandy.

A large crowd in a semicircle of mostly black faces lined the area around them, held back by armed guards. Many more people were watching from upper windows and the rooftops of the buildings lining the waterfront. Sailors on *HMS Imperious* lined the sides of the big frigate to watch it all from above while yet more people were watching from other ships tethered beside it. *HMS Alice* was the next ship in line beside the *Imperious* and her sailors had a commanding view as well.

Hubert Montdenoix was one of the faces watching it all from a nearby rooftop. Hedouville had ordered him to attend in the hope more information could be gleaned about Toussaint and the British. Montdenoix was all too happy to go, for his master seemed mired in a permanently foul mood ever since word of the British raid on Santo Domingo had reached them. When a hasty message from Roume himself arrived a couple of days later Hedouville had fallen into alternating moments of dark rage and sullen depression.

Some of his dark rage was vented on Montdenoix, as Hedouville railed at British spies obviously outwitting Montdenoix and his lacklustre efforts. The criticisms stung, but Montdenoix had to admit there could be no coincidence in a major British raid occurring at the same time as aid was being readied from Santo Domingo to Hedouville.

Even worse, Roume's letter carried a warning it would be a total waste of time to expect a new mission could be mounted in a hurry. The toll of death and destruction visited on the Spanish forces and the waterfront of Santo Domingo was sobering. More Spanish ships were available further up the river, but the local commanders were already adamant they would not be freed up to send men to Hedouville, claiming they were needed for the defense of Santo Domingo. Roume bluntly told Hedouville it would be weeks or even months before he felt confident he could realistically cajole any further help out of the Spanish.

Bare moments before Montdenoix rose to leave Hedouville had engaged in yet another fit of destructive rage by smashing a picture hanging on the wall with an empty glass.
The last Montdenoix had seen of him was of the man sitting slumped head in hands at his desk, a half empty bottle of brandy and a glass before him. He had waved a hand in dismissal without looking

up at Montdenoix.

"Go Hubert, just go. Find me something. I must have something to work with or we are finished here."

Montdenoix privately agreed and he spent his entire time riding from Cap Le Francois to Mole St. Nicholas in thought over the situation, but once he arrived he was as bereft of ideas as Hedouville. Having the British about to leave the island seemed on the surface to be a positive development, but British traders were already flocking to Cap Le Francois and Port-au-Prince with their wares. Montdenoix could picture their masters in the Directory back home and the sarcastic questions he and Hedouville could face from them. Trying to pretend the departure of the British Army from Saint Domingue while having them replaced with a host of British traders was a victory would not be a winning strategy.

Movement below and the murmur of the crowd drew Montdenoix's attention back to the scene before him. General Maitland and a number of his officers were marching off *HMS Imperious* and obviously doing it with all of the aplomb they could muster. At the same time Montdenoix could sense something was happening below, as the crowd right at the front of the table was being shoved back to make a path. As the General and his men came to a stop beside the table a group of black soldiers in their own colorful, matching dress uniforms came marching forward with Toussaint in tow, waving at the people as he slowly walked up.

The two smiling leaders met in the middle and

both men waved as the crowd cheered lustily in response. General Maitland opened the ceremony by emphasizing how grateful he was the handover was going so smoothly and that Toussaint's men were so cooperative. Toussaint expressed his own gratitude for the respect he was once again being shown and for the British commitment to keeping their word to leave in an orderly fashion and without strife.

Montdenoix realized there must have been agreement to keep the ceremony short, for soon enough the two men were finished their speeches. The General poured a measure of brandy into the two glasses and the two men toasted each other before downing the contents at the same time. The crowd clapped and roared approval as the two men shook hands and waved at the crowd one last time.

The General turning to face the waiting Marines was the sign it was over. The Marine Captain in charge of the file barked an order and the Marines did an about face as one, marching in good order back onto *HMS Imperious*. One by one the Army officers who had joined General Maitland on the dock followed them, leaving the General himself to be the last British Army soldier to take leave of Saint Domingue. The crowd's approval was thunderous and the General couldn't resist one last wave as he reached the deck, before finally disappearing from view below.

Montdenoix remained standing in silence as the raucous crowd finally began to disperse. As he stood watching them a sense of being watched himself stole over him. The sense was so strong he scanned the faces in the crowd with wary caution, but saw no one who gave concern. He turned his gaze to the British warship now releasing the lines tethering it to the shore before he realized it was the much smaller ship beside it that warranted attention. Standing on the quarterdeck was his one armed foe and Montdenoix instantly realized the man was watching him. Around him the small ship he was on was also coming to life and making ready to slip away, but his foe was motionless and staring intently at him.

As they locked eyes what Montdenoix found disconcerting enough to be instantly alarming was the huge grin on his foe's face. The two men remained staring at each other until the Englishman was interrupted by one of the sailors on the ship. The Englishman glanced back at Montdenoix one last time, still smiling, and waved before turning away for good to see to his ship.

Montdenoix frowned to himself, puzzled over why the Englishman had made a point of smiling. A sense of foreboding stole over him, although he didn't know the cause. He sighed as he turned away himself, knowing it was going to bother him until he learned whether or not he had cause to be wary.

The same night Montdenoix trawled the taverns of Mole St. Nicholas and put to use all of his skills in search of the information he needed and of the prey he knew would have it. His focus was the host of drunken men present who were Toussaint's soldiers, but his problem was there were far too many of them and most would not have what he needed. But fortune finally smiled on Montdenoix near midnight.

Montdenoix found what he was looking for in a large inn with a tavern away from the docks that was distinctly better maintained than those on the waterfront. This tavern had a separate room at the back for private groups and as the door opened and closed to admit servers he saw a number of Toussaint's senior military commanders in the group. Montdenoix smiled and went in search of the manager. The man's face lit with avarice the second Montdenoix showed him the French gold he was being offered and fifteen minutes later Montdenoix had what he needed.

An adjoining room at the back of the inn with a locked, but connecting door was all Montdenoix needed. Listening to the drunken crowd of men through the door was easy. He made himself comfortable and settled in to learn what he could. Two hours later the party was finally winding down as the men stumbled out, clutching the whores they had brought in as they made their way to their rooms. Montdenoix remained slumped against the door, willing himself to get up and leave, but not finding the will to do so. He had found what he sought, but what he learned was the worst news possible. A voice he was certain belonged to one of Toussaint's most senior commanders had given the secret away.

"Can you believe the stupidity of the British? They worry Toussaint will attack Jamaica and Toussaint lets them think he wants to. But he couldn't care less about it! He thinks this Hedouville is a madman to want an invasion of Jamaica. So the

British get their Treaty, agree to leave, and Toussaint gets what he wants. Then the British are so grateful they practically beg Toussaint to let them help by trading with him, which is also exactly what Toussaint wants."

As the laughter died down another voice spoke.

"But what about this idea of independence? Is Toussaint really going to do it?"

"Who knows? He told the British he wouldn't, but with the support of the Americans and now the British trading with us, he just might change his mind. I tell you, Toussaint is smarter than all of his enemies put together."

Montdenoix finally stood up and left to make his way to his own room for the night. He was looking forward to the bottle of brandy waiting for him. And he knew the smile on the face of the British spy would still haunt his dreams in the night regardless of how much brandy he drank.

***

Toussaint's face was flushed with anger as he flung the piece of paper in his hands down on the table before him.

"Is the man mad? What does he think he is doing? Listen, you can hear the crowds shouting in town even out here in Fort Picolet! And we have nothing to do with it. They are angry without any prodding from me."

The men sitting around the table nodded agreement, for they didn't have to strain hard to hear the distant sounds of strife coming through the open window.

"And what is this madness going on at the

garrison? Is this rumor true they tried to kill my commander?"

Julien Raimond nodded and spoke in response.

"Toussaint, it is true there has been fighting between your men and the French soldiers in the garrison. Your commander Moyse was involved and he survived, but it is not clear whether this was a deliberate attempt or something spur of the moment. We are still trying to find out if Hedouville actually ordered his murder. Even if he didn't it seems clear the fighting with your men is a direct result of Hedouville's orders. Moyse and his men have received minimal if any rations from the French for a while now and getting enough food to your men continues to be a real problem, too. It is no surprise this is all boiling over."

"Toussaint," said Baptiste. "It seems clear to me this man Hedouville is now completely desperate. We all know the British put a stop to any thought of help for him coming from the other side of the island, so his options are limited. He is reduced to taking great risks and it seems to me this poster is the greatest of all, for he is trying to force your hand. Once again, he does not understand Saint Domingue."

"And you say these are appearing everywhere?"

"Yes. A trader came into port just this afternoon and confirmed they are widespread in Port-au-Prince and Mole St. Nicholas. It seems the last to appear have been here."

Toussaint hammered a heavy fist into the table in frustration. Baptiste was certain Evan's plan was working and he was filled with elation at the thought. The poster Evan's clerk Jeanne had carefully forged so many copies of for wide distribution was doing its job. Using previous posters Hedouville had issued she had copied the handwriting of Hedouville's clerk so meticulously Baptiste was unable to see any material difference. The same style and format was used as well. With the posters announcing the formal reinstatement of slavery everywhere throughout Saint Domingue on the orders of Hedouville it was the all too believable message they conveyed. Baptiste himself had gone out in the middle of the night and put them up throughout the town.

Baptiste had no hand in whatever was happening at the garrison, but he welcomed it as one more development that would move Toussaint to act in the way Evan Ross wanted. By now Baptiste knew the signs of when Toussaint had made up his mind on something and the familiar look was on Toussaint's face as he shoved his chair back from the table and stood up. The men around the table did the same.

"We cannot let this madness continue. Julien, I want my own posters made and put out everywhere as soon as possible. They need to state this man Hedouville is disruptive and does not understand the needs of Saint Domingue or of France, for this action in not in anyone's interests. Everyone is to disregard any talk of reinstating slavery."

"I shall have them made at once, Toussaint. What will you do in the meantime?"

"In the meantime, I have had enough of this madness and continual jousting with this fool

Hedouville. The time for talk is over. I will now lead my army and we will deal with this once and for all."

***

Hubert Montdenoix returned to Cap Le Francois in time to finally understand exactly why the British spy in Mole St. Nicholas had smiled. Numerous French owned businesses were being looted and vandalized. Smoke could be seen rising from various parts of the town. Puzzled by it all as he made his way through the town, Montdenoix focused on a tense, milling crowd of people standing and looking at a poster nailed to a wall. On reading it he had torn it off the wall in anger and been forced to draw his sword to clear a path away from the equally angry crowd. After seeing what was happening he shoved his way through the teeming crowds to the army barracks and discovered he was bare moments ahead of his superior. Hedouville stormed into the room where Montdenoix was waiting when told of Montdenoix's presence.

"Hubert! These animals attacked our headquarters. If it weren't for our guards using hard steel on them I would be a dead man right now. We escaped out the back and they were on our heels the whole way here. So what is all this madness going on here? Why are these people so angry?"

Montdenoix handed the poster to his master and sighed.

"I found this posted outside. The soldiers here tell me there are more of them everywhere. Theodore, did you put these out?"

The Sugar Inferno

Hedouville looked at Montdenoix as if he was a madman before snatching the poster from his hands and quickly reading it. The look of horror on Hedouville's face told Montdenoix his answer. Hedouville groaned aloud in anguish.

"My God! Of course I didn't put these out. This is insane!"

Hedouville began muttering and pacing back and forth with the distracted, restless energy of a man caged by walls which were closing in from all directions and threatening to crush him, for no clear way out was at hand. Montdenoix sighed as he spoke again.

"Theodore, I am sorry to report this, but I do not have good news from Mole St. Nicholas."

Hedouville groaned again and slumped into a chair.

"Go on, I must know it all, as much as I do not want to."

As Montdenoix finished telling him what he had learned Hedouville stood up and went over to a side cabinet in search of a drink. He came back with two glasses and a decanter of cognac, pouring a glass for each of them. Montdenoix sighed as he reached for his glass.

"The other news, Theodore, although this is only a rumor at this point, is that these posters have already been put up around the rest of the island and the people are reacting in exactly the same way elsewhere. Our soldiers have heard this from a number of the madmen trying to kill us all."

"The scheming goddamn British are behind this, aren't they?"

The Sugar Inferno

"Yes, I am certain they are. I do not like to say it, but they have beaten us this time."

As he finished speaking a knock came on the door and a harried looking French army officer came in. He saluted in a rush.

"Sir? I am to report we fear being pressed badly. It would seem Toussaint himself is rallying his men. We believe we will soon be outnumbered beyond our ability to cope. Do you have orders for us?"

"Orders?" said Hedouville, his voice uncertain.

"Sir, if you ask us to defend the barracks we will do so to the best of our ability, but this is not a sound position for such a purpose. With the numbers we believe we will face, it is only a matter of time before we are massacred."

Hedouville sighed. " I will come. I must see what is happening."

All three men made their way to the roof of the barracks, which they knew would offer a commanding view of the town and the port. The senior French Colonel in charge of Hedouville's forces was already there with three of his junior officers.

The scene was worse than Montdenoix feared. Angry mobs were still roaming the streets smashing anything French owned indiscriminately. Even more fires with dense smoke could be seen rising to the sky. The barracks were surrounded, but the soldiers were holding the crowds back. A constant hail of stones and garbage was being thrown at the French defenders. Worst of all, it was obvious a large cohort of black soldiers were massing a few blocks away. The Colonel turned as Hedouville came to stand beside him.

"I am told the situation is not good."

"This is correct, sir. We are holding our own against the mobs, but the crowd forming over there in the distance look to be Toussaint's soldiers. The situation will change if they attack. There is a rumor Toussaint is leading them and they will indeed challenge us."

"What options do we have?"

"Very few, sir. We can stay here, but we will be annihilated, if only because of the sheer numbers they can throw at us. The best position to defend in this town is Fort Picolet, but Toussaint already occupies this. I know of nowhere else we could move to in Cap Le Francois that would change our fortunes for the better. We will defend here as best we can if you order it so, but the reality is if we wish to survive it is time to leave."

"Take ship and leave is our only real choice then."

"Sir, it is. The two frigates and two troopships in the harbor are the only way out. The ships will be seriously overcrowded, but perhaps we can commandeer a merchant vessel or two. And we will have to pray the damned Royal Navy isn't prowling offshore."

Hedouville turned to Montdenoix. "Do you see any viable alternatives?"

"I am sorry, Theodore. I do not."

Hedouville turned back and stood silent looking out at the town. After an uncomfortably long minute the Colonel finally spoke up.

"Sir. I realize this is a difficult decision, but I must point out time is not on our side. If we are leaving, we must do so now. Toussaint will not be waiting much longer to unleash his men."

"Yes, yes, I understand. I have only one question. Will the ships truly be a refuge? Can we simply get on board and leave?"

"Sir, we can. I have had conversations with the Captains of our warships. Given the tensions we have had lately with Toussaint's men we knew a situation like this could be a possibility. I assure you, they will be watching and waiting for us to make our move. We will do a fighting, but coordinated retreat. When the Marines on the ships see us coming they will help to cover us while we board the men."

"Then let us go and do it now. Hubert and I will go back downstairs and await your word for when to leave."

On their way back to the meeting room they were in earlier Hedouville called for a clerk to be sent to them. As they waited Hedouville poured himself another drink.

"Well, Hubert, I have tried, but it is time for me to leave and hand this over to someone who may perhaps do better. But before I go I must set the stage for whoever the Directory sends out to replace me."

"What do you have in mind, Theodore?"

"It is too late to stop this madness, but we must put out the truth. The people must be told we are not behind this announcement about slavery. And while we are at it, it is time to expose Toussaint as the practiced liar he is. We will put out posters telling everyone he is a British pawn and has agreed to leave Jamaica alone. We will tell everyone he is seeking independence and has forsaken France at the behest of the scheming British and Americans. And finally I will absolve both Rigaud and Roume of any need to follow Toussaint's lead on anything. We must make many copies of this and have them posted everywhere in Saint Domingue."

"I have contacts who will help distribute and post them, Theodore."

"Excellent," said Hedouville, as a clerk entered with writing materials. "Then let us do what we can before we must evacuate."

Montdenoix sat and watched as Hedouville organized the clerk. He reached for his glass of cognac and downed a large portion before putting the snifter down. As he stared at the remaining contents of his glass he vowed in silence that many would pay some day for what had happened in Saint Domingue. And at the top of the target list forming in his mind was the smiling British spy.

***

The ship's boat Evan was steering made its way toward the shore where the lantern was shining with it's light shaded to show only out to sea. As they came closer he could see the figures of two people waiting for them in the dim moonlight. To his surprise, Baptiste was not one of them.

"Sylvie?" said Evan, when they were within a few feet of the shore. "Where is Baptiste?"

Sylvie grabbed the line one of Evan's men threw here and she pulled the boat closer, making it fast to the small dock.

"Baptiste sent me to greet you, sir. He went to Cap Le Francois because of everything happening there, but he promised he would be back by sundown. He should be back any time now. This is Solange. She is the slave who helped us to expose Pierrot. We want to bring her with us. The small bag of belongings she has is all she is bringing with her. She can act as if she was caught up in what we are about to do. No one will have cause to think anything suspicious about her."

"I see. All right, we can make room," said Evan, stepping ashore with the four men accompanying him. "And your preparations? Are you ready to go?"

"Sir, we are. Baptiste freed all of our slaves and gave each of them a sum of money several days ago. He told them he wanted to be the first of Toussaint's advisors to do the right thing by freeing them once and for all as you suggested. He also told them the money was in recognition of their service, because to his mind they really should have been paid for it. As you predicted, most have stayed to carry on working. They will all be horrified at what is going to happen, but they will not be left to their own devices. The money was ample enough they will be able to start small businesses if they choose."

"Excellent. It is just a matter of time then for Baptiste to return and we can be away. I—ah, and here he is."

"Captain Ross," called Baptiste, making his way down the hill to the group on the dock. "I am sorry to keep you waiting. I simply had to learn what was happening in town. I bring good news."

"And?"

"Your plan has worked, sir. The French are evacuating as we speak. As you had hoped, they are making for the harbor and the French warships. Toussaint and the mobs and his soldiers are pushing them hard, but I think Toussaint has realized what is happening and is happy about it. Toussaint's officers told me the French sent word that Hedouville and all French soldiers are leaving and won't be back."

"Very good. Hedouville may be leaving, but I don't know we can expect the Directory to stop meddling in Saint Domingue. Those soldiers may well return in future, but it is a problem for another day. Then the only task left to you is to implement our plan here?"

"Sir, Sylvie and I are ready. Solange can leave her belongings here with the boat and join us. We will leave now and await you on our verandah."

Evan gave them ten minutes before following the same path back up the hill. They took their time, as it was pitch dark in the tree-lined path, but soon enough they reached the top and made their way to the mansion without seeing anyone. Baptiste had promised to dismiss all of the servants, who were now likely all in their quarters for the evening.

"Swords at the ready," said Evan over his shoulder. "Remember, please, we are not interested in harming anyone. We want to scare them off."

They reached an entrance door and although it wasn't locked the sailors kicked the door in with a loud crash. They stormed up the stairs to the upper floor, smashing furniture aside indiscriminately. They made their way to where Sylvie and Baptiste were waiting for them. In a voice loud enough to be heard in the nearby servants quarters Evan told them in French they were prisoners of the French administration and they would be coming with them. Baptiste demanded to know why and Evan proclaimed him a traitor to France. Baptiste and Sylvie shouted for help while Evan kicked more furniture around to make as much noise as possible. Baptiste cried out in pretend agony while Sylvie screamed in anguish, before they splashed a small container of pig's blood indiscriminately on the verandah.

As the three of them made their way fast out of the mansion shouts of alarm were coming from the servants quarters. Three of Evan's sailors who all spoke French formed the rear guard, waving their swords and threatening the first few servants that appeared. The servants stopped in their tracks and disappeared back into their quarters, but not before catching a glimpse of Baptiste clutching at Sylvie and Solange for support as Evan kept shoving him toward the path. The two women made a point of looking terrified at Evan.

They spilled yet more blood along the way to maintain the fiction. Evan's three sailors followed close behind. On reaching the boat they splashed the last of the pig's blood on the dock and shoved off. They were well on their way to *HMS Alice* by the time Baptiste's servants found the courage to go to the dock.

Once on board Baptiste grinned at Evan. "Do you think we pulled it off, Captain?"

"I think so. I'm sure they heard me shouting and our men speaking French would add to the fiction. Even if they didn't, with all this going on I am confident Toussaint will put it together as we planned and reach the conclusion Hedouville somehow managed a little revenge on you before he left. Well, we had to try this. We don't want Toussaint suspicious he was the pawn of a British spy, now do we?"

"Are we going back to Antigua now, Captain?"

"Not just yet, but soon. You two have done your part, though, and you have done it well. I must find a way to reward both of you. But for now, we have one last thing to do here. I must make certain the French really are leaving, for General Maitland will want to know."

Evan barked a series of orders that soon had them underway, following a course around the headland toward Cap Le Francois. Although their course would take them near Fort Picolet and the men therein would be alert, Evan felt it an acceptable risk, as it was unlikely they would fire on a small ship without cause. The wind was brisk enough they were offshore of the fort in thirty minutes. Evan was more and more in awe at the scene the closer they got to the port.

The destruction being visited on French businesses in Cap Le Francois had now extended beyond the boundaries of the town to the many sugar and coffee plantations surrounding the town. Large fires dotted the landscape in all directions and

Evan knew it was likely the angry mobs were hitting the French where it would hurt the most. An inferno of burning sugar stockpiles and the mills producing them were alight in towering pillars of flames and devastation. The raging fires sent thick smoke even higher into the night sky. Despite being as far out at sea as they were they could smell the stench from the burning sugar drifting across the water.

Weapons fire and distant screams of men fighting and dying were carried out to them, too. And even as Evan trained his night glass on the docks and the French ships he knew were moored there he saw the sign he was looking for. One by one the French ships were pulling away from the shore and making sail. He lowered his night glass and smiled, for his plans had all come to fruition. Baptiste was standing beside him with a night glass and he too lowered it as he turned to Evan.

"Congratulations, sir. It is a total victory."
***

The Captain of *HMS Imperious* and General Maitland were waiting for him in the Captain's cabin as the frigate swung at anchor in Mole St. Nicholas harbor. Evan could see both men had a look of anticipation on their faces and he smiled to let them know he bore good news. As Evan told them of what had occurred in Cap Le Francois both men grew their own broad smiles. When he was done the General nodded before speaking.

"Captain Ross, you have once again proved your reputation is well deserved. I will be sending a full report to the First Lord and will commend your efforts without hesitation. I can only hope they find a way to reward you. This isn't the outcome our masters were perhaps expecting, but I daresay they will be happy nonetheless. Jamaica is spared, our traders are very happy, and this meddling French administrator has been driven away. The flow of money from this island to France won't be resuming any time soon. We could not have hoped for better."

"I agree with the General, Captain Ross," said the Captain of *HMS Imperious*. "It is too bad I didn't have enough frigates to spare to take on the French as they left port in Cap Le Francois, but the frigate I do have waiting for them out to sea will harass them all the way to Guadeloupe or wherever they head for."

"Thank you for the kind words, gentlemen. Hopefully this will put a stop to French meddling here, at least for a while."

"Perhaps. Or perhaps not," said the General. "They have too much at stake on this island, I think. I fear Toussaint may face a rough time in future, once the French regroup. It's too bad he didn't want independence and a full treaty with us, but who knows what the future holds? The Royal Navy may be able to quietly help him when the time comes if the French return in force."

"What a lovely thought," said the Captain of the *Imperious*. "Let's hope so."

The three men laughed and Evan spoke as the laughter died down.

"Are you off for home, General?"

"Ah, the *Imperious* and I are heading for Barbados, Captain. I expect to be there a little while and then return home, yes. And you are returning to Antigua?"

"Sir, I am. I look forward to seeing my family. You know, General, you may wish to find reasons to stay in Barbados a bit longer. I've enjoyed my many visits there. It really is a wonderful island and it would still be bloody cold at home if you returned right away."

The General laughed. "I like your thinking, Captain Ross."

***

The warmth of the late October sun on his shoulders was welcome as Evan walked out of the Dockyard gate in Antigua and began trudging to his nearby home. They sailed into English Harbour in the morning and it had taken him almost all of the rest of the day before he had finally dealt with the last of the people demanding his time. Commander Cooke had for the most part dealt with the pile of paperwork sitting on his desk in Evan's absence, but it would still need Evan's attention eventually. With Evan was no longer directly in charge of the Dockyard the paperwork and correspondence pile was actually smaller than he was anticipating. But what was left could all wait for another day.

As he made his way up the path to their home Evan was unsurprised once again to find the only one waiting for him on the verandah was Nelson the dog. This late in the day the children would already have been fed and Alice would be inside preparing dinner for the adults, while her mother was likely minding the children. Nelson gave him a friendly bark of welcome and wagged his tail for some attention as he always did. Evan took a deep breath and looked around, drinking in the atmosphere and enjoying the simple, welcome feeling of being home. As he straightened up from scratching Nelson's ear he heard an inarticulate scream of joy behind him and he turned in time to have Alice envelope him in a crushing embrace.

"My God, lover man. You've been gone so long!"

Right behind her came the children and Alice's mother. They all needed plenty of hugs and attention too, and it was ten minutes before the celebration of his return finally died down. When he told them he was finished with Saint Domingue and not likely to return there anytime soon it became yet another cause for celebration. As Alice's mother took the children off to put them to bed and they all went inside Evan looked around, but saw no sign of Amelie Caron or her daughter. Knowing he would have to broach the subject sooner or later, Evan decided to get it over with and asked for their whereabouts.

Alice stopped what she was doing in the kitchen and turned to face him, hands on her hips. Evan groaned inside, for it was never a good sign when his wife did that. Alice arched an eyebrow at him as she spoke.

"Ah, yes, the most beautiful French lady you found. How is it you seem to attract beautiful women like flies, lover man?"

Despite James's warning, Evan had not managed to come up with anything other than the simple truth to respond to Alice. Still, Evan stood openmouthed for a long moment, desperately trying to think of a response safe enough to keep him out of trouble. In the end his answer seemed lame even in his own mind.

"Umm, she needed help, my love. It was the General who told me to help her. My God, Alice, what could I do?"

Alice gave him a stern look. "And you had to send her here to me, did you?"

Evan held his hand out in supplication, still unable to think of anything to say. He finally tried one more time.

"My dear, you are still the most beautiful woman in the Caribbean or anywhere, for that matter. I have eyes only for you."

As he spoke Alice doubled over laughing before finally coming over to wrap him in her arms.

"I am sorry, Evan. I couldn't resist teasing you. Even I have to admit she is a very beautiful woman too, although I'll take your word for it I am still the best."

Evan smiled in relief. "You absolutely are. So I take it they are not here?"

"Yes, they have indeed left. As it happened they were only here a few days. I had Commander Cooke pull a few strings to get them on a trader leaving for America and then on to Canada. After all, there is room for only one stunningly beautiful woman around here and this would be me. We actually got to know each other well during the short time she was here and I like her. She assured me you were the perfect gentleman the entire time and the happy news for you is I believe her."

"I love you, Alice. Thank you for taking care of her."

"Thank you for being the true gentleman you are, lover man," said Alice, before giving him one of the broad grins he had come to know and love for so many years.

"Just keep remembering you are *my* gentleman and it will all be fine."

The End

Author Notes

As always, I have attempted to ensure the historical elements blended into the fiction of *The Sugar Inferno* are as true to the record as possible. Having said this, historical fiction authors do have the luxury of taking occasional liberties with the truth when it suits our purposes.

For the most part the historical characters, the events, and the timelines in this book are very close to the record. General Maitland, Toussaint L'Ouverture, Philip Roume, Theodore Hedouville, Jean-Jacques Dessalines, and Andre Rigaud were all real people who more or less behaved as depicted. Hubert Montdenoix was a real French spy in the Caribbean, although I have no idea whether he actually plied his trade in Saint Domingue.

The only major elements of the action in this work where I deviated from the historical record are mostly towards the end. The raid by British warships on Santo Domingo as described never happened and Roume's efforts to scrape together Spanish soldiers to fight in Saint Domingue actually went nowhere, because Spanish support for their French masters was as tepid as the story portrays. The poster proclaiming the return of slavery was real, but it was not a product of British intrigue. Hedouville himself actually put this proclamation out and it inflamed the blacks so much Toussaint L'Ouverture seized the opportunity to rid himself of the Frenchman once and for all. The setting of Admiralty House in London is real, as were the politicians at the meeting, but of course the meeting with my fictional characters Evan Ross and Sir James Standish never happened.

As a minor aside, Lieutenant Thomas Pitt, the second Baron Camelford, was in fact real and behaved as described in the story. His erratic behavior was evident both before and after the events in Antigua, and at various times in his life he was suspected of being insane. Although he is not directly linked to the story of what was happening in Saint Domingue, I couldn't resist including reference to him. The murder he committed in what is now known as Nelson's Dockyard did happen at the time right before *The Sugar Inferno* begins. He is yet another of the colorful characters populating Antigua and the Caribbean in this era, all of which continue to fascinate me. He was killed in a duel a few years after returning to England.

If there are any historians reading *The Sugar Inferno* it is possible they may take issue with how the motivations of the real characters and even some of the events are presented in this work. Any errors are mine alone. I expect some of you may have found the twists and turns of allegiances in the story more than a little convoluted in nature. But if anything, I think the reality was even more complicated than I depicted it and I expect people familiar with this era and this particular island will agree with me. I justify the approach I've taken in the name of simplicity, with the thought it is never a good idea to lose your reader in a morass of complex details.

The reason for the complex nature of the situation at this point in history is the context of the times. Many forces came together all at the same time on the island of Saint Domingue to create the outcome. The French Revolution and a patriotic, but torn people, British imperialism, a global war for domination, the scourge of slavery, and above all the overwhelming greed stemming from the vast wealth brought about by the production and sale of sugar were all at play. The metaphor that is the title of this work is no mystery to me.

As a small note of interest for those of you not terribly familiar with the geography of the Caribbean, the French half of Saint Domingue is what we know today as Haiti. To complicate matters the British often referred to Saint Domingue as St. Domingo. The Spanish side of the island, now known as The Dominican Republic, was at the time known as Santo Domingo. To make it all worse, the capital city was and still is known by the name Santo Domingo. To minimize confusion I decided to keep it simple and not use St. Domingo in the narrative. The island in its entirety is still known as Hispaniola, which is another element I have chosen to minimize use of.

Geography had much to do with motivations in this story. If you look at a map of the Caribbean it is easy to see the much prized island of Jamaica is relatively close to the southern part of the country and in particular the western peninsula where Jeremie is located. Because of this close proximity and the aggression of the French, the British had reason to fear an invasion. Before becoming reluctant allies to the French, the Spanish would have been elated to make the entire island their domain to complement their holdings in Cuba to the west and Puerto Rico to the east. Taking Jamaica back from the English would have made the Spanish even happier.

Patriotism and a lust for power were also motivators driving some of the key people in this story. As I researched the history I found it fascinating that the common denominator of the patriotism of Hedouville, Rigaud, and L'Ouverture was not enough to find common ground and overcome the lust for power all of them clearly had.

People not familiar with Haiti and its history can be forgiven for perhaps thinking, after reading this, that matters could not possibly have gotten worse or remained as complicated as it was in 1798. Sadly, the reality is it did, enough to rival anything a fiction writer could drag out of their imagination.

The coming confrontation alluded to in *The Sugar Inferno* between L'Ouverture and Rigaud came to be known as The War of Knives, taking place in 1799 and 1800. Because Rigaud was allied with the French, who in turn were still at odds with the Americans, the United States Navy aided Toussaint's forces by blockading Rigaud's ports. Toussaint won the war, but as General Maitland feared the French and Napoleon Bonaparte decided to reclaim Saint Domingue in 1802. Bonaparte sent over twenty thousand soldiers and an equally large number of sailors to do it and promptly reintroduced slavery on the island. But fever took a heavy toll on the French, as it did with the British before them.

Toussaint L'Ouverture was captured and sent to France, where he died in a cold French prison in

1803, but Toussaint's commander Jean-Jacques Dessalines took charge and defeated the French forces. Dessalines was particularly brutal with his use of scorched earth policies. Meanwhile, the British Royal Navy was a thorn in the side of the French invaders throughout.

History was made January 1, 1804 when Dessalines proclaimed independence of the first black republic in the world effectively created as the result of a slave revolution. Geography once again made this of particular interest to the Americans, given the relative close proximity of Haiti to the continent.

President Thomas Jefferson of the United States greeted the event with some alarm, given the large population of slaves in his country, but at this point they were in no position to do something about it. The United States would not recognize Haiti as a country until after the American Civil War. But America remained interested in Haiti and as American power grew so did their willingness to use it. Americans occupied Haiti in 1914 and remained there for nineteen years.

Throughout its history Haiti's leaders have, for the most part, been what can only be described as a series of dictators. Corruption and enormous greed continues to be the bane of this country. Adding to the misery of the people, a 7.0 magnitude earthquake devastated the country in 2010. Despite massive efforts and many millions of dollars in aid by foreign donors over many decades, Haiti remains one of the poorest countries in the world and wears the dubious mantle of poorest country in the western hemisphere.

For Haiti to have fallen as low as it has is a sad irony. Times were hard in France in the late 18th century and Saint Domingue attracted many young people seeking their fortune and a better life. Before the Haitian revolution Cap Le Francois, now known as Cap Haitien, was even known as the Paris of the Antilles. I can only hope a day will come when the long suffering, ordinary people of Haiti find a way to rise above the devastation of their island created by greed, corruption, and natural disasters.

So what is next for Captain Evan Ross? *The Sugar Inferno* is the fifth book in this series and the sixth book, *The Admiral's Pursuit,* will be the last. The Caribbean is a wonderful, diverse part of the world, but I have other projects in mind to pursue and it is time to move on. But given how much I love it, the possibility exists one of those future projects may take you back to the sunshine and amazing islands and people of the Caribbean.

So please do watch for *The Admiral's Pursuit,* coming soon. Horatio Nelson, now Admiral Lord Horatio Nelson, will reappear for this one and you won't want to miss it. Nelson was always in the thick of the action and this story won't be any different. I do hope you have enjoyed reading *The Sugar Inferno.*

Made in the USA
Middletown, DE
04 July 2019